Heaven Scent

Heaven Scent

Trilogy

A Fantasy
by

J.K. Maxwell

To order additional copies of this book, contact:
Xlibris Corporation
1-888-795-4274
www.Xlibris.com
Orders@Xlibris.com
31511

To my granddaughters Jolan and Brette Boockvor,
and my great nieces Erin and Heather Vanderhoof all of whom
keep me writing until the book's completion.

GRETCHEN DANDRICH, a young socialite and sometimes writer, happened upon an unusual situation. Along with her best friend

KRISTIN, who owns an antique shop, the two set out to solve a mystery Gretchen unwittingly became entangled in. While having dinner with her attorney-husband,

HARLEY DANDRICH, a quiet, bespectacled, intense young man given more to realism than his wife's excursions into past lives and fantasy, at

SHAMAN'S PUB, a noted eatery—a replica of an Olde Irishe Pub—in the small town of Ridgecrest, Connecticut, when they are approached by one of Shaman's customers,

PROFESSOR IPSWITCH with his new invention—guaranteed to keep the young, the youthful, and the old contented—which is sold by Kristin in her antique shop until he tangles with Gretchen and her alter ego, a white Persian cat that introduces Gretchen into the cat world.

SHAMAN, a bartender of some notoriety, fashioned his pub reminiscent of an Olde Irishe Pub. The ambiance of Shaman's Pub—and his two Siamese cats, Ming and Einstein—makes it a favorite watering hole among youthful adults as Shaman regales his customers with stories about past lives, legends of Ireland, and the little people with whom he seems to have an intrinsic acquaintance. No one knows how many years Shaman has been on earth. Many suspect he's been a fixture for centuries as no one can remember him as a youth—or remember a time before his arrival.

When the first baby laughed for the first time, the laugh broke into a thousand pieces and they all went skipping about. And that was the beginning of fairies.

—J. M. Barrie

PART I

Heaven Scent

Chapter One

Spirit whose breath is in the four winds: Breathe, breathe on me.

Gretchen Dandrich put the finishing touches on her new novel in preparation for sending to her publisher. Her best story yet—even **Harley**, her husband, agreed. Usually, he never wanted to read her stories, but this time he took her manuscript to work and read it from cover to cover. She wondered about his sudden interest in this particular story, but decided not to investigate too deeply. Enough that he read it. Nevertheless, today being Friday—her weekly luncheon engagement with **Kristin Sanders**—she closed up her desk and took off for **the Brass Ring**, her friend's antique shop. She couldn't wait to tell her about her new novel—how her fictional phantom sleuth had uncovered an espionage plot that had successfully eluded the FBI for years. Her college friend, **Lauren Calloway,** worked for the FBI in Washington DC and had been her advisor in setting up the plot.

After feeding her cocker spaniel, she patted Amber on her head. "Take care of the place for me while I'm gone, Amber." Amber barked her assent—as well as her indignation at being left behind—and Gretchen bounced down the well-trodden path to meet Kristin and lunch at **Shaman's Pub.**

Shaman, a recent immigrant from Ireland, had purchased **Grumman's Bar and Grill** from Mr. Grumman's heirs when the old man died. His sons had no desire to continue in the food business, and Shaman purchased the restaurant shortly after his arrival. Missing the cordial camaraderie of hometown Irish pubs, Shaman restored **Grumman's** to an attractive replica of an ancient Irish pub. He kept the name because of its past *goodwill* value, but the establishment unofficially became known as **Shaman's Pub.**

Shaman had added his own individual touches, and the pub had achieved a certain distinct ambiance. He'd tossed out bar stools, but kept a brass rung that served as a footrest for customers—*to discourage women from drinking at the bar,* he'd tell customers. Instead, he served wholesome meals at charmingly arranged tables in a crisp, immaculate dining room. Winters, he kept a roaring fire in the huge stone hearth, where Ming, his Siamese cat, yawned and stretched for her public. Ming, his seemingly ageless Siamese, seemed entirely too wise and knowing for an ordinary cat, and talk of her being a witch's *familiar* made the rounds of speculation.

Shaman's own rotund self also defied age designation, as he could be anywhere from fifty to one hundred, and some of the tales he told to the customers caused them to believe he had lived for centuries. Usually an amiable bartender, with twinkling blue orbs and a ready smile, he could turn indignant in a moment if he suspected mischief in his pub. Gretchen introduced Harley to Shaman, and Harley adopted the attractive Irish pub as his second home. He and Shaman had developed a congenial rapport— Shaman regaling Harley with tales of past lives in his Irish homeland, and Harley using Shaman's age-old wisdom in determining resolutions to his sticky cases.

Today Gretchen breezed along the sidewalk this brisk October morning intent on her purpose and unaware of what lay ahead of her before the day's end. The tall, willowy New Englander turned heads wherever she went although she pretended to be unaware of this ability. She still thought of herself as a shy, gawky teenager—all arms and legs—worried about acne, and her sudden thrust into popularity during her college years presented a challenge to her earlier, almost puritanical, upbringing. Sometimes she often felt as though she had a foot in two oddly contrasting worlds.

Today, though, she believed she'd conquered her two worlds and lived now at peace with her life. Her worldly college roommate, Kristin, helped her overcome her shyness and introduced her to all kinds of new and exciting adventures. Kristin's upbringing had been considerably more indulgent than Gretchen's; she took profound pleasure in experimenting with the new and the untried.

"That's what college is for," she'd assured Gretchen. "So you can make sane choices for your future lifestyle unencumbered by social mores."

Gretchen envied her friend's liberal British approach to life, in sharp contrast to her own restrictive Quaker roots. Kristin shocked the staid Connecticut College and, in an attempt to temper her impulsiveness, the college thrust the two opposites together as roommates. However, the two girls connected immediately as each found in the other what they lacked in their own lives. After college graduation, they maintained in contact in spite of diverse lifestyles—Kristin, an entrepreneur, and Gretchen, married to her attorney-husband, Harley, happy in her role as a Connecticut housewife and filling her spare hours writing mystery novels.

Gretchen had met Harley when he helped her settle the intricacies of her mother's estate. They'd hit it off immediately—like soul mates who'd known each other in previous lives—sharing a common belief in the complexities of reincarnation. She had the same feeling of déjà vu when she met Kristin, but unlike Harley, Kristin thought her belief of reincarnation crazy—a sort of wishful thinking or product of a vivid imagination. But Harley understood. They both believed it so natural—a solution to all those questions the King James Bible never answered for them.

Today Gretchen reveled in the crispness of a beautiful New England autumn day as she breezed along the tree-lined street leading to Kristin's antique shop, dodging the falling leaves that reminded her of colder weather to come. She loved this attractive old town, one of the oldest in America, with its huge elm trees and well-kept attractive shops, and loathed the huge trucks that had begun using Main Street as a shortcut from the parkway to the interstate. The pavement, unused to heavy traffic, had begun to crumble in spots, keeping town officials busy making repairs.

"Ready for lunch?" she asked the young, vivacious British shopkeeper as she entered **the Brass Ring,** her friend's antique shop. The young woman facing her carried herself with distinction, her short stubby hair bristling with energy as she caressed the stock she so lovingly maintained. Gretchen realized that Kristin had deep affection for all this old furniture and ancient bric-a-brac that cluttered every available inch of her attractive little enterprise. She gazed around the shop, feeling very much at home. A new item on a gift counter caught her attention.

"What's this, Kristin? I don't remember seeing this display before. Is it new?"

Kristin laughed as she shrugged into her English mackintosh and slapped a snazzy brown fedora on her shaggy curls. "It's a new line I'm trying out. My gift area seems to attract teenagers. They're some of my best customers. You know how kids are—they love intrigue. It's all in fun, but they seem to hunger for the mystic."

She picked up one of the bottles and handed it to Gretchen. "I call this particular bottle *Heaven Scent.* Would you like one?"

"What's in it?" asked a curious Gretchen.

"It's a love potion created by a professor at the university, and one of my best sellers."

"Really? And the kids fall for this?" Gretchen read the verse on the tag attached to the potion: *Spirit whose breath is in the four winds: Breathe, breathe on me.*

"Not only kids. I sold some to Shaman over at the pub. Plans to give it to his wife." Kristin chuckled. "Sure hope it works for him—might change his disposition."

"Why the old coot"—Gretchen smiled—"but, hey, if he believes in it . . ." She read the label. "What's the secret ingredient?"

"I've no idea," said Kristin, her eyes twinkling. "But it does add to the intrigue, doesn't it?" She appraised the tall, slender blond with her sparkling blue eyes—eyes as blue as a summer sky. An intelligent person, but slightly gullible—*imagine believing in reincarnation*—although Kristin found this characteristic in Gretchen intriguing at times.

"Ever hear the legend of Magus?" she teased, hoping Gretchen would bite.

Gretchen didn't disappoint her. "Magus? No, who's he?"

"You remember the magi, don't you? You sing about them at Christmastime . . . the visitors at the manger of the Christ child. In its singular form, *magus* means wise man or clever one. Today, he'd be your *shrink.*"

"Really? I've heard that England is full of stories about witches and ghosts. Does Magus deal in any of that?" Gretchen pocketed the love potion Kristin offered her, thinking, *if she sells it, it's got to be safe.*

"Sure, according to legend, Magus had good spirits and bad spirits around who appeared to him as men," Kristin said, bemused by Gretchen's sudden interest in the occult. She slipped on her gloves and headed for the door. "There's a third kind of spirit we call *ghosts.* Spirits separated from the body, but still roaming the earth. After that, the legend becomes rather complicated and murky—dealing with sorcery and witchcraft—but everything begins with Magus and his magic drum.

"Aha—a magic drum—of course." Gretchen wondered if she was being teased, but Kristin looked totally serious, so she continued, "And pray tell, how *did* Magus use his magic drum?"

"Why, to exorcise fiends who roamed the four corners of heaven, my dear. How else?" Kristin checked her watch, turning the sign in the window that read: Out to Lunch—Back at 2:00 PM. "Let's go, Gretchen, the **pub** will be crowded, and we're running late." Locking the door behind her, the two exited the shop, Kristin hurrying Gretchen into the crowd of hungry workers heading to one of the many scenic cafés dispersed among a proliferation of antique shops along Main Street.

On reaching **Shaman's Pub**, Kristin suddenly stops to warn Gretchen. "I've asked an old friend to join us. I hope you don't mind."

"Kristin, you know I hate surprises. You should have warned me."

"You'll like this surprise." And Kristin dragged a reluctant Gretchen into the **pub** to a table already occupied by a handsome young redhead.

"Oh, good, he's saved us a table." Stunned, Gretchen's eyebrows arched, and she looked questioningly at Kristin. *Kristin? A cop? I can't believe it.*

"Gretchen, let me introduce you to an old friend of mine from my days in *Merrye Olde England,* Sergeant Gregory Baggette. Roscoe, meet my friend from college days, Gretchen Dandrich. Gretchen recovered from shock in time to acknowledge the introduction.

"What a surprise." Gretchen looked from one to the other. "How long has this been going on?" she asked.

The friendly face spread into a mischievous grin, his freckles struggling to stay in sight among crinkly laugh lines. Gretchen took in the steel blue eyes revealing a ready humor he had difficulty hiding. A slight man at first glance, his biceps and pectorals tested the seams on his police uniform and belied any frailty a casual observer might envision.

"Since I visited an antique shop for a desk she had advertised," the hunk answered, "imagine my surprise to find Kristin in charge."

"Why did she call you *Roscoe?*"

Before he could answer, Kristin interrupted. "A high school nickname. Can't quite get used to calling him Gregory or Greg . . . or Sergeant Baggette for that matter. He's always been Roscoe."

"You knew each other in school?" Gretchen asked.

"Yes, in Britain."

Kristin's cop friend laughed as he told her, "She's an army brat whose parents thought an English education would be good for her."

"Then they shipped me off to America for college . . . before I became too British. He followed me," Kristin teased.

"I got an opportunity to work here after college," he explained to Gretchen. Studying the face of the attractive blonde facing him, he added, "I meant to call her as soon as I got settled."

"So you say."

Kristin turned to Gretchen and explained, "We've more or less kept in touch all through college."

Roscoe had the same delightful British accent so much a part of Kristin's appeal and seemed genuinely fond of Kristin. Toasted by the wine, the ambiance, and the company, Gretchen found herself warming to Kristin's friend when a sudden draft from an open door startled the group, and a chill wind blew into the room. All attention turned to the door as a strange man entered. He headed for the bar, but not before letting in a second stranger that sneaked past him and headed for the warm fireplace, curling up on the hearth alongside Ming.

"Oh, look," said Gretchen, "Ming's found a new friend. Isn't he beautiful?" The three glanced at the hearth where two matching Siamese cats shared space. As Shaman approached their table, Gretchen asked about the new feline.

"He be hangin' around the pub and don't seem to belong to no one far's I can tell, so I sorta adopted him," he said warily, glancing at the hearth. "I call him Einstein, he's that smart. Little devil . . . comes and goes as he pleases . . . doin' his own thing, so to speak." He looked at the two cats affectionately. "Ming seems to have taken a shine to 'im."

"He's a real beauty, Shaman," agreed Gretchen, feeling the same strange eeriness with Einstein that she felt with Ming. *No wonder Shaman calls him Einstein.* The cat turned and locked eyes with Gretchen. "He seems almost human."

"That he does—wise beyond his years, he is," Shaman agreed, picking up a few of the dirtied dishes on the table. "You be wantin' more wine?"

"No, thanks, Shaman, I'm meeting Harley here for dinner. I'll save it for later."

"And we're on our way back to work," Kristin said. "But we'll be back, you know we will . . . the food's delicious and the service superb."

Gretchen gave a parting glance to the pair on the fireside as she left. Kristin paused to speak to the stranger at the bar. Later she explained that the stranger she'd spoken to, Professor Ipswitch, had created *Heaven Scent,* the potent Gretchen had in her pocket.

"Really? Doesn't look like any professor from our days," Gretchen said. Kristin agreed. "The new, modern look, no doubt."

Gretchen knew she referred to the spiked hair and weird glasses that bridged his immense nose making him look more like an owl than a professor.

"He's a regular at Shaman's," she added. "Says he has a lab at the university."

"Things have changed since our college days."

"That's for sure."

Chapter Two

The source of the existent and the nonexistent is but one.

Professor Ipswitch clutched his notebook close to him as he headed for the campus laboratory. He considered the day he bailed **Jake Dunbar** out of jail, and earned his friendship, to be one of his luckiest days. Yes, Jake had surpassed all expectations during his latest incarceration when he perused the prison library and read up on little known facts. His research uncovered an item of immense interest to the professor—a remarkable recipe obtained from an inmate presently in residence at the Connecticut House of Corrections.

Professor Ipswitch had managed to secure a position at the local university—not as a professor per se, but as assistant to a legitimate professor in the chemistry lab. And what an interesting place that turned out to be, especially when he discovered he had access to laboratory facilities after hours.

One of his jobs included cleaning up what students left behind each day. He'd even managed to befriend one student who gave him access to paraphernalia he needed for his own personal research.

Then he had the good fortune to meet that young antique dealer, **Kristin,** at **Shaman's Pub**, and the pieces fell into place. The recipe Jake found in the archives of the prison library helped the professor concoct a potion that proved quite popular among the younger crowd. Kristin, a terrific marketer of the unusual, agreed to sell his product in her gift shop. She called the potion *Heaven Scent—a Love Potion* and assured the professor that the name alone would attract any teenager's love for mystery.

"It's all in the marketing," Kristin convinced the professor. "We can expect to gain considerable profit if it's marketed correctly. I'll have my attorney friend draw up an agreement."

Her attorney friend, **Harley Dandrich,** assured them there would be no problems. Everything looked on the up and up. They agreed, and Harley extracted a percentage of the sales as his fee.

After that little venture, Professor Ipswitch accepted the moniker of *Professor*—as the students had begun to dub him—without guilt. No one bothered to investigate the source of the product—a harmless scent—and he proved exceptionally successful in maintaining discretion.

Today, slipping into the laboratory, he saw **Morgan** already hard at work. Morgan, a short, ugly, gnomelike man—who looked all the world like one of the Seven Dwarfs that so beleaguered Snow White—had been a find for Professor Ipswitch.

The professor kept Morgan pretty much out of sight—in the woods behind his cottage. He's been thoroughly vexed when he entered **Shaman'**s last evening and saw Morgan sitting at the bar listening to one of Shaman's Irish tales. Morgan knew how dangerous it could be for him to be seen in public. He could only hope that no one would remember him, but that seemed highly unlikely as Morgan's strange appearance made an indelible mark on most minds.

Morgan merely said—*not to worry*—that he could make himself invisible if the need arose. *Humph, a lot of malarkey*, the professor huffed. *I'd need proof before I'd believe that far-fetched story.* The professor knew Morgan to be a chap full of unbelievable tales—like Shaman and his weird tales of past lives in Ireland—and marveled at the ease with which Morgan silently came and went as though walls didn't deter him. He claimed to have an ability to come and go from this world to the next whenever he pleased. He did seem to disappear into thin air at times, a worry to the professor as he needed some kind of contact with him—a phone number, an address or something—but Morgan merely said he'd pick up his messages without the inconvenience of a telephone.

Morgan claimed to have met Jake Dunbar in prison—the thief Harley Dandrich sent up the river—claiming Jake introduced him to the prison library where he'd discovered a recipe that when taken, promised entry into the *Netherworld.* The professor didn't believe him. Morgan didn't elaborate, but refused to use Jake's recipe claiming his own version vastly superior. Thus, the professor allowed Morgan to create his own concoction and kept Jake's recipe in reserve in a place no one knew of except the professor himself.

Professor Ipswitch entered the laboratory to find Morgan already hard at work on his latest concoction. His test tube bubbled and foamed as Morgan peered and sniffed, stirring his concoction with deep concentration.

Kristin intended to market this one as *Resurrection,* a youth potion created to extend the aging of young women far into their mid-eighties. The professor envisioned riches beyond all expectation.

"What do you have there?" the professor asked him. "Anything interesting?" Morgan turned slowly and looked at the professor with his catlike yellow eyes, blinking his disapproval at the unexpected interruption. *The man seemed almost catlike in his demeanor, even speaking a sort of guttural sound hard to follow.* When Morgan worked on a new product—one he said would far surpass *Heaven Scent* and revolutionize the world—he disliked interruption.

"Time to test," groaned the gnomelike little man. He turned to face Professor Ipswitch. "Your job." He slid down from the high stool at the lab table, handed the professor a tube filled with a liquid solution and uttered his last remark, "Done." He shuffled from the room. The professor watched his departure from a window until he disappeared into the forest. The professor knew he would not reappear until the professor willed him, and then only at his own discretion.

Professor Ipswitch took the vial Morgan left with him to his cottage at the entrance of the university, then called Kristin to ask for her assistance in bottling and marketing the new product. She agreed to his terms, but first wanted assurance the potion would do no harm. "You need to test it," she told him.

"Do you have any ideas?"

"I suggest an animal test," she replied. "If the animal survives, the substance is harmless. Otherwise . . ."

"What kind of animal do you suggest?"

"Any animal . . . maybe a cat or a monkey . . . then I'd have no qualms about marketing your product. I refuse to be responsible for consequences that may develop from inadequate testing."

Professor Ipswitch hung up the phone. "Damned female," he grumbled. "I need something larger than a cat." He looked at the vial in his hand. "Shaman has a cat, and that place of his is always good for an evening of entertainment. Maybe I'll find me a willing *guinea pig.*" He slipped the small vial in his pocket and left the cottage. "Yeah, that's what I'll do," he decided.

Chapter Three

For whatever purpose a man bestows a gift
For that same purpose, he receives in his next birth . . . its reward.

Shaman was in his cups. It had been a long night at the pub, and he'd drunk more than usual. He felt as though his head would split. *Why did I take that last drink?* The Dandriches, Gretchen and Harley, had been there all evening, along with that crazy Professor Ipswitch. Gretchen, one of his favorite customers, loved hearing his Irish tales of leprechauns, etc., and tonight he'd outdone himself with his tales of Irish lore. Even Harley Dandrich seemed intrigued with the professor.

The professor—now there was a character. Shaman didn't know if he really were a professor or if he'd tagged the name on himself to bolster his self-esteem. He never seemed to have a class at the university, but kept talking about his experiments. If his experiments really did what he claimed they did, he'd turn the world upside down. The professor and Harley had discussed the pros and cons of investing all evening until Shaman thought they'd never leave.

Shaman knew he shouldn't drink in front of customers, but that night, he'd broken his own rule. *Why? Was it that gnomelike little man who'd come in near the end of the evening? Where have I seen him before?* He'd been in the middle of his latest Irish tale when the man entered, sat at the opposite end of the bar from the professor, and proceeded to drink heavily, glaring at Shaman as though he knew him.

The gnomelike little man reminded Shaman of a tale he'd once told—that is, until the tale became too personal and kept him awake at nights—a tale of his boyhood in Old Ireland, of cats he knew who talked to people, of tales of the *Netherworld,* and where Morgan moved easily between the two worlds of life and death. *Could the professor be* **Morgan**—*his archenemy of many centuries ago? No, that's crazy. I'm imagining things again, like the night he'd tested too many of his unique concoctions and told too many of his weird stories.*

He remembered that night he'd tested too many of his unique concoctions and told too many of his weird stories, and Ming spoke to him as plain as day. He hadn't had a drink since; that is, until tonight when Morgan, that gnomelike little man, appeared out of nowhere in his very own pub, like a message out of his past. *What's he doing here?*

After everyone had left and he'd locked up for the night, he'd stumbled into the back room where he kept a couch for just such occasions as this. Passing out, he drifted into an uneasy sleep.

*   *   *

He's a child again in Olde Ireland and his nanny sends him out to play. In those days, he loved to wander through the woods behind his house and listen to the songs of the different birds or watch a spidery web spill from dew-soaked vines. There were animals in his world, too—graceful cats that sprang from limb to limb and wolves that howled taunts at animals out of their reach. Every day the scenery changed. He never knew if it were the same spider or the same animal—that was the wonder of it all. Every day he watched spidery webs grow and flowers bud then burst into bloom. He'd learned to study the ways of the forest.

One day, darkness came to his young world. His mother died, and his father remarried. He no longer had a nanny, and his stepmother barely tolerated him. Doubting very much they'd even miss him, he left his home behind and made his home in the forest with his animal friends. He talked to the little people in the forest, and they took care of him. He became skilled in locating animals in the trees and snakes in the grass. He knew how to find help—which plants he could eat and which he could not.

During his wanderings he discovered the Feast of Shaman in progress. He'd heard about its wonders from the little people—how only a door separated his world from the Netherworld, and how the doors would open during the Feast of Shaman and allow people to wander back and forth between the two worlds. Curious about this custom of Shamanism, he decided to attend and arrived at Tara, the castle of the little people, in time to join them and partake in the feast. As he wandered among the guests, he learned how they performed this feat—how some people could wander through the two worlds and glean wisdom on the

*other side. Shaman wanted knowledge and wisdom more than anything else
and really believed that if it were possible for one to see into the past, one could
surely see into the future. Not many were allowed this privilege, and he wanted
to be one of them.*

*The night of the Feast of Shaman, he meets Fionne, an Irish laddie who
claimed to have lived centuries ago. Fionne had eaten of the Tree of Knowledge
and told Shaman he would teach him all he knew if he would return to the
Netherworld during the Feast of Shaman every year. Shaman agreed, and every
year thereafter, he would return with Fionne to the Netherworld during the
Feast of Shaman to gain more knowledge.*

*After one feast, Fionne takes him far into the Netherworld. "You have until
morning, when the Feast of Shaman ends, to find your way back to your world.
I have taught you all I know. If you can do this, you will gain the knowledge
you desire from the fisherman who has the knowledge you desire." Otherwise,
you must remain in the Netherworld until the next Feast of Shaman," he tells
Shaman and departs.*

Shaman stirs restlessly in his sleep as he recalls his encounter with Morgan
in the *Netherworld. Unknown to Fionne, Morgan has followed the pair into
the Netherworld, hiding behind a tree until Fionne departs. Then he follows
Shaman as he wanders along the river until he sees a fisherman fishing along
the banks of the River of No Return. He does not know that the fisherman is
Morgan who has gotten there ahead of him.*

"What are you fishing for?" he asks the old man.

*"I'm fishing for wisdom," the old man tells him, looking around at
Shaman.*

"How long have you been fishing?" Shaman asks.

*"Forever," the old man answers. "You see, I must fish until I find someone
worthy of eating of the fish I catch. Are you worthy?"*

*"I want wisdom more than anything else in the world," Shaman answers
him.*

*Morgan pauses in his fishing and turns to Shaman. "I am weary of seeking
someone worthy of knowledge, but I cannot stop fishing until I find him."*

*The fisherman reminded Shaman of Father Time, with his wrinkled and
worn face, his aged, red-rimmed eyes sunken in a haggard face, and his hair
drooping in strings beneath his cap. "I'm running short of time," Shaman tells
the old man. "I must return to my world before morning or remain until the
next Feast of Shaman."*

*"I understand. If you are the one worthy of wisdom, you will have time," the
old man assures him. He points to a path behind him. "Do you see that cottage*

*there in the woods? Go there and build me a fire. The flesh of the fish contains
the wisdom you desire."*

"How can that be?" Shaman asks.

"It is so," the fisherman tells him. "From a Sacred Bush overhanging a
secret pool in a sacred place. The Sacred Bush overhanging the secret pool drops
its berries into the water and they float on the river. The fish eats of the berries
and becomes wise beyond all things. If you are the one, the fish will be ready
when you are."

"Why not eat of the berries of the Sacred Bush?" asks Shaman.

"The berries can only be eaten by the fish," says the fisherman.

"We wait for the fish," agrees Shaman and wanders down the narrow path
toward a thatched cottage nestled among the trees. He gathers twigs to build a
fire and looks inside the cottage for a pan for roasting—all the while, watching
the fisherman fishing on the banks of the river. He lights the fire and works
to keep it burning, wondering if he will be found worthy of the wisdom that
eludes so many.

"Will I ever be wise enough to learn all the answers to all the questions
everyone asks? Can wisdom really be absorbed into the flesh from eating a fish?
Will I learn why some people are happy and some people are not? Why the moon
comes up at the same time every day? Why people fight, and men make war?
Will the old man catch the fish because I am here and have built a fire?"

The fire burns brightly, and Shaman can almost taste the flesh of the fish.
The fisherman continues to fish, and Shaman becomes anxious. "Time is running
out. I must return to my world. I cannot wait another year to gain wisdom." As
Shaman waits for the fisherman to return, he falls asleep by the fire.

When the fisherman catches his fish, he returns to the cottage and places the
basket near Shaman. "Look in the basket," he tells Shaman when he awakens.

Shaman looks in the basket and sees a huge fish. He cleans the fish and bakes
him in the roasting pan. The fisherman refuses to partake of the fish. "How can I
thank you?" he asks the fisherman. Shaman eats his fill of the truculent flesh.

"There is no need," the fisherman says. "You are late and must remain my
guest 'til next Feast of Shaman."

"Oh no!" Shaman cries. "You've cheated me. Where is Fionne?"

"He is gone." As he speaks, he strips off his disguise and stands before Shaman,
his hunchback in evidence, and his cruel lips curled in a sneer. "I am your old
friend, Morgan. We'll see how far your wisdom takes you."

Shaman leaves the cottage, his hopes shattered. He meets up with a small
tiger that listens to his tale of woe. "Morgan does not know all exits," the tiger
assures Shaman. "Come with me. I will lead you home."

"How can I trust you?" asks Shaman.

*"You must. I will guide you home. Close your eyes and repeat after me.
'Spirit whose breath is in the four winds breathe, breathe on me.'" Shaman did
as the tiger requests. "Trust me. It is so," the voice continues. "When you open
your eyes, you will be home."*

*Shaman does as the tiger requests, repeating the phrase over and over as if in
prayer until he sees Fionne in the distance. "Tell Fionne you have accomplished
your mission," the tiger says.*

*As he approaches, his friend Fionne says to him, "Morgan deceived you.
He has been captured and will spend many centuries across the River of No
Return."*

"Thank you for your help, Fionne. Will I see you again?"

*Fionne's voice floats off in the distance. "When next you need me," the voice
floats back. "When next you need me . . ."*

Shaman felt a paw tapping his shoulder. He struggled to awaken. Fionne's
voice drifted off into the distance. The tapping paw became more urgent as
Ming hesitantly attempted to awaken him.

"What is it, Ming?" he asked, stroking the Siamese affectionately as he
struggled to awaken. He opened his eyes and groaned, surprised to be in
the back room of his pub.

He tried to remember. *Didn't I go home last night?*

"Mirreeow," Ming wailed.

Then Shaman heard the sound that had caused Ming to seek his
assistance. A scratching noise at the front door of the pub got his attention,
and he arose to investigate. Opening the door, a shadow darted between his
legs. He turned in time to see a cat—the spitting image of Ming—parking
itself beside her on his hearth.

"Where did you come from?" he asked the new intruder.

The two bookends stared silently from their place on the hearth. *Am I
still dreaming?* He returned to his cot recalling his dream of seeking wisdom.
He wondered what it meant. As he stared at the two cats watching over him,
he leaned back and immediately fell sleep. An overwhelming sense of peace
and tranquility enveloped him.

Chapter Four

Imagination is the eye of the soul.
—Joseph Joubert

Harley had consumed his first glass of wine by the time Gretchen arrived at **Grumman's Bar and Grill** that Friday evening. She'd agreed to meet him there after he left the office and had walked the few blocks from their home on Main Street. Harley had struck up a conversation with a strange-looking gentleman at the bar, but when Gretchen arrived, he left the bar and joined her at a table near the fireplace.

"An interesting man, that professor," he told Gretchen as he helped her off with her coat. "Does a bit of experimental work in his laboratory at the university. Seems he's made up some concoction that he sells to shops here, and it's going over big."

"I know, I have some," Gretchen said, pulling out the bottle Kristin had given her from her coat pocket. She read the inscription to Harley. "Catchy, isn't it?"

"Let me see that." Harley took the bottle from her and read the label. "What's the secret ingredient?" he asked.

"It's a mystery. Why don't you ask the professor?"

"Later," he said and slipped the potion into his pocket.

"It's a scent. You might at least take a whiff and watch his reaction."

But when Shaman approached to take their order, Harley asked him, "What do you know about that fellow at the bar? Is he for real?"

"I'm not one you should be askin'," he said. "Seems a likable enough chap. Pushin' his latest snake oil, methinks." More than that he refused to say, leaving them to arrive at their own conclusion.

"Doesn't seem to think much of the professor's creation, does he?" Harley commented. "What does Kristin say?"

"She feeds into the mystery, tells me old English tales of Magus, magic drums, old wives' tales," Gretchen answered.

"You believe her?"

"I'm a writer. I don't discount anything. Introduce me to him, then I'll decide."

After they had eaten, Harley takes Gretchen to the bar and introduced her to the eminent **Professor Ipswitch**. She'd only had a glimpse of him at lunch today and now examined him up close. This evening she saw a weird-looking chap with big owl eyes framed in huge octagon-shaped spectacles, giving him the appearance of a big hoot owl. Even his hair, chopped short and gelled into spikes, emphasized this oddity. Harley couldn't remember ever having seen him before, but Shaman seemed to know him, so he must be an okay guy.

"I'm associated with **Brohaugh's Conservatory of Arts and Science**," the professor told them. He ogled Gretchen over black-rimmed specs and attempted to entice her. "You'd make a terrific prototype for my new invention."

"Really?" Gretchen's eyebrows made a definitive arch. "What is it?"

"A potion introducing the wisdom of the ages, one I call *Resurrection,* for want of a better name," the professor said. "Especially suited for one so young."

"What does it do?"

The professor glanced at Shaman before answering, but Shaman appeared busy with another customer. "True wisdom comes only with age. Wouldn't it be wonderful to have that which usually comes only with age . . . and yet remain young for decades to come. Are you interested?"

"Who wouldn't be?" Gretchen smiled. Harley watched, amused. "Is it dangerous?"

"No more dangerous than most experiments," the professor replied. For just a flash, Gretchen registered a chilling glimpse into his ice-cold eyes and pulled back.

"I don't think so," she said. The professor shrugged. Gretchen turned to Harley. "I'm a pussycat when it comes to taking chances," adding for the professor. "You should try Kristin. She's always up for an adventure into the unknown."

Harley laughed, and the two returned to their table. Gretchen forgot her glass of wine. A few moments later, the professor brought it to her and joined them at the table. The three talked into the evening. Harley was seemingly mesmerized by the professor's plans, and eventually their conversation delved into patents, marketing, etc. Gretchen tried to concentrate, but the room suddenly felt stifling. She needed air.

"Harley," she said, "it's so warm in here. I'm going outside to cool off."

Harley looked at her. "You do look rather flushed. Go ahead, I'll join you shortly." Gretchen remembered her last thought as she went through the door—*once a lawyer, always a lawyer.* Then all memory for Gretchen Dandrich stopped at that point.

Chapter Five

To imagine is everything, to know is nothing at all.
—Anatole France

Roscoe crossed the road looking both ways before darting between the cars. He'd promised Gretchen he'd be at their favorite lunch spot behind the Fisherman's Wharf. He'd met Gretchen quite by accident one day and had never completely recovered from the shock. Roscoe, a large varicolored cat with glossy green eyes, had been engaged in his usual skullduggery under the overpass. He and his cronies had been rooting through the garbage debris vagrants left behind when he stumbled on a tightly bound sack.

"Hey, fellas," he called out. "Can any one of you help me with this sack? There's something in there. I can smell it." He waited until the alley cats crowded around the sack, eager to see what had attracted Roscoe. Each one grabbed a corner in his sharp teeth and pulled at the worn gunnysack. As the bag started to rip, a fluffy white tail poked out, tickling Roscoe's nose.

"By God, it's one of us," Roscoe said. "Who do you suppose tied her up and dropped her off here? Is she dead?"

"No," answered Einstein, a Seal Point Siamese and self-appointed leader of the alley cats. "She's moving. Get back and give her some space." The cats gathered around and watched as the gunnysack came to life. A strange white cat poked a pink nose out and struggled to speak.

Gretchen closed her eyes and tried to concentrate. She looked around at the curious cat faces surrounding her. *Where am I? What happened to me?* She looked down and saw hairy paws instead of hands and turned around in time to see a long white fluffy attachment flipping back and forth over her back with no effort on her part.

"Damn that devil! What's he done to me? I'm not a cat." The motley crew of cats stared in disbelief. "Am I?" The newcomer glared at Roscoe. "Did you do this to me?"

Instead of being pleased at being rescued, this cat was mad. Roscoe tried to step in, but the white cat took a swing at him.

"Did you? You filthy feline." Roscoe ducked and hissed until Julian came to his rescue. He jumped on the white cat and held her down.

Einstein watched the scene in disbelief. "Calm down, Matey," he advised. "Roscoe, here, is a gentleman. Whoever did this to you is not one of us, but one of those unreliable creatures we call *humanoids*."

"What do you mean? You're not a cat?" Roscoe shook himself off and glared at the intruder. "What do you call yourself? You look like the rest of us, even if you do have blue eyes and long white hair. And what's that silly chain doing around your neck?"

"You could hang yourself with that, you know, if you're not careful," Einstein cautioned. He'd selected himself as advisor *extraordinaire* to the Cat Monger's League and prided himself on getting his entourage through some rough scrapes. *What's one more cat? And this one looks sadly in need of my services.*

"You apologize to Mr. Roscoe," he instructed Gretchen, "or it's no dinner for you tonight." The white cat ignored him. The onlookers watched. The newcomer had an accent like the *humanoids* they avoided, but they understood her.

Einstein sat back on his haunches and observed the white feline. "You're a cat," he decided, looking at the confused intruder. "You're complaining?"

"Yes, I'm complaining. I'm not a cat, that's for sure," the white metamorphosis said.

"What do they call you?" asked Roscoe, smoothing the fur she'd ruffled with his rough pink tongue. "You do have a name, don't you?"

"I'm Gretchen, and I'm a *humanoid*, if that's what you call us." She looked at her paws and added, "At least, I thought I was." Gretchen pushed herself back into the gunnysack as though seeking some kind of solace and stared at the puzzled cat faces around her.

"Honest," she told them. "I really don't know what happened to me. The last I remember, there was this weird-looking cat—oops, I'm sorry—I mean chap in the pub. He bought me a few drinks." She dropped her head on her front paws and looked up at them, her eyes welling with tears. "That's all I remember, and I wound up here."

"What were you drinking?" asked Roscoe. "Some of that stuff they throw out here can really curl your hair."

"Maybe you should give it a rest," Einstein advised. "Try not to remember everything all at once. Let it come back gradually. If you are a person, as you say, and you were tossed over the side of the overpass, you're not supposed to be alive. Luckily, you didn't land in the water. The question is, 'When did you become a cat?'"

Yes, how did I suddenly change into this beautiful white Persian cat? Vaguely, she remembered an odd-looking guy at Shaman's who promised to show her his laboratory. *Did I go?* Gretchen closed her eyes, the better to concentrate, and to keep out the staring eyes of those strange felines surrounding her. *Oh, Harley, where are you when I need you?*

These cats, what do they want from me? Einstein appears to be the leader—he with the sleek dark fur and intelligent face, but what's a Siamese cat doing out so late at night? I thought they were pampered pets—too precious to roam streets and alleys after dark. Einstein seemed like a king on his throne, and the other cats, his subjects.

That big black cat with the cold green eyes—the one who held me down, I know him. He lives down the street from me, and is forever chasing Amber. He seems to be the friendliest cat here, although he looks mean. And the one they call Roscoe—he's big and muscular like a Maine coon cat—but seems a likable pet too. I don't know the other three—they seem to wait for Einstein to make their decisions for them.

"Oh," said Einstein, "I suppose I should introduce you. I'm forgetting my manners. He extended a graceful paw in the direction of the black cat. "This cat's Julius," he said. "Roscoe is the cat that found you, and these cats"—his paw swept toward the remaining three—"are Methuselah, Antonio, and Kristin."

Gretchen blinked at the three she didn't know, acknowledging Einstein's introductions. Methuselah, a quiet, playful Ragdoll; Antonio, a gray tabby who looked very much like Einstein; and Kristin, a short-haired British tabby, all watching the proceedings in silence, happy to be part of a group.

*   *   *

Some hours later, Harley Dandrich pulled into his driveway. He vaguely remembered stopping off at **Grumman's Bar and Grill** after he got off work. Maybe he'd only dreamed it, but he could have sworn he'd met Gretchen there although his memory seemed pretty fuzzy. He hadn't drunk any more than usual. Two glasses of wine, that's all he ever had, but he remembered Gretchen consuming the entire bottle of Kriter's Brut de Brut that weird young man brought to their table. *Did Gretchen leave alone, or did she go with that chap?* He tried to clear the cobwebs from his brain. *Damned if I can remember.*

"Called himself a professor," Harley vaguely remembered. "Professor Ipswitch from **Brohaugh's Conservatory of Arts and Science.**" He'd promised to take Gretchen by his laboratory and show her how innocent combinations of supposedly mild elements could produce the strangest results. Gretchen appeared fascinated. *Had she gone?*

Harley literally crawled up the stairs to his and Gretchen's room. He didn't see Gretchen. *Is she mad at me?* His brain failed to cope. Feeling drugged, he fell across their king-size bed. Sleep came immediately, and he drifted into a nightmarish dream. Usually his dreamlike sojourns crept into some wilderness of his reveries, and he survived them, but tonight he discovered Gretchen acting in a most peculiar way, more like a house cat than a housewife.

Harley wasn't a strange person, as people go, but he did have strange ideas—like believing in ghosts and the hereafter, reincarnation and time travel. Most of his friends thought him crazy when he advised them to shape up in this lifetime or run the risk of returning as one of their archenemies. Sometimes in his dreams, he'd see Julius, the young chap who lived down the street from him in the form of a big black cat. He didn't know Julius and seldom saw him, but he could have sworn that big black cat he'd seen Gretchen feeding some mornings was his spitting image. *Julius reborn? But that couldn't be. Could it?* Harley tossed and turned. Gretchen attacked him. He feinted. *What's wrong with her?* He slept on.

Chapter Six

Inasmuch as body is not the self . . . it is impermanent . . . so it is with feeling.

Gretchen's head ached. Her world had turned upside down. She needed to fill in the blanks and tried to remember. *What happened! It's all so frustrating, and I'm too tired to think.* She'd dreamed of being home in her own bed, a dream so vivid; she swore she heard Harley growling in his sleep beside her. But when she awakened, her cat body remained, still there. Tears rolled down her cat face, and she brushed them aside with her paw.

"I want to go home," Gretchen informed her new friends. "I'm hungry."

Einstein took over. "It'll be daylight soon," he informed the cats. "Can one of you take Gretchen home with you and get her something to eat?"

"No," said Gretchen. "I'm going to my own home. I know where the food is."

"Do you think that's wise? Houses are locked up during the day when owners are at work." Einstein looked at Roscoe. "Take her home with you, Roscoe. She's not used to scrounging and could run into trouble. We really shouldn't leave her alone until she becomes oriented to the dangers associated with living in a people world."

"No," a determined Gretchen said. "I can handle it. I've a doggy door for Amber. She knows me. She'll let me in."

"I live down the street," Julius piped up. "I can watch out for her."

"It's settled then," Einstein said. "After you've eaten and napped, we'll meet behind the Fisherman's Wharf." Einstein looked at Gretchen. "Try to remember how you spent your last hours as a *humanoid*, Gretchen. We need a lead of some kind."

The motley crew drifted apart, Einstein keeping watch until the cats safely crossed the road. Then he trotted nonchalantly toward the last place Gretchen could remember, the **Grummans Bar and Grill,** popularly known as **Shaman's Pub**. *Maybe Ming knows what happened the evening past.*

*   *   *

Einstein had made the acquaintance of a certain feline wonder of his own ilk—her moniker, Ming. Ming resided at **Shaman's Pub** and could always be depended on to keep Einstein up on the latest village gossip. *Maybe she knows what inhumane sorcerer wreaked his magic on an unsuspecting humanoid.*

Shaman had sort of adopted Einstein since he'd hung around the pub so much and seemed to enjoy his hearth and companionship with Ming. Einstein had complete freedom to roam the village green, while Ming, being a female, stayed close to hearth. Shaman didn't believe males—being the scavengers they are—should be so confined. Besides, he suspected Ming and Einstein had a romance going.

Einstein found Ming curled up on the hearth at **Shaman's Pub**. He nuzzled her until she awakened. "Psst," he whispered into her twitching ear. "I've a job for you." He stood by as Ming stretched the length of the hearth, yawned sleepily, and with half-closed eyes put out a paw to meet Einstein's. The two curled up close to each other on the fireside. An outsider would believe them asleep, but they were passing messages between them.

"I've need for your powers of observation," Einstein began. "An odd occurrence took place this evening past in this sanctuary after I left, and I'm wondering if you happened to observe an odd-looking gentleman seated at the end of the bar, buying drinks for a good-looking young lady with husband in tow."

"I saw them," answered Ming. "A gentleman with glasses and spiked hair. I wonder how he does that. I prefer my hair smooth so I can clean it easier. What do you suppose is wrong with these *humanoids?*"

"I don't know. 'Ours is not to wonder why . . .'" Einstein said, then remembered himself. "Did anything strange occur? I mean, what did this gentleman do?"

"Why, nothing that I saw. Why should he? He's the eminent Professor Ipswitch from the university. He's working on some new potions to revolutionize disease control," Ming informed him. "The pretty blond and her husband seemed most interested. In fact, he wanted to take her back to his laboratory to pick up some potion he'd invented—guaranteed to preserve youth and endow wisdom in beautiful young women."

"She fell for that old line?"

Ming looked at him, her ears back, tail twitching in anger. Einstein backed off. "How dare you?" she hissed. "We women do whatever it takes to stay young and attractive to the opposite sex." She sniffed. "Men certainly fall for it every time, so what's a girl to do?"

"Okay, okay, don't hiss at me. Did she go with him?"

"She did consume quite a bit of wine. I remember her going outside at one point. Why do you ask?"

"If she got slipped something on the sly, that might explain it."

"Explain what?" Ming questioned. "What do you know?"

"Gretchen now has nine lives."

"You mean she's a cat?" Ming turned to look at Einstein, her eyes wide and alert. "How can that be?"

"Don't know exactly. She's one of us now, and no one seems to know how it happened, or why. Certainly, she'd prefer to turn back into a female, if she only knew how."

Einstein put his head down on his paws and opened one eye the better to observe Ming's reaction, but Ming seems distracted. She sits upright, her attention focused on the entrance to the pub. Einstein followed her gaze.

The pub door opened, and the esteemed Professor Ipswitch entered. His eyes darted around the room as though looking for someone. He ordered a drink from Shaman and asked, "Has Gretchen Dandrich been by today, per chance?"

"No, Matey," said Shaman, noting the man's nervousness. He shoved a Rob Roy in front of him. "She's not much for comin' in on Saturdays. Why? You be needin' of her?"

"She's supposed to meet me here." The professor took a swig of his Rob Roy, his feet tapping an irritating rhythm on the brass rail. He checked his watch and tossed Shaman some change. "Can you let me know if you should see her?" he asked Shaman. "It's very important I contact her." He gulped down the rest of his Rob Roy and headed for the exit.

"Sure," said Shaman to the departing back as he continued to mop the bar top, intending to forget the matter. Something about the professor bothered him. "What's he up to?" He mumbled something that sounded like, "Does he think I'm his bloomin' secretary."

Einstein turned to Ming. "Something's amiss," he told her, "and I think I know what it is. You keep a lookout here. I'm going to follow the professor—see if I can find out something about what went down last night. Evidently, something's backfired."

Einstein slipped out the door between the feet of incoming customers in time to see the professor climb aboard his motorcycle. He raced down the street following the sound of the fast disappearing machine. One good thing about being a cat, you didn't have to follow the roads. Einstein leapt across yards and over fences, following the sound of the motorcycle. It headed toward the university, but instead of continuing toward the institution of higher learning, the professor stopped at the caretaker's cottage located inside the university grounds.

Einstein located a comfortable spot under the surrounding shrubs outside the cottage and watched as the professor entered. Later he heard the professor speaking to someone he couldn't see.

"Something's gone awry." Einstein heard the professor say. "I know it." The professor listened. "You never told me there were possible side effects. Some sense of humor, you have—What form? You don't know, but you *think* some type of animal? Well, I've got to find her, whatever shape she's in." Einstein couldn't see to whom the professor spoke.

"There's fifty million animals in this town," the professor informed his listener, "and we haven't a clue which highly intelligent animal lurking around is Gretchen. I can't go around talking to all the animals in town. They'll throw me in the loony bin."

Einstein had heard enough. He figured he had the winning hand because he *knew* the animal concerned. He raced back across the housetops and slipped in beside Ming.

"There's someone else in on this," Einstein told Ming. "I have to find out who."

Ming merely raised her cat eyebrows. "You mean, the professor may have a partner?"

"It's a likely possibility," Einstein said. "And I need to find out who it is."

"What do you want me to do?" Ming asked. "The professor may be back. It's Saturday night."

"If he does, get as close to him as you can, and keep your ears open. I'm going back stick close to the professor and try to find out who else is in on this, then find Gretchen and tell her what I learn. Maybe somehow, it will jog her memory," Einstein instructed her and slipped into the night.

Ming stretched the length of the hearth, yawned, turned around twice, and resettled, tail curled around her body, and ears in alert mode. She catnapped and waited.

Chapter Seven

There is a superstition in avoiding superstition.

Einstein positioned himself outside Professor Ipswitch's window. He heard the professor talking to someone, but only the rhythmic creaking of a rocker indicated another presence in the room. So far, Einstein didn't have a clue. He had no yearning to face the consequences of a surprise visit and considered it indelicate to drop into the room uninvited.

"Which are the smart animals?" Professor Ipswitch asked his companion.

"Who the devil is he talking to?" Einstein wondered. "I wish he'd turn around." His desire to learn the identity of the professor's cohort did not surpass his cat sense.

"Oh yeah! Cats!" he heard the professor say. "You mean Shaman's stray Siamese that hangs around the pub? That the one you mean?" Einstein strained to hear, but the man only mumbled.

"Yeah, there were two of them today—sleeping on the hearth. The female's been there for years. That stray cat couldn't be Gretchen. It's a male."

(Mumble, mumble, mumble, came from the chair.)

"You may be right," the professor agreed. He leaned back in his chair as though contemplating his cohort's latest words. "Yeah, that's right. The stray may lead us to her—he's the bait . . . we can move in on the female later when Shaman's too busy to notice. Yeah, 'til the male leaves." He placed a slim elegant slipper foot on the coffee table.

(Mumble, mumble, mumble came from the chair.)

"Okay, you go after that stuff for the formula. I'll go grab the cat." The professor picked up his helmet and looked around for a sack. Leading his cohort to the back door, he headed for his trusty Honda.

Einstein faced a dilemma. *Follow the professor or his partner or stick around and look for the professor's formula?* He sent a mental message to Ming warning her to keep out of sight as she's about to have a visitor of the nastiest kind—a catnapper.

As the professor's motorcycle roared away, Einstein tailed the stranger at a safe distance. The man shuffled off in the direction of the university building—*to the laboratory?* No, the man veered right, slipping into shadowy shrubbery surrounding the main building on the campus. As swift as Einstein considered himself to be, he couldn't outpace this stranger. Before he could catch a glimpse of his face, the stranger vanished into thin air. Einstein sniffed with his keen nose, but the trail ended short of the forest.

Baffled, Einstein returned to the cottage, slipping in through the open window. Keeping one cat antenna on Ming back at the pub and the other on instant alert in the cottage, Einstein looked around the room, wondering where to start first. *Might as well see what's here—I'll figure out what to do about that guy later.*

He crept his way among the papers on the table nosing one piece of paper this way and another that way. *Amazing what clutter these humanoids live in.* A book fell off the desk onto the floor. Einstein jumped down beside it, trying to interpret the title, but to no avail.

"Gretchen needs to see this," he decided. "I can't read, and that picture on the cover means nothing to me."

Grabbing the book in his strong jaws, Einstein jumped out of the window and headed for the overpass, hoping Roscoe and Gretchen had returned. They hadn't. The place was deserted. Sitting on the small book he carried with him, he fell fast asleep.

*   *   *

"Einstein," a soft voice whispered in his ear some time later, "we're back. What have you learned?" Einstein opened one eye and saw Gretchen and Roscoe watching him. He stretched his long legs and curled his tail back over his body and yawned, shaking off fatigue.

"Ahhr," Einstein purred, fully alert and facing his two friends. "I found something on the professor's desk, but I don't know if it's what we're looking for." He pushed the book toward Gretchen. "If it isn't, I'll have to go back."

"Let me see," said Gretchen, sitting on her haunches and attempting to read the book. "Roscoe, you hold the book down on your side, and, Einstein, you hold down the other side. I can't do this alone." She studied the book while the two cats attempted to hold it steady.

"You mean this may be it?" Einstein asked, his tail flipping in anticipation. He held the book down securely on his side while Roscoe struggled with the other side. Gretchen stepped back from the book.

"Hold it up a little more, would you? I can't read if it's too close," she said. "I seem to be farsighted anymore. Must be my cat eyes." She began reading. Einstein and Roscoe watched her, impatient for a verdict. "This isn't it," Gretchen said, hitting the page with her front paw. "This is a recipe for clam chowder." She turned a page, then turned another page. Puzzled, she looked up from the book and faced the two waiting cats. "These aren't lab notes," she determined. "It's a cookbook."

Einstein and Roscoe looked at each other. "But why would he have a cookbook on his desk?" Einstein asked, puzzled. "Are you sure that's all it is?"

Gretchen glared at Einstein, fur bristling, her tail twitching. "I may look like a cat, but I can read. Why should I lie to you?"

"It's okay, Gretchen," Roscoe said, "I'm sure Einstein didn't mean it. Maybe there's something else in the book." He picked it up and shook it. Something fell out from between the leaves. "Oh, my! Oh, my! What's this?" he asked, dropping the book and nosing a loose slip of paper toward Gretchen. "There's some writing on it, Gretchen. What does it say?"

Gretchen purred with pleasure, pushing the paper smooth with her paws. "This is it, the formula. How clever of the professor . . . to hide it in a cookbook. But look at all those ingredients. I've never heard them . . . and certainly wouldn't know where to find them."

"What are they?" Einstein asked.

"They must be in the professor's laboratory, else, how could he have mixed the potion?" Roscoe asked. Occasionally, Roscoe came up with real insight.

"You're right, Roscoe. They must be in the lab. We'll have to go back there. Gretchen, you read out the ingredients, and I'll memorize them," said Einstein. "We have to return this book to Professor Ipswitch before he finds it missing."

Gretchen began to read. *Transmogrification . . . Sole property of Erichtho of Lucan.*

"What's that?" Roscoe interrupted. "And who's Erichtho of Lucan?"

Gretchen tried to explain. "He's the devil. Quit interrupting. Who else would have a recipe like this? And Transmogrification is . . . Oh no!"

"What is it, Gretchen?" Einstein asked. "What scares you about trans-mo-m-m-m what? This isn't the antidote?"

"I don't know. If this is what the professor gave me, I've already been transmogrified."

"Didn't he call the potion, *Resurrection?*" Einstein asked.

"Oh, that's right. Then this has to be the antidote." She continued to read the incantation, and as she read, Roscoe and Einstein repeated the ingredients after her, concentrating as hard as they could to remember.

> Mingle together to confect a charm,
> The bloods of black animals in a remote, solitary place.
> Burn entrails, feet and claws, the head, the skin, or feathers.
> Except a black cat.
> Scatter some ashes far and wide and others in a quart of wine.
> Roast over a slow fire or on charcoal embers 'til air is full of smoke.
> And in its midst,
> Set a pristine bowl of crystal clear water before the fire.
> Gaze into the water as you drink the wine and cry out the words,
> Boil and bubble, toil and trouble.

"Ugh, gross," commented Gretchen. "I can't do this. Surely there's a better way."

Einstein and Roscoe looked her in bewilderment. "We do this all the time," Roscoe said. "How else do you plan to be transformed? Are you going to be a squeamish female?"

"'Course if you're beginning to have second thoughts . . ." Einstein mused. "Yeah," added Roscoe. "If you prefer being a cat . . ."

Gretchen shuddered. "No, I have to get back to my original form." She looked at her two accomplices with affection. "Let's go." And the three raced back to the professor's cottage to return the book. No sooner had Einstein replaced the book in its proper place than he felt the vibration of the professor's motorcycle returning from his mission. Einstein scooted out of the cottage to join Gretchen and Roscoe.

"You two stay here and keep an eye on the professor. I'm going back to the pub to check on Ming."

Leaving them hidden outside the cottage, Einstein raced over the housetops. He found Ming safe and sound, sleeping with one eye open, invisibly taking in the activity of the pub.

"Did the professor ever come by, Ming?" he asked.

"He did, but I joined Shaman behind the bar. He didn't dare make a move on me," Ming answered, shifting her cat body to give Einstein space to curl up beside her. "Einstein, I just remembered. Gretchen never returned that night after she left, and Harley and the professor didn't leave 'til after closing time."

"You're sure?" Einstein mewed.

"Of course, I'm sure," Ming snapped. "I wouldn't say so otherwise."

Einstein put his head on his paws and stared at her. "That puts an entirely different slant on the project," he said. He closed his eyes to reflect.

Chapter Eight

Such as we are made of, such we be.
—Shakespeare

Harley Dandrich returned home that evening disappointed. With Gretchen's car still in the garage, he knew she hadn't been home. He'd tried all weekend to find her, certain she would contact her best friend, but Kristin hadn't heard from her either. The cops allowed Gretchen forty-eight hours to return before Harley could file a "missing persons" report. After all, Gretchen was an adult and in full charge of her faculties.

"She'll show up when she's ready," a burly, disinterested policeman told Harley, and that's the best Harley could do.

Harley looked around, thinking there might have been activity around the house since he'd left early that morning, but except for the stray cat he found on his doorstep, nothing seemed out of the ordinary. He tried to shove the wayward animal aside, but the cat hissed at him, determined to enter the house. Alarmed at the cat's ferocity, Harley hesitated, and Gretchen slipped between his legs and into the house.

Harley reviewed the situation. *Maybe it's best I make friends with this cat.* He poured the cat a saucer of milk and set it on the kitchen floor. The cat drank the milk eagerly, and Harley settled down with his newspaper. Having finished the milk, the cat jumped on Harley's lap and began to purr. She snuggled up on Harley's warm chest.

"Don't let him know you can speak or that you understand him," Einstein had warned her. "Until we know what happened to you, we need to take all necessary precaution."

"But it's Harley, my husband. We can trust him," she said, but Einstein insisted. Gretchen knew he was right. She'd say nothing until they knew for sure what had happened to her. *If only they could find that antidote.*

Harley watched the cat purring peacefully, kneading her furry paws into his chest, and had a change of heart. Normally a cat hater, he actually began to stroke the intruder rather fondly, thinking her as unusually friendly despite having hissed at him. Then it happened. Harley began to sneeze and sneeze and sneeze. He couldn't help it—and he couldn't stop. He picked up Gretchen in a most unfriendly way, strode to the door, and tossed the puzzled cat out into the front yard. Brushing cat hairs from his dark suit, he remembered why he hated felines. They made him ill.

"Damn cat," he grumbled. "That'll teach me. Can't get near the damn things." He returned to his comfy easy chair and again attempted to read his paper. He had no trouble being around the cats at **Shaman's Pub**, but then he never touched those cats. This one insisted on jumping on him. He couldn't have that.

Outside, Gretchen groomed her ruffled fur, disgruntled at being dumped so unmercifully, when she heard the phone ring. She perked up her ears, moving closer to the window by the telephone. *Why didn't that happen when I was inside?* Unable to hear through the thick pane of glass, she moved closer to patio door that Harley had left ajar and pushed close against the screen in time to hear him say, "A cat? You think she's a cat? Well, I admit, there were times—oh, you mean, literally." He listened. "Look, Professor, that's impossible." He shook his head in disgust. "You're crazy," he said and hung up.

Harley resumed reading his newspaper—thinking over what the professor said. Then it registered. He threw down his paper, walked out on the patio, and called to the cat, "Here, kitty, here, kitty. Come to Papa. I'm sorry I put you out."

But Gretchen had heard enough and disappeared. *I think I know who called Harley. Thank God, he tossed me out in time. I need to talk to Einstein and convince him Harley can be trusted. We'll need his help.*

She found Einstein occupying his usual spot next to Ming on the hearth at **Grumman's Bar and Grill** and hissed at him from the protection of the kitchen door. Shaman watched Einstein leave Ming when he caught sight of Gretchen by the door and mused about cats and their strange behaviors.

Once outside, Einstein asked, "Where's Roscoe? You're not supposed to be alone."

"I know. I went home to see Harley," Gretchen confessed, adding in a plaintive voice. "Einstein, we can trust him. He can help us."

Einstein shook his head. "No, not yet, Gretchen. We need to find the ingredients for that potion before we start adding accomplices."

"I nearly told him, but his allergies hit, and he threw me out. I can't stay a cat, Einstein. Harley's allergic to me," she said, nearly in tears.

Einstein felt empathy for Gretchen and her peculiar plight. "Maybe you're right. I'll think about it. Where will you spend the night?"

"At home. I've a nice comfortable chaise lounge on the patio. I'll stay there," Gretchen decided. "Don't worry about me."

Einstein hesitated, then agreed, "All right. I'll have Julius look in on you."

He intended on returning to the fireside and Ming, but Gretchen, about to return home, spied Harley's car pulling into the parking lot.

"Einstein," she warned. "Harley's here. That must have been the professor he talked to on the phone. Is he inside?"

"No, but maybe they're meeting here. I'd better warn Ming." And Einstein disappeared into the pub.

Gretchen chilled at the sight of the professor arriving from another direction. He joined Harley at the entrance. From around the corner of the pub, she watched the two enter. *Maybe Einstein's right. I can't trust Harley. Not yet, anyway.*

*   *   *

"Evenin' fellas," Shaman greeted the two new arrivals. "What'll it be? The usual?" and placed a Rob Roy in front of the professor, a beer in front of Harley. "World treating you right, is it?" He followed the professor's gaze in the direction of the fireplace, noticing that Ming and Einstein had disappeared.

"That cat of yours," Professor Ipswitch began. "He ever display unusual characteristics?"

"The cat's a *she,*" Shaman informed the professor.

"Sorry," said Professor Ipswitch. "Does *she?*"

"Not unless you want to call bein' a witch's *familiar* an unusual characteristic," Shaman said, his eyes sparkling as he chuckled.

"Huh?" asked the professor, white knuckles grabbing the edge of the bar. "What did you say? You know about witches?" Professor Ipswitch had nothing against witches, except that they charged a horrendous fee for their services. Already indebted to one witch, he had no desire for assistance from another.

"Can't you tell a joke when you hear one?" Harley teased. "Is she a witch's familiar?" he asked Shaman.

"No," Shaman said. "Ain't nothin' unusual about my cat that doesn't apply to every other cat. Why?"

"Because, Shaman, we've got a problem. Remember when we were here last Friday night, and the professor had some kind of potion he wanted to give to my wife?"

"Yeah?" Shaman stopped in midstroke of cleaning the bar counter to glare at the two. "What happened to her?"

"She's disappeared," Harley said. "We think she may be under the influence of that potion. The professor needs to check on her reaction, but we can't find her."

"And you think she might 'ave turned into a cat?" Shaman chuckled. "And 'tain't even Halloween. You guys been drinkin' yer own potions, ha' ye?"

The professor and Harley looked at each other, Harley feeling foolish. Professor Ipswitch had learned all about *Shamanism*. He knew it to be an old religious belief in an unseen world inhabited by gods, demons, and ancestral spirits. *If Harley weren't here, I'd challenge the old goat on that.* The two hurriedly finished their drinks and left the pub.

Outside, they were surprised when confronted by a brace of six ferocious cats barring their escape. One of them is the cat Harley remembered petting in his living room just hours before. He pointed to her.

"That's the one, professor," he said. "That's Gretchen. I know it is." As he approached, Gretchen hissed, and the other cats circled around her.

"She's gone from your world," the professor told Harley. "And she seems to have found allies to protect her. Leave her be."

"But I can't leave her here," Harley insisted.

"Look, we can't bring her back. My formula has disappeared. Maybe that old hag, I bought the recipe from, will return Halloween night to redeem her just dues."

"You mean it's not even your invention? You experimented on my wife with a potion you bought from a witch? How dare you!" Harley took a swing at the professor. The professor ducked.

"I didn't know," the professor defended himself. "Not 'til after I went back to find her, and couldn't . . . not until Halloween, anyway." He shuffled his feet, his hand deep in his pockets. "There's something else you need to know," the professor said.

"Don't tell me. I've heard enough." Harley sits down on the curb, holding his aching head in the palms of his hands and ignoring the professor. Gretchen and the four cats watch the pitiful sight, unable to understand what made Harley flare up like that. Einstein, hiding behind the shrubbery, listened intently, but the professor said no more.

What else does the professor know that Harley needs to know? He watched them leave, Harley in his Daimler, and the professor roaring out of the parking lot on his Honda, scattering rocks in all directions. Einstein rejoined the cats.

"You did good tonight," he told the group. "Evidently the professor doesn't remember where he put the recipe, but we have it now. We're the only ones who can help Gretchen return to her world." He looked at Gretchen, pity in his blue cat eyes. "Although why she wants to return is more than I can figure out."

He turned his back on the cats and reentered the pub.

Chapter Nine

Nothing is so strong as gentleness, and nothing so gentle as real strength.
—Saint Frances de Sales

Gretchen snuggled down onto the patio chaise behind her home on Market Street. She'd always loved her garden and looked around it now from a new perspective, a position of quiet solitude. Fall blooms in a dazzling array of nature's colors—amber, gold, and rusts—intermingled with a scattering of brilliant reds and yellows.

As a cat, Gretchen could wander through these plants, brush against them, sniff the aromas at close range, absorb the moisture of morning dew, and nibble at her late blooming strawberries. The *humanoid* Gretchen had to bend to be this close to nature, and Gretchen realized she seldom did that. Tonight she listened to the chirping of crickets in the night air, watched the flickering of fireflies dancing before her eyes, and swatting at them with her paw when they came too close.

An evening breeze chilled the October air, but Gretchen didn't feel the cold through her heavy white fur coat. Lazily, she roused and took a few licks at a burr she'd picked up during her travels that day. She thought about Julius, the black cat down the street, and wondered what skullduggery he planned for tonight. He and Einstein were hoping Professor Ipswitch would lead them to his lab so they could sneak in and await their chance to find the ingredients for her antidote. Gretchen knew the errand Julius and Einstein undertook would benefit her, but she didn't know that Julius had plans of his own for the drug. So Gretchen dozed in peace, secure in the knowledge that her problems would soon be over, and she'd be back with Harley.

Julius had told her he'd once been a *humanoid* and *morphed* into a cat the same way she had, but Gretchen was skeptical. If that were true, why couldn't he read the way she could? She dozed on until approaching footsteps interrupted her thoughts. She sprang up, alert and ready. She jumped from the chaise and scurried into the bushes in time to see Harley entering the garden. He headed for the storage shed.

What's Harley doing in the garden this late at night? She watched him enter the shed and return to the garden with a spade. He took the spade into the garden Gretchen had planted in early May and began to dig up one of her strawberry plants. From the ground, he retrieved a plastic-wrapped article from under one of her prized strawberry plants. He placed the object on the patio table and returned the spade to the shed.

Gretchen came out of hiding when Harley took the retrieved object into the house. She jumped onto the window box and peered through the kitchen window as Harley opened the oddly shaped plastic packet. A revolver tumbled out onto the counter. She continued to watch as Harley cleaned the gun.

"So that's what happened to my protection," Gretchen mused. "He told me he'd sold it—that he had no more use for it." Then she began to worry. *Why does he need a gun? Is he in trouble?* She remembered the last time she'd seen that particular gun. Harley bought it for her the time he prosecuted a scam artist who threatened to get even. The client claimed Harley reneged on a deal he'd made with him, and Harley, fearing Gretchen might be vulnerable, purchased the gun for her protection. When the scam artist went to prison, Gretchen gave it back to Harley. *Why did he tell me he'd sold it when he didn't?*

The phone rang. Harley stopped cleaning the gun and picked up the phone. She heard him say, "Yeah, I found it [pause]." "Seems in pretty good shape considering its long sleep [pause]." "Yeah, about thirty minutes. Okay, see ya." He hung up and continued cleaning and polishing the revolver at the kitchen counter.

Gretchen pondered the situation. *Is it because of my disappearance from the people world? Tomorrow is Halloween, the night of witches and goblins. Who is this mysterious partner—and why the gun?* First, she feared for Julius. Now, she feared for Harley.

"Ooh, we've got to create that antidote before tomorrow night," she said to no one in particular as she raced across backyards and streets toward the pub. She found that Einstein and Julius had already left, chasing after the professor to the university. Ming had refused to leave. Not knowing what else to do, Gretchen headed for the overpass. Maybe Roscoe will be there. She stubbed her paw on the curb in her rush. "Ouch," she complained.

This running around on cat's paws tires me. And they say, all a cat does is sit around and sleep all day. Hah! I've had sooo little sleep since I became a cat.

Gretchen sat down and licked her bruised paw, then took off again, running as fast as she could, leaping fences and gardens until she reached the underpass. There she crawled behind some shrubbery near the concrete underpass, and waited for one of her cat friends to return. *Maybe I should have gone by Fisherman's Wharf. I might have found Roscoe there with Kristin. He seems to spend an awful lot of time with her.*

She stretched out her long, agile cat's body, wary eyes scanning the nearby parking lot, listening and enjoying the night sounds. A car pulled into a deserted parking lot across the road. Its lights shone brightly for a moment, then disappeared. Silence returned. Gretchen dozed as she waited. She'd already discovered that being a cat required frequent catnaps. Minutes later, she sensed movement nearby, and her cat antennae sailed into full alert mode. Hearing voices, she slipped deeper into the shrubbery. The voices became angry, disturbing her solitude. She peeked out from behind her secluded spot.

Then it happened. In one quick movement, a figure pulled away, and Gretchen saw the flash of a knife and heard the muffled thud of a body dropping to the ground. A car drove by, its headlights flashing on a scene close by Gretchen. The man with the knife panicked. He ducked under the overpass, tossing his weapon into the shrubbery and barely missing Gretchen as she scrunched behind a bush against the concrete. She closed her eyes—afraid the killer might detect her presence—then opened them as she heard the footsteps running toward the parking lot.

A couple walking across the bridge leaned over and shone a flashlight on Gretchen. Blinded, she scampered away and the light followed her. "Only a cat," a voice said, and the couple continued their journey. After they leave, Gretchen heard footsteps running toward the parking lot. A car door slammed, and an engine roared. The lone car in the parking lot departed. Gretchen raced to investigate.

"Please, God," she prayed, "don't let it be Harley." But she'd never seen this man before. *Maybe Einstein knows him. He meets a lot of people at Shaman's.*

Gretchen raced for home. She had to be sure Harley wasn't the other man. *What if it is Harley—and the man he called is the dead man? Oh, dear, I don't know if I can stand being a cat much longer. It's sooo frustrating!* She found Roscoe and Kristin rummaging in an overflowing garbage can behind the cats' favorite restaurant.

As soon as Gretchen approached, Kristin takes off. "Did I scare her off?" asked Gretchen.

"Nah, she had to go home. Time to watch *Tom and Jerry* with the kids."

"What?" *Hmm, there's more to this cat business than I realize.* She looked at Roscoe. Compared to Gretchen and her immaculately maintained self, Roscoe's rough, untidy fur could never be termed *slick* no matter how much grooming it got. Tonight was no exception. He looked scruffy. *No wonder Kristin left.*

"Roscoe," Gretchen informed the raggle-taggle tomcat, "I witnessed a murder tonight."

"Oh? Did you recognize the killer?" he asked, pausing over a delectable portion of leftover salmon he silently thanked some generous customer for leaving. Roscoe eyed her with suspicion, chewing the piece of salmon in his jaws. He believed Gretchen to have a terrific imagination—also exceptionally acute senses. Maybe having been *humanoid* did that to cats. He decided to go along with her fantasy.

"No, but I'm on my way home. I want to be sure Harley isn't involved."

"What do you want me to do?" Roscoe asked, wondering if she had plans to track the killer.

"Would you help me rescue the knife?" Gretchen asked. "I pushed it way into the bushes to hide it, but it's too heavy for me to carry. I need your help."

"Me?" Roscoe asked. "You ask for my help?" He eyed her with suspicion.

"Yes." Gretchen's eyes tear up. She sat down to wait. Roscoe watched her.

"Really, you're entirely too polite for a cat," Roscoe mewed around the salmon clutched in his paws. "You must be more aggressive. All us cats are, you know."

Gretchen ignored his comment.

"Well, at least, let me finish my salmon." He motioned toward the salmon. "Aren't you having any?" He tempted her, pushing a piece of salmon in front of her. "It's delicious."

Gretchen looked at the salmon. She hadn't eaten tonight. "Well," she conceded, "just a bit while I'm waiting. We really can't afford to waste time." She tasted the morsel Roscoe pushed toward her. "Hmm, that is good, a delectable flavor. Wonder what seasoning the chef uses?" The two greedily finish off the salmon.

Half an hour lapsed before Gretchen remembered the knife. "Oh, my goodness, Roscoe, we've got to hurry. What if someone's already found it?"

Roscoe pulled himself away. "I'm sorry, Gretchen. We should have saved the knife first instead of being so greedy. Let's go."

"It's probably already too late," admitted Gretchen. "Poor Harley!" The two cats head back toward the overpass.

"What do you mean, poor Harley?" Roscoe meowed, trailing along behind Gretchen. "Is he one of the men you saw?"

"I don't know, but he has a gun."

Roscoe stopped and stared at her. "We're looking for a knife. Isn't that what you said?"

Gretchen stopped running, her front paw poised in midair. "Oh, that's right. It couldn't have been Harley, could it? Unless—"

"Unless what?"

"Nothing," she mewed. "Let's hurry. Damn you and your salmon dinner!"

"Me? Seems you enjoyed it pretty much too." Roscoe stopped to pull a plastic bag free that had blown against the fence. He locked the sack in his jaws.

Then, leaping in tandem, the two cats scampered away to the scene of the crime. They found the knife where Gretchen had hidden it. After a few failed attempts, the two succeeded in bagging the knife—Gretchen holding the bag open with the help of a nearby rock, and Roscoe nosing the knife into position and into the bag.

Julius and Einstein, having failed in their mission to locate ingredients for the potion, espy Gretchen and Roscoe at the foot of the embankment, and rush down to investigate.

"Einstein," Roscoe bragged to the Siamese, "look what we found."

"A knife? Collecting souvenirs, are you? What do you plan to do with it?"

Roscoe shifted the blame to Gretchen. "It's her idea. She seems to think it's important."

Einstein turned to Gretchen. "Why do you need a knife, Gretchen? Last time I looked, you were still a cat." Gretchen looked at Roscoe in disgust. He ignored her.

Suddenly, a shout is heard from the bridge. All the cats go into alert mode. Someone had discovered the body. Einstein and Julius raced to investigate, and Gretchen and Roscoe struggled to drag the knife back to the safety of the bushes. Gretchen nears panic stage.

"Let Einstein handle this, Gretchen," Roscoe told her. "He'll know what to do." When Einstein returned, he faced the two cats. "You two know something about that body someone found up there?" he asked.

Gretchen looked at Roscoe. "Meow," she said.

"Don't look at me," Roscoe answered. "I was only helping."

"Gretchen?" Einstein accused. "Where did you get this knife, and why are you hanging on to it when it is obviously the murder weapon?"

Gretchen confessed, giving Einstein a hasty description of her adventure under the overpass. "I witnessed the murder and found the knife, Einstein. But I can't let the police find it 'til I know for sure Harley's not involved." Her blue cat eyes welled up in tears. "Please, Einstein. It may have his fingerprints on it."

Einstein made a hasty decision. He looked at the sack containing the evidence, nodded to Julius, and they grabbed the sack. Between the two of them, they tossed the knife into the Cat Monger's cache of memorable keepsakes. Relieved, Gretchen raced for home, hoping to find Harley tucked in their bed fast asleep, mercifully unaware and innocent of Gretchen and her excursions.

*   *   *

A nearly full moon lit the path as Gretchen sneaked home, her heart pounding, afraid Harley would not be there. She passed the hole in her garden where she'd seen Harley digging up the gun—a gun she thought he'd sold years ago—and gave it a cursory glance before entering Amber's doggy door.

Once inside she listened for noises or movement. Amber, asleep in her basket, opened one eye, then went back to sleep. Hearing nothing, Gretchen moved farther inside the house, racing upstairs. She crept into the bedroom—their bedroom where Harley now slept alone—and jumped on her dresser. Seeing a sleeping Harley in bed, she suppressed a desire to crawl in beside him.

Her cat eyes penetrated the darkness. That's when she saw the bottle on her dresser—set on a sheet of white paper with writing on it. Jumping on the dresser, she recognized the incantation that fell from the cookbook Einstein found on the professor's desk. Believing it to be the antidote that would reverse her undignified existence in the cat world, she moved in closer to read the prescription on the bottle. *Did Harley kill for this bottle?*

She put out one paw and tried to pick up the bottle, but only managed to upset it. She thought about knocking it off the dresser, and rolling it down the long steps, but didn't want to awaken Harley. She left the bottle on the dresser and jumped down onto the carpet. *Finding the gun and getting rid of it is more important than facing the impossible task of opening a bottle with only cat paws. I might break the bottle and all would be lost—the potion worthless.*

Gretchen raced downstairs, looking in all the places Harley might possibly have stored the gun, but couldn't find it anywhere. Frustrated, she resumed her spot on the chaise lounge knowing she wouldn't sleep much that night. She contented herself by keeping an unrelenting vigil over the garden—particularly the disturbed plot of ground where Harley dug up the gun. Occasionally, she catnapped, welcoming the opportunity to rest her eyes.

Sensing movement, she opened one dilated blue eye in time to observe Julius moving stealthily along the garden fence. She watched him as he crept along the fence, marveling at the symmetry of his movements, like a cat dancing to an unheard melody. Silently he jumped off the fence onto the chaise beside Gretchen. She transmitted a mental question to him. "You hear what happened?" she asked.

"I did," transmitted Julius.

"I found the potion," she purred silently.

"Where is it?" he purred back.

"On my dresser, in my bedroom."

Gretchen turned to look in Julius's green eyes. *He's really quite handsome; that is, if I were really a cat.* "I left it there. I'm more concerned about the gun. I can't find it"

"You didn't take any of the potion?" Gretchen swore he actually smiled when he asked that. "Getting to like being a cat, are you?"

"Cool it, cat. That'll be the day." She sniffed her displeasure.

"Then why?"

"Afraid, I suppose. What if it works? How could I explain what's been going on?" Gretchen laid her face on her front paws. "We've got to find the gun. No one's safe until we do. Besides"—she raised her face and turned to Julius—"how can I be sure the bottle of potion and the recipe are the same?"

"Probably isn't," Julius answered. "Halloween's tomorrow. Didn't the professor say he wouldn't have it 'til then?"

"I know." She turned to the black cat, concern in her blue eyes. "Halloween. Julius, you know how dangerous that day is for black cats. What will you do?"

Julius's eyes twinkled. "I plan to take a certain white cat to the witch's coven for protection—a sort of good-luck charm, so to speak."

Gretchen stretched to her fullest and glared at Julius. "How dare you!" she hissed and slapped at him with a sheathed claw. "I'm not your Lady Luck."

Julius caught the paw and pulled her down. "Oh, come now," he purred. "Admit it, we could make beautiful music together . . . you and me."

Gretchen shivered. The night had suddenly turned chilly.

*   *   *

Chapter Ten

A likely impossibility is always preferable to an unconvincing possibility.
—Aristotle from *Poetics*

Gretchen and Julius are awakened by the sound of someone opening the garden gate. In unison, they jumped from the chaise and hid under a lilac bush by the side of the house, peering in the direction of the sound. A man entered the garden, walking directly to the hole Harley dug in the garden and retrieved the gun that had miraculously been returned to its original hiding place. *No wonder I couldn't find the gun in the house, Harley put it back in the garden.* Pulling something from his jacket pocket, the man dropped an object into the hole. Using his hands, he replaced the disturbed strawberry plant, tapping the soil firmly around the plant. When he finished, he quietly left the same way he'd arrived. Julius and Gretchen immediately entered conference mode, hoping to contact Einstein. But Einstein doesn't answer.

"He's out of range," decided Julius.

"What do we do?" asked Gretchen to Julius, aware they are now on their own.

Julius thought a while before he said, "There are two of us and one of him. I could follow the interloper and you could retrieve the gun."

"We don't know if it's a gun he dug up, Julius. Let's follow the guy. We can worry about what he planted later. It won't go anywhere."

Julius looked at her with pride. "I knew your brains would come in handy," he praised her. "Come on, let's go." And the two flew out the garden gate tracking the fast disappearing lights of a pickup truck.

"Julius, I can't go much farther." Gretchen implored a few blocks away. "I don't have your stamina. Maybe you better go on ahead." She sat on her haunches to rest. "I'll go back and wait for you."

Julius slowed for a moment, transmitting his sympathies when the truck stopped at the only stoplight in town. Rested momentarily, Julius and Gretchen caught up with the truck and the two cats scrambled onto the truck bed.

"No sense running when we can ride," Julius said as the two cats struggled to catch their breath. The run had affected Gretchen most, not being as used to exercise as Julius. As the two positioned themselves under the cab window—Gretchen to the right, and Julius to the left—Gretchen glanced into the rearview mirror. She recognized the driver.

"Oh, Julius," she said. "It's Shaman." Julius looked skeptical. "Look, if you don't believe me." Julius did.

"Why on earth would he be digging in your garden?" he asked.

Shaman caught Julius peering in at him through his rearview mirror. He continued to drive down the darkened lanes toward his home. Musing at the versatility of animals in hitching rides, a thought hit him. *Could one o' them cats be the one Professor Ipswitch be alookin' for? Might be a bounty on its head. I'll give 'im a call.*

On reaching home, he pulled the truck into his open garage and immediately hit the button to close the garage door. Julius, realizing what happened, jumped from the truck bed and scuttled under the door before it closed completely. Gretchen—tired and not as alert as Julius—took a second too long to react and got caught in Shaman's garage.

Shaman grabbed the white cat, intending to bag her until he could contact the professor. He picked her up by the scruff of the neck, rendering Gretchen helpless. That's when Shaman felt the chain around her neck.

"What's this?" he asked, examining the collar around the cat's neck. "Well, b'gorra, what do you know. I do believe they be real diamonds."

And for the second time in her short cat life, Gretchen found herself tied up in the limited confines of a gunnysack. She put her head on her paws and wept real cat tears. Gretchen did not make it home that night.

*   *   *

Roscoe, partaking of his favorite pastime—eating—is interrupted in the middle of a delectable dinner of crab pasta by the appearance of Kristin. Kristin, the British tabby who complicated his bachelorhood, expressed disapproval of his recent interest in Gretchen. She cornered Roscoe behind the Fisherman's Wharf and snarled at him.

"Look," Roscoe explained to Kristin, "she's a people cat. I've no interest in her at all. I'm merely trying to help her get oriented to living in the cat world. She doesn't know how to avoid *humanoid* pitfalls."

"I should warn her about you then," Kristin countered, nosing a piece of crab that had slipped from Roscoe's mouth as he turned to defend himself. "You've never been a good judge of character." She mouthed another morsel of crab as she continued to pick at Roscoe about his shortcomings.

"Kristin," Roscoe consoled her, "you know Gretchen means nothing to me. Surely you understand. She'll return to her own way of life someday, and our lives will return to normal."

Kristin melted somewhat. Roscoe could always do that to her. Ever since she'd met him, his raggle-taggle, totally British countenance attracted Kristin as had no other cat. Certainly not Einstein with his snooty ways, nor Julius, an alley cat if there ever were one. No self-respecting female was safe from his catting ways. He had absolutely no respect for decent felines.

"She's disappeared, you know," Roscoe informed Kristin.

Kristin stopped eating. "She returned to the people world?"

"Don't know. If she's become a *humanoid* again, we'd have no way of knowing," Roscoe surmised. "She was last seen with Shaman. Maybe he dumped her somewhere."

"Good riddance," said Kristin. "She's entirely too consumed with herself and her own welfare. Even Julius fell under her spell." *Ah, retribution, how sweet it is.* A sudden thought struck her. "If Einstein and Julius find the antidote and discover the potion, we may all be subjected to the *humanoid* world. I know you wouldn't resist becoming a *humanoid* if you had a chance." She turned to look at him and realized her stab in the dark bore some validity.

Roscoe stopped eating long enough to face his antagonist. "Dont tell me you wouldn't be the least bit curious, my dear Kristin," he said snuggling cozily against her. "Bet you'd make a honey of a female *m' cherie.*" He used his favorite word for a *femme fatale.*

"Hmm, maybe," Kristin agreed.

＊　　＊　　＊

Meanwhile back at the pub, Shaman checked out the gun he'd dug up from Gretchen's strawberry patch. Harley had concealed it in a plastic cover after cleaning it. *Exactly what I need . . . so nice of Harley to find it for me . . .*

*strange man . . . all he wants in return is a signed picture of Professor Ipswitch
and his partner. Wonder why? Ah well, none of my business.*

He dug into the gunnysack, exposing Gretchen's head and tied the
sack firmly around her neck with a piece of string. He then removed the
collar from around the neck of the helpless cat and checked the validity of
the stones on a piece of glass. *Ah, that's what I thought—real diamonds.* He
untied the string and dropped Gretchen back into the gunnysack, placed
the necklace in a small jewelry box, and tossed the sack and Gretchen into
the back of his pickup.

Once back at the pub, Shaman dumped the sack in the back storeroom
and headed for a telephone. For the second time in her short cat life, Gretchen
found her nightmare repeated. She struggled to get out of the sack, her sharp
teeth trying to break through the heavy burlap, all the while, sending silent
cat messages to Ming, Einstein, Julius, or anyone who would listen.

*   *   *

Julius watched Harley leave for work early the next morning, then
scampered through Amber's doggie door. He raced upstairs. The bottle
was still on the dressing table, but Gretchen was nowhere to be seen. Julius
worried. *Where is she?* Racing back downstairs, he headed for **Shaman's Pub**.
Maybe Ming knows. But Ming hadn't seen Shaman, although she did give
Julius some interesting information.

"If you look in the back storeroom, you'll find your white cat," she
told Julius. "Better hurry though. Professor Ipswitch is on his way to pick
her up."

"You sure?" asked Julius. "Why would Shaman turn her over to the
enemy?"

"I'm not sure the professor is the enemy," Ming said. "Isn't he the one
with the potion to return her to her own world?" She looked closely at
Julius. "You're smitten with her, aren't you? You want to keep her in the cat
world."

Julius had to admit Ming's guess hit close to his heart. He hadn't realized
how fond he'd become of Gretchen. "How do I get into the storeroom?"
he asked Ming.

Ming shrugged her cat shoulders and shook her head. "If you must,"
she said, "follow me." She took a quick glance at Shaman behind the bar
before she said, "Meet me at the back door. I'll let you in from there. We'll
look too suspicious if we trail through the pub together."

Julius departed through the customer door, turned the corner, and waited by the back door where Shaman's white truck was parked. A few minutes later, Ming pushed the door open from the inside, and Julius entered.

"Follow me." Ming led Julius by a circuitous route that ended in the pub storeroom. She had her own secret path to the storeroom without having to go through the pub. They found Gretchen still struggling to bite her way out of her gunnysack prison.

"Oh no, not again, Gretchen. Is that you in that sack?" Julius scolded. "Can't leave you alone for a minute, can I? You get yourself all tied up again. Haven't you learned yet? You can't trust *humanoids?*"

"It isn't *my* choice," Gretchen sputtered between bites. "Shaman stole my necklace and dumped me here. I don't know what he plans to do to me with me. My opinion of him is slowly disintegrating."

"Shaman?" asked Julius as he gave the last rip to free Gretchen. "Why on earth would he steal your collar? Is it worth stealing?"

Gretchen tumbled out on the floor of the storeroom, shaking herself and licking at her ruffled fur. "The crazy nut thinks they're real diamonds." She looked around her. "Where am I?"

"In Shaman's storeroom," Julius answered automatically, his mind still on the necklace. "Are they real diamonds?" he asked.

"Impossible. Harley gave me that necklace for my birthday. He can't afford diamonds." Gretchen continued grooming her white fur coat as Julius watched.

"Well, whatever," he said. "We have to get you out of here. Shaman has already called Professor Ipswitch to tell him he's found you. He'll be here soon." He led Gretchen outside by the same circuitous route Ming led him in, but instead of following Ming into the pub, Julius led her out the back door and into the alley.

"Getting tied up is becoming a habit with you, isn't it?" Julius commented as the two scurried home to safety.

"Sorta looks that way, doesn't it?" she purred, her blue eyes shining their gratitude. Once home, Gretchen jumped onto the chaise and turned to face Julius who had jumped up beside her. She placed an appreciative paw on his. "Anyway, thanks for the rescue."

"It'll cost you," Julius purred lasciviously as the two cats cuddled down for a well-deserved nap—a portrait in black and white.

*　　*　　*

Later, awake and rested, the two scoot through Amber's doggie door and tear up the stairs at full speed. The bottle Gretchen had seen still sat on her dressing table. The two eyed the bottle from all angles, trying to decide how best to accomplish the task at hand.

"I think we can handle it," Julius said, looking over the situation. "But you'll need to use your mouth for something more than complaining."

Gretchen glared, ignoring his snide comment. "It's too heavy." *How can such a kind, considerate cat be so sassy at times?* "I tried, and merely succeeded in upsetting the bottle. We need something to wrap it in, then we can drag it."

Julius conceded, and Gretchen looked around to see what they could use. Her eyes fell on her makeup pouch on the dresser. "This might do it, Julius. Help me dump it out."

Julius shook his head. "Too flimsy," he decided. "We need to pad the bottle—that is, if we want to get it across town in one-piece."

"You're right." Gretchen jumped down and headed for the bathroom. "This should do it," she said dragging back a monogrammed guest towel and dropping it in front of Julius for his approval.

"Mighty fancy," Julius commented. "Now, how about a little help. I can't go it alone."

Gretchen jumped up on the dresser. "Tell me what you want me to do."

"Take hold of the pouch on your side, and I'll take hold of the pouch on this side, and when I say *dump*, you pick up your end, and I'll pick up mine. Ready?"

"Ready," purred Gretchen, and simultaneously the two dumped her makeup onto the top of the dresser. They stuffed the guest towel inside the empty pouch and then tackled the bottle. Julius pushed it close to the pouch.

"Oops," he said as the bottle starts to roll.

"Careful." Gretchen admonished. She pushed the open pouch to a different angle so the bottle would roll into the pouch rather than off the dresser. Successful the second time, Julius nudged the bottle into the pouch with his paws. Mission accomplished, they pulled the pouch drawstring with their teeth.

"So far, so good," Julius breathed. "The hard part is over. Now to get it off the dresser with breaking or spilling it. Any ideas?"

In answer, Gretchen jumped off the dresser and ran to the bed, pulling at the feather pillow on her side of the bed. She grabbed a corner, her teeth tearing the cover.

"Hey, okay. Can you handle it alone?" Julius asked from the top of the dresser. Gretchen flipped her tail in response. *Amazing how expressive a tail can be. Saved words.*

Dragging the pillow off the bed, she maneuvered it close to the dresser while Julius nosed the makeup pouch slowly off the dresser in the vicinity of the pillow. "Catch," he said as the pouch dropped from the dresser, hit the pillow, and rolled off onto the floor.

Julius jumped down, and the two cats grabbed the pouch by its drawstrings then bounced it down the long carpeted staircase through the doggie door and into the backyard. They hid the pouch behind a lilac bush to be retrieved later and headed for a meeting of the Cat Monger's League.

Chapter Eleven

We do not understand Hope until confronted with doubts.

All Hallows Day is an important time of the year for cats, a time to pull together to ensure a safe Halloween for all. The cats had organized the Cat Monger's League so that all cats, regardless of breed or color, could have an equal chance in the world of *humanoids*. All year long they'd collected their arsenal of precious items to ensure their safety on Halloween Night when night goblins and ghosts were free to roam the earth. Sometimes the cats had to buy their way out of weird situations in order to survive another year.

Tonight, Einstein listened to Gretchen and her tale of woe—her escapade in the gunnysack, her stolen collar, and her rescue by Julius. "You were supposed to look after Gretchen," Einstein chided Julius. "Why did you leave her alone in the truck? She hasn't yet acquired danger-sensing skills."

"I thought she was right behind me until the garage door slammed," Julius said. "Even then, I knew Shamus to be her friend, and I didn't worry. He surprised me."

"Doubtless, she did, too, but in this instance, he proved not to be a friend."

Julius eyed the ground and flipped his tail in embarrassment. He said nothing, knowing he was amiss in exposing Gretchen to additional trauma.

"We protect our felines," Einstein continued. "They perform admirable services for us tomcats, and it's our duty as males to care for them." He turned his attention from Julius and faced the other cats.

"Tonight," he informed the ragtag crew, "we've been requested to put in an appearance at the Witches' Coven. I hope you all know how to protect yourselves, for it can sometimes be dangerous." He glared at Julius as though reinforcing his charges of ineptness.

Gretchen took pity on him. "I'm sorry, Julius," Gretchen said. "I didn't mean to get you in trouble. I *will* learn. I've nearly got that *slick slide* down pat, but I didn't think I'd need it with Shaman." She looked at Julius. "Do you think I really had a diamond collar?"

"If it's true, your necklace is probably in some pawnshop by now. What say we check a few before closing time?" Roscoe offered.

"Could we?" Gretchen turned her blue eyes to Roscoe in gratitude.

"Sure," agreed Julius, "but first, let's practice your yowls. You need to have some ammunition to defend yourself. Let me hear you do it."

"Meoow," said Gretchen in her loudest voice.

"Not good enough," Julius warned. "Here, watch me." He arched his back, exposed his claws, and bared his sharp fangs. Then he let go with a *yeeooww* that rent the air with an earsplitting crescendo. Julius sat back on his haunches and purred his self-satisfaction. "That's how," he said.

"Ohhh," answered Gretchen, "I can do that." She aped Julius's tenor performance with an equally ferocious performance of her own in a high soprano key.

"Now, you've got it," Julius approved. "You know that, you can go anywhere. Helps too if you add a little *spit* to that *yeow*. Scares the nastiest of felons—cat spit does. It's our poison, you know, and it can kill."

"Why didn't you teach me this before?" Gretchen asked. "I'd still have my necklace."

"We sorta like you the way you are—sweet and innocent," Roscoe said

"Yeah," said Julius, "but in this world, it's not the safest way to be. Come on. Let's go check some pawnshops."

And the three cats sneaked around buildings, down back alleys, and over wooden fences, ducking into selected hockshops, but their trip proved futile. They returned to the overpass because, as Julius reminded them, "We've a date tonight, at the Witches' Coven."

And Gretchen, feeling brave and invulnerable, trotted alongside Julius and Roscoe into the night air ready for an exciting adventure. They headed for Cat Monger's Cave—the entrance to a night of terror.

Chapter Twelve

Happiness comes through doors you didn't know you left open.

Shaman set out for the coven meeting wearing the clothes of a seventeenth-century fakir, an ancient pistol tucked in his belt. His silvery hair blew in the wind as he piloted the horse-drawn chariot down the narrow, twisting streets of Dublin. He visited his home once a year on Halloween—the one day he could go back in time—the one night a year he could enjoy the wilds of Ireland and be with his one true love, Elise. The moon darted back and forth among the dark clouds as Shaman headed for the graveyard and his rendezvous with his Elise.

Now, it isn't that Shaman is not a satisfied man—what with his American pub, his wife and his wee *bairns*—but for this one night a year, he achieved his nirvana. Shaman steered the span of black horses through the wide iron gates of the cemetery, opened wide once a year for the annual meeting of little people, the imaginary people of Ireland. Shaman could hardly wait. The horses seemed to crawl although he knew they did their best.

Centuries ago when he first knew Elise, he'd made a pact with the devil in exchange for eternal life for himself and Elise, but somewhere among the good intentions and incantations, he'd lost Elise. All his eternal lives since consisted of his efforts to find her again. He never knew what happened— what went wrong—or why the devil tried to atone for his failure by allowing Shaman to visit Elise once a year on Halloween night. Shaman treasured these visits, but had to forfeit his life and the lives of others to the devil in order to be with her.

As centuries passed, the devil took over more and more control of the country. Except for Halloween night, when he availed Shaman with his visit to Elise, the devil pretty much left him to his own devices. He had more important ventures to occupy his time. Evil had become a way of life in the world, and the devil and his minions worked hard to keep it that way. Tonight, Shaman would discuss with Elise his plans to rid himself of the devil's curse. He had the equipment he needed to reverse the original pact, but it would take two to accomplish this and Elise may not agree.

Then he saw her, perched on her tombstone, as young and beautiful as ever. Her long, tawny hair flowing over a gown of floating chiffon, her blue eyes sparkling under black lashes, and her smile—the smile that lit up his world and caused his heart to beat so rapidly he felt a need to hold it still. He placed his hand on his chest to steady the pounding, fearful of its leaving his body. When Elise caught sight of him, she flew to him, arms outstretched, and the two renewed their acquaintance.

*   *   *

Meanwhile, Professor Ipswitch and Harley also had plans of their own for Halloween. They met the professor's accomplice in the woods behind the professor's cottage. The gnome-shaped little man pulled back some shrubbery, and the three entered what appeared to Harley to be an oversized rabbit hole. Inside, a vast cold marsh with coiling weeds greeted them. Tough snaky growth held out splintery arms that attempted to grip and trip him, as though ready to pull him into its depths. The place of darkness reminded Harley of Erebus, he of the underworld on his way to Hades. He shuddered. The gnome-like little man led them into an area where the trees grew so thick and the undergrowth so dense that one could scarcely pass through. But the little man located a path through the overgrown woods, a deeply scooped-out hollow place that ran the entire length of the forest. Moving down the gloomy trail, the three made slow progress, seeming to penetrate deeper into the forest. As the air became more and more suffocating, Harley felt as though he would scream. *Will we ever get out of here?* He swore he heard thumping sounds overhead.

What's that? The little man leading the way stopped and mumbled something only the professor could hear, and the two looked back at Harley. Harley waited while the two make some sort of decision regarding him.

"We have to chance it," the professor finally decided. "He can't do anything. He's powerless out of his own environment." The little man mumbled again.

They continued their journey until suddenly an opening in the forest appeared directly in front of them. The little man exited the opening, and Harley and the professor followed close behind. Beyond the opening, Harley saw a large expanse of clear land that appeared to be on the edge of a graveyard, a very active graveyard.

Little people danced all around, meeting and greeting each other as though at a festival. Unobserved at the edge of the forest, the three newcomers witnessed a reunion between Shaman and his Elise, and Harley realized the thumping sound he heard came from the stomping of the four-in-hand leading Shaman's ancient chariot.

"Where is this place, Professor?" Harley asked, looking around in amazement. He felt as though he'd been dropped into another century. Professor Ipswitch, busy viewing the scene transpiring in the graveyard, ignored him. Even the gnome-like little man seemed engrossed in watching the reunion between Shaman and Elise.

Harley pulled at the professor's sleeve. "What do I call him?" Harley asked to the professor, indicating the gnome-like figure in front of them.

"His name is Morgan," said the professor, "a very great magician from the House of Kahn. You can learn a lot from him tonight. Pay attention."

"Morgan, the magician for the King of Tara? How can that be? He existed centuries ago." Harley looked behind him and noticed that the entrance to the forest had closed behind them.

The professor ignored his question. When he did finally speak, he said, "Morgan has an exceptional ability to enter and exit past lives, not only his own, but all souls. I, myself, am privileged to enter once a year because of my acquaintance with the keeper of lost souls."

"Lost souls? Weird." He looked hard at the professor before he asked, "Where are we? Have we traveled back in time?"

"You do not need to know. Tonight, you are here as my guest, but only because I need your assistance."

"My assistance?" questioned Harley. "You appear to be an expert in the field of *Transmogrification*. What are your plans for me?"

"You want the antidote, do you not?" asked the professor turning to Harley. "Where else do you expect to find the source?"

"You came here for the antidote? The one you bought from the witch?"

"Yes, the same one, and if you are unwilling to participate in its creation and brewing, you may never return the way you came."

"I'm not complaining . . . merely interested. I will continue," said Harley, remembering the whitewashed skulls he'd seen along their path. *Is this my destiny?* The three continued their surveillance of Shaman. For Harley, at least, they had headed into unknown territory.

"He has the power," Professor Ipswitch advised Harley. "Do not underestimate him. If anyone can bring Gretchen back, it is he. We follow his lead."

"Lead on, I see no other way," agreed Harley, fearful he could not find his way back alone.

*   *   *

"Elise," Shaman said, enamored by the fury of their reunion. "I have a plan for us to be together for all eternity, but I'll need your help." He took her by the hand, and led her to his chariot.

"But your wife and *bairns*?" Elise's blue eyes showed her bewilderment. "How can we be together without causing misery to them?"

"Don't be worryin' about that, Elise." He led her to the waiting chariot. "Get in," he instructed, helping her climb onto the high-seated chariot. "We've only one night to do this . . . lest we need wait another year. I don't know about ye, my dear, but annual visits be not enough for me."

Shaman climbed up beside Elise and grabbed the reins of the four spirited horses. "I have the evocation we need to get out of my pact with the devil."

Elise looked at him in admiration. "What has happened, my love?"

"Remember Professor Ipswitch? Well, he charged me an arm and a leg for the potion, but I had a bit o' good luck, a diamond necklace that accidentally fell into my possession."

He turned to Elise. "It has to work, this time, my beloved . . . it's our last chance to right a wrong. Evil has spread over the earth faster than even the devil believed possible. He gets lax when he loses control of his minions, to our advantage." He kissed her. "It's now or never, Elise."

"Professor Ipswitch?" asked Elise. "Is he the same Professor Ipswitch who sold you the first incantation so many centuries ago?"

"The one and only," Shaman assured her. "I fair went into shock when he entered my pub, but he didn't appear to recognize me. I have made good use of him because of that. Nevertheless, his evil cannot be allowed to rule our world. He must go. He has infested my life for the last time." Elise peeked at him, her eyes sparkling in understanding, and kissed him on his ruddy cheek. "My darling, I've waited so long for this time. Of course, I will help you, now that I know your heart is true." She checked the packages in the wagon behind them, and asked, "You have everything?"

"I do. I've spent days collectin' the required ingredients. Tonight, we rid the devil of his power. Let us go." The chariot and *four-in-hand* tore through the iron gates, Elise clutching her lover's waist to keep from falling, Shaman's strong hands directing the chariot. He stopped at the entrance of a deserted barn outside Dublin—the place where it all began.

Halting his team, Shaman sat and stared at the structure, dumbfounded by its prime state of repair after so many centuries. He couldn't believe it still survived, untouched by time and the elements. *Well, why not? Is it not himself who is the miracle—transported into the seventeenth century by the will of the devil? The barn remained—as it always has—dark and dreary with an aura of evil.*

Shaman collected the many mysterious packages he'd brought from the rear of the chariot, and the two enter the barn. He proceeded to arrange the contents according to the instructions of Professor Ipswitch, remembering a similar scene many centuries ago. Tonight, he would reverse that procedure. Instead of the devil, he would call forth an angel to remove the devil's incantation. Instead of darkness there would be light. Shaman lit a glowing fire in the middle of the room—a fire huge enough to reflect a shimmering light and fill every corner of the room—from floor to rafters.

The scenery set, he filled a basin with sparkling water secured from a nearby brook. He hung a lantern from an overhead beam in such a way as to reflect on the surface of the water. From his pocket, he pulled out the professor's potion—the very potion that eluded Gretchen and Einstein—and began to sprinkle it into the water. He repeated an incantation—not the one Professor Ipswitch gave him—but one he believed would reverse evil. He instructed Elise to do the same.

Spirit whose breath is in the four winds, breathe, breathe on me.

Then from his pack of supplies, he pulled out a bottle of red wine, added a healthy dose of potion to the wine, and poured the mixture into two glasses. He set them by the fireside as he once again dug into his pack of treasures. This time he pulled out a box and poured its contents onto the roaring fire. The fire flared, casting orange flames to the ceiling and illuminating brilliant light into every corner of the room.

Shaman picked up one glass of wine from its place on the hearth and handed it to Elise. Elise hesitated a moment then accepted the offering, her soft eyes puzzled. Entranced by the proceedings, Shaman glimpsed her moment of uncertainty. He hastened to reassure her.

"If we do this right," he told her, "we will be able to see an angel. The angel will speak to us and tell us how to right the devil's wrong." He lifted his glass to hers. "Gaze into the water, my dear, as you drink the wine," he instructed. The two drank of the bitter wine, all the while, gazing deeply into the basin of sparkling water.

Then Shaman pulled out two silk shawls from his pack of goodies. One he draped lovingly over Elise's entire being, refilling the glasses with the remaining wine. He wrapped himself in the other silk shawl and handed Elise one of the glasses of wine before partaking of the remaining glass of wine.

"Drink it all," Shaman advised her. "To the last drop, then we wait."

Elise did as instructed, and the two quaffed their second draught as they sat in silence before the roaring fire, awaiting the arrival of their guardian angel.

Chapter Thirteen

Such as we are made of, such we be.
—Shakespeare

Gretchen followed Julius through the Cat Monger's Cave into a labyrinth of circuitous routes, any of which could cause Gretchen to lose her way, but she followed Julius, confident he knew the way to wherever they headed. The route they traveled reminded her of a haunted house she'd visited, decorated by the PTA to scare the kids on Halloween night although the cobwebs and bleached skulls she saw along this path were definitely real.

The spidery vegetation gave Gretchen an eerie, surreal feeling, and she swore some of the foliage moved in uncanny ways as though it had lives of its own. Gretchen moved in silence along the path to *somewhere* with her newfound friends. Twice rescued by her feline friends, she felt a kinship to the cat world she'd never before appreciated. In fact, as a *humanoid,* Gretchen seldom gave cats a second thought, preferring the friendliness of Amber and the dog world to the haughty cat world. She had definitely developed an understanding of how the feline mind worked and a much deeper appreciation of the cat world since she'd become a feline. Cunning in the ways of survival and independent of *humanoids,* they accepted few *humanoids* into their world.

Totally lost in thought, Gretchen failed to notice that the other cats were far ahead. She hurried to catch up, but suddenly realized she faced a dilemma. There were too many paths, and she could detect no cat trails. Uncertain which path the others took, she panicked and began to meow in her loudest voice.

"Meow, Meow, where are you?" she called plaintively, and sat down to wait. No one answered. "Use logic," she scolded herself. "You're not a cat, you know." She eyed the two likely pathways in front of her. The path in one direction looked too overgrown, the other path, less so. Thinking logically, she chose the path of least resistance. Surely the other cats wouldn't attempt the overgrown path. Gretchen didn't realize that no matter which direction she chose, the path would open up—that her chosen path appeared more open only because she faced it.

Moving as rapidly as she could down the clearer path, Gretchen tried to catch up with her friends. Too late, she realized she'd lost her way in a cave that had too many scary paths and no exits. Sniffing the trail, she sensed no feline odors and feared she'd chosen wrong. *I should have sniffed first before I chose a path.* She turned around to retrace her steps, but the path had changed direction, leading her to an opening ahead.

A bright light glimmered in the distance, and she moved cautiously forward toward the light, her cat eyes adjusting to the change. Reaching the opening, she peered around the edge to see if the other cats waited there for her. Instead of her cat friends, Gretchen saw two shrouded figures seated before a roaring fire in a lighted room. No, not a room, more like a medieval barn, complete with a loft filled to capacity with bales of dry hay. A lantern hung from a rusty nail above the rafters, casting a strange light onto a vessel of water placed in front of the fire. Engrossed in a world of their own, the shrouded couple did not notice Gretchen.

Gretchen crept in closer keeping a wary eye on the two figures seated in a trancelike state. Seeing the vessel of water Shaman had prepared and feeling thirsty, she stopped for a drink. She tried not to emit the lapping sound cats were wont to make for fear of alerting the couple of her presence. As she drank her fill from the vessel, she sensed movement from under the shawls and crept behind the couple looking for an exit. *I certainly don't need another humanoid confrontation tonight.*

As she moved away, Gretchen began to feel strange. Her paws had turned to hands, and her tail gone, and she realized her cat persona had begun to disappear without any warning. *It's the water! It must contain the antidote. It's changing me!* One of the shrouded figures moved, and Gretchen recognized the exposed face of Shaman. *What's he doing here?*

Shaman, seeing Gretchen in her transformed state reflected in the water, believed her to be the angel he and Elise awaited. Not wanting to disturb the angel, he quietly nudged Elise, shushing her to silence. And Gretchen, remembering her experience in Shaman's truck, exhibited surprise when Shaman began to speak reverently to her image in the water.

He's asking me to grant his wish? Asking me to release him from the devil's curse so he can be with Elise for all eternity?

Amused, she asked Shaman, "What in heaven's name do you expect from me? You're the one who stole my necklace, and now you want me to grant you your wish? Why ever should I?"

Shaman, continuing to watch the angel image in the water, answered. "Professor Ipswitch has your necklace, his fee for the potion. I needed the potion to break the devil's curse and free Elise and me from eternal life. I didn't know you were an angel. Please forgive me."

"Professor Ipswitch has my necklace? You sold my necklace to him in exchange for a potion?"

"And an ancient pistol," he answered. "Here." He pulled the pistol from his tunic pocket. "It has magic bullets to protect its owner in the *Netherworld.*"

"You fell for that old ploy?" Gretchen asked. "That old relic came out of my strawberry patch. It has no magic, and I have no magic, only a stick I picked up by the fire. I can't destroy your curse, but maybe you can."

"How?" asked Shaman, as he caressed Elise. "You have a plan?"

Elise had returned from her trance and watched the angel's reflection in the water.

"Yes, you must find Magus and his magic drum. He can lead you out of the devil's lair and the evil that surrounds you." She lifted her arm to show him she carried only a stick. "See? No magic wand." But the stick changed. Instead of a stick, she held a sparkling scepter.

"Where the devil did you come from?" she asked the scepter. "Oh well"—accepting the wand as another unexplainable happening in an unaccountable evening—"if I must, I must!"

Gretchen waved the wand over Shaman and Elise, remembering from somewhere in her fairy tale days that that's how magic wands worked.

Gretchen waited to see what magic the wand wrought, staring in wonderment as a dense vapor smoke engulfed the room. Through the smoke, she looked up and saw Einstein, Julius, and Roscoe viewing the scene. She waved the scepter at them; they seemed unfazed by her new persona.

"Follow Einstein," she instructed Shaman. "He will lead you through to the other side."

Shaman rose from the fireside, helping Elise do the same, and drawing her close to his side, instructed her, "Come, my dear. Stay close." He led her to the shield, protecting the cats from the *Netherworld.* Elise disappeared into the smoke and vapors, but Shaman hit a hard surface. He couldn't move beyond the shield.

He panicked. "I can't make it." He lamented, turning to face Gretchen. "What shall I do?"

"Get rid of the pistol," Gretchen answered. "Customs, you know." Shaman dropped the pistol into the water. It disintegrated, and Shaman disappeared into the void.

"Well, what do you know," Gretchen said, stroking the scepter. "It works. Must be my newly acquired feline abilities." She sat down on the hearth, dipped the wand into the water, and asked of the wand, "Harley, I have returned. Where are you?"

A strong gust of wind blew the barn door opened; and Harley, Professor Ipswitch, and Morgan, the gnome like little man, entered the barn. "Where is he?" demanded the professor. "I know he came in here—he and that witch of his." He stopped as he saw Gretchen sitting on the hearth, her gossamer white gown glowing and a sparkling scepter in her hand, looking every bit the angel Shaman conjured with his incantation.

"Is she for real?" he asked Harley, but Harley saw only the Gretchen he knew, not the angel seen by Morgan and the professor. He started toward her, but Gretchen motioned him to step away, apart from Professor Ipswitch and Morgan.

Morgan, knowing instantly what had happened, attempted to creep behind Gretchen, moving toward her as though to push her into the fire. Professor Ipswitch grabbed Gretchen, causing Morgan to lose balance, and the fire swallowed up Morgan instead, pulling him into its bosom. A stunned Harley could only watch as Morgan slowly disintegrated in the blazing fire.

"He's all right," the professor told Harley. "Fire is his nourishment. You've detained him for only a moment. He'll be back." Then he turned to Gretchen. "And you, young lady, your power won't last much longer. It's nearly midnight. You must return from whence you came or be forever trapped in the *Netherworld.*"

Gretchen watched Harley's reaction. "Can you believe that?" she asked him.

"It's Halloween," he said. "Witching hour is nearly over. We must leave before the witches do . . . otherwise we'll be stuck here." Harley checked his watch. "We have fifteen minutes."

In the distance, the drums of Magus could be heard in his annual quest to rid the four corners of heaven from evil. "Come, Harley," Gretchen said. "I can lead you out, but the professor had to find his own way."

"Maybe we can make a deal," the professor appealed to Harley. "You owe me, you know."

"I owe you nothing. Except for you, we wouldn't be here. Why should we help you?"

"I can't go back without you. Please, Gretchen," the professor pleaded, knowing his guide no longer existed. Morgan would not revive until after midnight—too late for him.

But Gretchen didn't listen. She's drawn to an empty bottle discarded by Shaman when he prepared his ritual potion with Elise, the ashes purchased from the proceeds of her necklace. She knew her power had nothing to do with midnight or the witching hour, but lay in some ingredient in that vessel of water—water in which she dipped the stick, and the vessel from which she drank.

Secretly as Harley and the professor argued deals and terms, she filled the bottle with water from the basin and slipped it into her tunic pocket. She dipped the wand into the water once more, tossing the remaining water onto the fire to put it out. But instead of snuffing out the fire, the fire blazed up anew, reaching and engulfing the dry hay in the loft. Panicking, she screamed, and Harley, seeing Gretchen in danger, grabbed her and raced out of the barn.

The two piled into Shaman's chariot as the sound of Magus and his drums grew louder in the distance. The *four-in-hand* stomped their impatience, excited by the sounds around them, and eager to distance themselves from the fire. Professor Ipswitch heard the drums too, but his fear of the fire raging in the ancient barn exceeded his fear of Magus, and he opted to join Gretchen and Harley in the chariot. He pushed them aside and took up the reins himself. The *four-in-hand* tore down the rutted road heading toward the graveyard as he tried to escape Magus who was rapidly closing in on them.

As the chariot neared the *Netherworld* exit, the professor leapt from the wagon and darted toward the opening, blocking the entrance from Gretchen and Harley. "You can't return," he told the pair behind him. "You are doomed to eternity."

Entering the exit from the *Netherworld*, he sealed off their escape route. Gretchen waved her wand, but it didn't work. She's powerless. The escape area remained sealed. Frantic, she remembered the magic water hidden in her tunic pocket, but as she started to take a drink of the potion, Magus appeared before them in all his power and glory. She returned the bottle to the pocket of her gown.

Magus wore a breastplate and helmet of gold. A mantle of blue satin swung from his massive shoulders, and a wide-grooved, blue-hilt sword hung from his silver-studded girth. A sash, slung around his massive neck, held a large purple drum deeply embossed in silver filigree, and in his strong hands, drumsticks made from the dry white bones of a large animal. His drums beat rhythmically, accompanied his songs condemning evil. He commanded a horse-drawn carriage as adorned and ornate as he, and a team of chargers whose thundering hooves barely touched the ground.

"Magus," Gretchen called out to him, "help us. We must return to our world before midnight. Professor Ipswitch deserted us."

"Wave your wand, Gretchen," Magus commanded. "Wave your wand."

Gretchen did as he said, and magically, the seal broke and the entrance opened. Magus entered the exit, and his long tentacles reached in far enough to reel in Professor Ipswitch. He deposited him in Shaman's chariot, and the *four-in-hand*, eager to do Magus's bidding, charged out of the graveyard, manes and tails flying over galloping hooves, back to the *Netherworld* with their cargo, back to the tomb that housed all evildoers of the world.

The professor, shocked at the sudden turn of events, waved and called to Harley and Gretchen from the rear of the chariot. "Harley, I didn't mean it. We can make a deal—we can make a deal!" His voice diminished as the *four-in-hand* raced to the ends of the earth.

Epilogue

Gretchen awakened next morning in her own room, Harley sleeping soundly beside her. She looked at her hands, no longer paws, and felt around her neck for her necklace. *It's gone. I know I wore it. Did I lose it?* She lay back down trying to piece together her scraps of memory. *How did I get here? I surely can't remember.* She thought about the funny-looking man at Shaman's—Professor Ipswitch he called himself. We talked about a love potion Kristin sells in her shop, and he offered me a chance to test his newest invention, *Resurrection. Did Harley bring me home?* She nudged him. He aroused sleepily.

"Harley," she said, "I had the strangest dream last night."

PART II

The Cat Monger's Cave

Trilogy Two

Chapter One

Let the past be content with its self, for man needs forgetfulness as
well as memory.

Shaman's Pub crackled with vitality that cold November morning as **Gretchen Dandrich** hurried to meet **Kristin Sanders** at **The Brass Rail,** Kristin's antique shop, for their weekly lunch date at **Shaman's Pub.** Gretchen had just put the final touches on her new mystery novel that morning. **Harley**, her husband, never bothered to read her stories using the excuse that he had enough reading to do what with law books, writs, depositions, etc., and didn't have time to wander into the realm of fiction. Today, he surprised her by asking to read this one. Maybe Harley half-believed her strange stories.

The morning after her dream, Harley had listened, then told her she attached entirely too much significance to a dream. "Forget it," he'd said, dropping the newspaper in his briefcase. "Aren't you meeting Kristin for lunch today?"

"That's Friday," she'd reminded him. Today's Sunday." She hesitated, noticing Harley dressed for the office. "Isn't it?"

"Hey, I'm the one who was out of town all week working on a case for Dr. Morgan. You were asleep when I came in last night." Gretchen remembered his look that morning when he'd asked her, "Are you all right?"

He seemed genuinely worried about her as she strived to absorb his vision of what happened. At the time, she'd shaken off her fears in hopes her mind would clear so she could connect the dots in some semblance of order on her own.

Now, heading for **Shaman's Pub,** her feelings of apprehension returned. *If today is Friday, where have I been all week? Harley said, "Forget it," but I* *can't*. She turned her thoughts to Kristin and their luncheon date, a ritual set up during their college days as a way to keep up-to-date in their varied world. *I'm going to have to spend more time in the real world and stop delving into the supernatural.*

In the beginning there'd been three of them—she, Kristin, and Lauren Calloway—rendezvousing at **Shaman's Pub** every Friday. Then Lauren had taken a job with the FBI and spent most of her time in Washington, DC. She'd seldom returned to Ridgecrest after her parents died and the old homestead sold, and Gretchen missed her. Kristin was flighty and devil-may-care, but Lauren had a level head. She could talk to her.

Shaman, their infamous Irish bartender, held court at his pub in the small village of Ridgecrest, Connecticut. Rumors abounded among his customers of his having wandered the world for centuries. Shaman didn't mind the rumors, and neither accepted nor rejected the fantasies that followed in his wake.

"Great for business," he would say, the sum total of his comments.

Ming, his Siamese cat, and Einstein, her newly acquired mate, seemed part of the mystique his pub attracted. Shaman left it to his customer's imagination to determine the authentic from the fantastic, but everyone agreed his two Siamese cats, wise beyond their years, knew more than anyone suspected of Shaman's past lives. Gretchen wrote them into her mysteries— Shaman and his Irish folk tales and his Siamese—recreating his stories and intertwining them with weird memories of her subconscious dreams. She'd introduced Harley to Shaman—an odd combination of personalities—and they'd developed a strange sort of rapport.

As Gretchen rounded the last corner, she saw Kristin entering the pub and called her. Kristin didn't hear and continued into the pub. When Gretchen entered, she found her engrossed in reading the headlines of the *Hartford Courier*, a courtesy copy Shaman kept on the counter for his customers. Gretchen stared at the headlines over her shoulder, and her blood chilled when she recognized the man in the picture. The caption asked, **"Who Is He?"** Her hair at the nape of her neck seemed to crawl up her scalp as she recognized **Morgan,** the fantasy creature of her dreams. It could*n't be*.

"What's wrong, Gretchen," asked Kristin, observing her friend's ashen face. "You look as though you've seen a ghost."

"I think I have. That man, Kristin, he's the one I dreamed about."

"Sure you did, Gretchen." Kristin laughed. "Come back to reality. You're still in your fantasy world."

"Probably," Gretchen agreed, shaking off her weird feelings. *It's as though I've been on a weird LSD trip and become completely detached.* She glanced around Shaman's totally Irish pub, a replica of seventeenth-century Ireland, and reality began to take shape again. *I've got to stop this nonsense. I'm in* **Shaman's Pub.** *Shaman tends bar here—his customers clamor to hear his wild Irish tales of sorcery and witchcraft.* The reality of the pub took over, and she relaxed. The two selected a booth and Kristin put aside the newspaper.

"Did you try the potion I gave you?" she asked her after Shaman had taken their order and brought their wine.

"Not yet. Harley's having it analyzed. He's as curious as I am about that secret ingredient. Professor Ipswitch refused to tell him . . . 'his own secret recipe,' he said."

"Can't blame the professor. That recipe might be worth its weight in gold if it does what he claims it does."

"No doubt." Gretchen sipped her wine, drifting away from the subject at hand and wondering how much of her crazy dream to tell Kristin.

"Something's on your mind. What is it?"

Gretchen pulled herself together. "You read minds?" she asked.

"I know you. Remember? And I worry about you."

"I worry about me, too, sometimes," Gretchen agreed. "In fact, I woke up this morning and swore it was Sunday and I'd lost a week of my life. That scares me."

"I know. Sometimes, I've had days like that."

"Not like this." She took a sip of her wine before she announced, "I dreamt about Magus last night."

"The power of suggestion?" Kristin mused, wondering where Gretchen drifted in her reveries. "How do you do that?"

"Do what?"

"Disappear into a world of your own, I suppose. Maybe that's how your week disappeared. You do it quite often, you know. Is it because you're a writer?"

"Maybe. I don't know. Tell me about Magus. I think I met him last night."

"Wow, you were interested? Doing research for another book?"

"Something like that. Tell me!"

"Later, let's order." She shook her head. "You do create a fantastic life."

Shaman brought their order, and they dug into his special Irish soup, ordering another glass of wine before Kristin began her story of Magus. She eyed Gretchen suspiciously, her eyes amused. "It's an ancient Irish fairy tale. You've probably already heard it since Shaman has told the story many times."

"I need to hear it from you, Kristin, and learn how it all started."

"Okay. It started in Central Asia, back in the early days when old hags performed horrible witchcraft practices like loitering around graveyards and hanging trees and gathering up body fragments and rotting limbs of the dead. They would burn the pieces of flesh and use the ashes in their rituals. Some of the potions they used as punishment for the damned with weird consequences, such as turning people into some form of animal."

"Animal?" Gretchen's eyes widened. "Ashes of dead people?"

"Right. According to legend, Magus had enormous powers. In fact, some folks swear he really did exist."

Gretchen glanced at Einstein, suddenly aware of his intense interest in the story. She recognized his stance from her dream—ears in alert mode while appearing disinterested. He turned away from her, giving her an abrupt snub. Kristin stopped talking to watch the byplay.

"You okay?" she asked. Gretchen nodded and turned her attention back to Kristin. She continued. "The witches used the ashes of the dead to create mysterious potions, then used them to attract the devil."

"Why? Didn't they have enough troubles?"

"In those days, people liked the idea of living forever and kept the devil busy performing his rituals and muttering his incantations. As the legend goes, the devil appeared to anyone who knew how to create the special ashes. When he chanted specific incantations and the ashes were scattered on water, it would attract the devil, the only one with the power to grant wishes for eternal physical existence."

"Strange."

"Not really. Magus was sort of like our modern-day shrink, except he also had the power to perform sacrifices and exorcise evil. He'd alert people of his presence by beating a magic drum and singing his magic songs, chasing the devil out of the four corners of heaven. Can't you just envision it?"

"I'm sure he had his hands full," Gretchen commented remembering the Magus of her dream. *Why do I have the feeling that my dream wasn't a dream?*

"Be that as it may, Magus held sway over his legion of guardians, both good and bad. They'd assist him in his quest to dispel evil, and he'd spend his days crying out against the devil and chanting his incantation, '*Spirit whose breath is in the four winds, breathe, breathe on me.*'"

Gretchen shuddered. "The incantation on the love potion you gave me."

"The very one. Good and evil never changes, does it? I hope Harley gets the potion analyzed. I'd love to know what's in it."

"I think I drank some of that water, Kristin. Maybe that's why I lost a week of my life."

Kristin laughed aloud, startling the two cats on the hearth. "You really take those legends seriously, don't you?"

Gretchen is not amused. "You don't understand. I've been there."

"Sure you have," Kristin hastened to assure her. She reached across the table and patted her hand. "Don't worry. We'll figure it out. I doubt you've lost track of time, probably had one of your out-of-body experiences." She smiled. "You know what I mean—one of your subconscious nighttime flights of fancy."

"You're teasing me."

"Maybe. I'm more inclined to believe someone slipped you a Mickey last Saturday night."

"Or maybe I really did *morph* into a cat." Gretchen laughed. Then became serious. "You're right, Kristin, there's usually a logical answer."

"Sure there is. But enough of Magus, I want to hear about this mysterious dream of yours."

Gretchen related the highlights of her dream—from the time she met Harley at Shaman's 'til she woke up in her own bed. As she talked, she noticed Einstein paying particular heed to her words, listening intently. As she ended her story, Kristin sat back and looked at her friend in disbelief.

"You witnessed a murder?" Her grin widened. "As a cat?"

"You're laughing." She drew back. "You don't believe me."

"I didn't say that." She picked up the newspaper she'd tossed aside earlier. "You didn't read this?" she asked. "Your dream made page one."

"You mean that picture?"

"No, the article." Kristin read the article accompanying the picture that had startled Gretchen when she'd first entered the pub.

Police are trying to solve a mystery surrounding the death of an unidentified body found under the old highway overpass entering the town. A search for the murder weapon is being conducted. Anyone knowing the identity of the victim is asked to contact the local police department.

Police believe the murder occurred sometime during the night of October 31 and may have been a prank that went awry. The

victim is male Caucasian, about five feet, two inches, and has a
noticeable humpback.

"No wonder Harley warned me not to get involved," Gretchen said.

"But if you know where the murder weapon is, Gretchen, you need to
tell the police."

"How can I? Harley calls it my *loony tunes* defense and says if I say
anything, I may wind up being the accused."

"He's probably right." Kristin laughed. "*Loony tunes*, that's funny."

"I'm glad you're amused. Harley thinks I should see a shrink."

"Really? Now, that's serious."

Kristin looked at her empty glass and signaled to Shaman for a refill.
Shaman brought the wine and cleared away the empty dishes, noting
Gretchen's puzzled expression. "Everything okay here?" he asked.

Kristin concentrated on the wine in her glass. "We're fine, Shaman."

"You think it's amusing, and Harley thinks I've flipped, Kristin."

"You know," Kristin suggested, an amused impish gleam glowing in
her eyes, "before we get too caught up in this, we might do a little advance
sleuthing on our own. Then if we turn up anything worth reporting, that
is, if we locate the weapon, we can bring Roscoe in on it."

Gretchen perked up. "Hmmmm, that sounds logical. Not even Harley
could object."

"Does he need to know?" The two chuckled as Gretchen got into the
mood.

"Do you think we can swing it?"

"Why not? There are people with psychic powers—those who see things
others can't. We could tell the police you're a psychic." She grinned. "Maybe
you could become a phantom sleuth."

"Phantom sleuth," Gretchen mused. "I like that." She sipped her wine,
deep in thought. Kristine toyed with her glass.

"They don't have to know the particulars," she said suddenly turning
morose.

"You mean . . . does my dream has any validity?"

"You don't want me to come across as a *loony tunes*, too, do you?"

Gretchen laughed. "Would it bother you?"

"Of course not. I've been accused of worse." Choosing her words
carefully, Kristin added, "Look, I will talk to Roscoe. He could use a good
lead. As far as the police know, the suspect's a transient."

Gretchen glanced up as Professor Ipswitch entered the pub, taking his usual position at the end of the bar. She stared at him as though seeing him for the first time. Kristin turned to see what caught her interest.

"Why do I feel there's something evil about that man?" Gretchen asked.

Kristin laughed. "You're letting your dream influence you. Professor Ipswitch is Magus's bad guy, not yours."

"You're right. Shaman's the one who stole my necklace and traded it for a gun and a potion to use on Elise."

"Why not check with Shaman? Maybe he found your necklace."

"It's a dream, Kristin."

"But you did lose it, didn't you?"

She caught Shaman's eye as he approached their table. "Shaman, Gretchen appears to have misplaced her necklace. She didn't leave it here, did she?"

"Well, you know, come to think o' it, some gent did bring in a bauble he found in the parking lot. I'll get it for you. Might be the one."

Trudging back to the bar, he returned carrying a necklace. "The clasp's broken, but with a little fixin' and cleanin', it'll be good as new."

Gretchen thanked him and vowed to take it in for repair before she lost it again.

"So much for my dream," she assures Kristin. "We probably won't find the murder weapon either. Time to get back to reality."

Kristin agreed. "The legend of Magus hardly belongs in the twenty-first century."

"But you know, Kristin," said Gretchen as she pocketed the necklace, "it was rather fun being a cat."

"Who knows, maybe you were, Gretchen. Maybe you were."

*   *   *

Chapter Two

There are none so deaf as those who won't hear.

Kristin did call Sergeant Baguette as promised. When she told him about Gretchen and her psychic experience, without divulging her psychic's name, he laughed at the idea and explained his experiences with psychics.

"You know, Kristin, police have attempted to use psychics in many of their cases. Some have proved to be valid, but most of them have no basis in fact because they're too vague. Psychics see symbols, but usually have no earthly idea how to read the symbols they profess to see, and their locations are usually nebulous. It's a miracle if psychics and police actually team up and create useable evidence."

"But it does happen, doesn't it?" Kristin argued. "Maybe this is one of those times."

"I doubt it. Whoever your psychic friend is, humor her, but don't involve the police. We tend to be leery of psychics."

"Not the police . . . you." Kristin said. "If we locate anything, will you help us?"

"That depends on what you find. So far, you've given me nothing solid to work on, and I have no intention of following up on some psychic's meandering into an ethereal world."

"Maybe it does sound like a chase down the *yellow brick road*, Roscoe, but I really think you should check this one out."

"What makes this psychic so special?" he asked. "Give me a good reason for going along with your crazy scheme."

"Because I'm asking . . . you don't have to tell anyone." Then teased, "'Course, if you're afraid of being teased by the boys at the station . . ."

"That's enough. What do you have in mind?" Roscoe asked.

"I've a plan."

"Why doesn't that surprise me? Okay, what is it?"

"I thought we could plan a picnic by the scene of the crime and sort of casual—like check out that cache Gretchen dreamed up?"

"Gretchen? You mean she's your psychic—the one married to that attorney fellow? My God! Don't get me involved with any attorneys."

Realizing her mistake, Kristin panicked. "Don't hang up, Roscoe. I'm sorry. I guess I blew it, but it's not what you think. Harley isn't in on this . . . just Gretchen. All I ask is that you listen to her story. Please, Roscoe, give her a chance. I'm convinced she really did witness your murder, and you don't have any other leads."

Roscoe relented, a sucker for anything Kristin wanted. "Okay, Kristin, set it up, but no attorney."

Kristin grinned. *All right!*

*   *   *

Later that day, at Kristin's bidding, Gretchen narrated her dream sequence to Sergeant Baguette. Feigning contempt for venturing into someone else's dream world—although in some deep recess of his mind it redeemed his *sixth sense*—Sergeant Baguette convinced himself that a clandestine rendezvous might uncover something of value. In his world, stranger things had happened. If nothing else, his uncertainty did need satisfying; thus Roscoe consoled himself, believing that this little venture might even be therapeutic for Gretchen.

According to Kristin, Gretchen did seem to be in an absolute state of confusion, trying to come to terms with her dream. Was it prophetic or merely wishful thinking? Regardless of the ribbing he might expect from his fellow cops, Roscoe decided to satisfy his curiosity.

Later, when Gretchen talked to Roscoe, she deliberately withheld information about her journey into the *Netherworld*—her status as a cat, or her conversion into an angel. Kristin nixed that part of the dream, concerned that Roscoe might reconsider and pull out. Besides, after that incident yesterday, she doubted her own sanity.

Gretchen returned home after telling her tale to Roscoe and tried to discuss the visit with Harley, but he *didn't want to hear about it.* Amber entered her doggie door and placed her head on Gretchen's lap, looking up at her with her sympathetic brown eyes. Gretchen ruffled her shaggy fur.

"You understand, don't you, Amber? You were there." She gave Amber a final pat and headed upstairs. *Maybe a shower will clear my head.* Under the relaxing spray of the shower, she reviewed the past week. *Harley says, "Forget it," but I can't. I've got to find out. Maybe if I return to the scene of the crime . . .*

She finished dressing, grabbed her car keys, and headed for the overpass, not knowing what to expect. Leaving her car in the parking lot by the bridge, she walked toward the overpass, reminiscing on how Roscoe and Einstein tossed the knife in the Cat Monger's Cave. As she reached the ill-fated spot along the underpass, she spied Julius sunning himself on the grass. He raised his head and watched her warily as she approached, but didn't move when she sat on the grass beside him.

"I lost you the other night, Julius, you and the other cats. I must have taken the wrong path, and it led me *somewhere* into a barn. Did you know where the cave would lead me?"

As she wondered if the black cat understood her, Julius transmitted his thoughts to her in cat language. "You took the path into the *Netherworld*," he meowed. "We, cats, do not go there."

Surprised that she still understood him, she continued her questioning. "Did you let me lose my way deliberately?"

"You needed to go there to get the antidote."

"Did you know Shaman would be there?"

"Yes, Shaman isn't a bad guy. He explained his activities to us when he came through the shield, but we couldn't reach you. We had to find you another way out. I see you made it. Are you all right?"

"Yes, but I'm having difficulty understanding the time lapse." Gretchen looked around hoping no one saw her talking to a cat. "I'm beginning to feel foolish," she told Julius, "not knowing how to explain my actions for a week. What shall I do?"

"You'll think of something. We'll help if we can."

"I'm not so sure. Einstein ignored me at the pub yesterday."

"That's because you were with one of them," he explained.

"Would you get the knife for me?" Gretchen asked.

"Knife? What knife?"

"The one in the Cat Monger's Cave, the murder weapon, don't you remember?"

Julius placed his paw on her hand, reminiscent of her days as a cat, and ignored her question. "Maybe we could meet on the chaise tonight and discuss old times?"

"Why you, old fox!" She cuffed his head with her hands and placed a kiss between his ears. "The knife. You'll get it for me?"

Julius turned serious. "What did you do with the antidote, Gretchen?"

"I don't know. I must have lost it on the way home. That's all right. I don't need it any more. I'm my old self again," she assured him. "Will you help me get the knife, Julius?"

"That is not wise," Julius transmitted. "All is not as it appears."

"Are you warning me? 'All is not well?' I know that. Tell me what to do."

Julius walked away. "Tonight, on the chaise?" He meowed his defiance, or maybe his dare.

Gretchen gave up. *He's not going to help me.* And returned to her car. *I wonder what he meant—all is not as it appears.* She scolded herself, shaking off an intangible feeling of having reentered the *Netherworld. What does he know? He's only a cat.*

Chapter Three

Dreams are the touchstones of our character.
—Henry David Thoreau.

Saturday morning in the light of day, she'd nearly forgotten her visit with Julius. Harley had left for his office before Kristin and Roscoe arrived, dressed in their oldest digs and ready for serious work. She'd decided not to tell them of her return visit to the overpass. *They'll think I really do need a shrink. Even I can hardly believe I actually talked "cat talk" with Julius.* Armed with a variety of tools and a hamper of goodies, they packed the trunk of Roscoe's beat-up Chevy Blazer.

Gretchen doubted that Harley would return from the office before they left on their excursion, but as luck would have it, he showed up unexpectedly as they were loading their gear. Unable to get into his driveway and curious about the strange-looking automobile blocking his entry to the garage, he called out, "What's going on, Gretchen? You heading somewhere?"

"We're going on a picnic," she told him with her usual candor. "You're welcome to come along, but please don't say I can't go."

"Oh no," she heard Kristin groan, but Harley ignored it.

"Hi, Kristine . . . and, Sergeant Baggett," Harley greeted them. "What's up?"

Roscoe shrugged, but before he could speak, Gretchen interrupted. "They're helping me recreate my dream," she told Harley.

"What dream? You mean the one you told me the other day?" Concerned, he looked at her. "Are you sure you're up to it?"

"I'm fine." Gretchen looked to Kristin and Roscoe for confirmation.

"Wouldn't it be better if you talked to Dr. Morgan, first?" Harley continued to press her.

She ignored his question. "We're making an outing out of it—a picnic. You're welcome to come along, you know. It's your choice, but please don't try to stop me."

"I understand—I think," he reassured her as he folded his lanky frame into the backseat of the Blazer next to Gretchen. He looked at Roscoe and shrugged. "I won't say anything to your cop friends, Roscoe, if you don't spread this around my office."

"It's a deal," Roscoe agreed, breathing easier and thinking Harley a real good sport about the whole venture. "At least," he told Harley, "the food will be great, whether we find anything or not."

"Do you expect to?" asked Harley of Roscoe.

"Not really." Roscoe grinned. "It's a long shot, but I'm stalled in my investigation. Sort of hoping we do find something. I need answers. So far, I've only got questions."

The ride was short. The town wasn't that big. Arriving at the crime scene, the four found a grassy knoll near the overpass, and Gretchen and Kristin spread out the picnic lunch. Harley and Roscoe watched a softball game going on in a nearby open field. Amidst small talk and banter, they ate their fill of Boston Fried Chicken and Kristin's crunchy potato salad and finished the meal off with ice-cold lemonade from the cooler as the two men discussed how best to play out the next scene. Gretchen and Kristin offered intermittent suggestions making the occasion appear both festive and intriguing. The game over, the boys and cars having disappeared, Gretchen decided the time had come. She led them to the entrance of the Cat Monger's Cave.

"You do the honors, Roscoe," Harley suggested as Gretchen pointed out the cache where the cats kept their trophies. "I'm not dressed for digging. I'll supervise."

"Spoken like a true attorney," Roscoe commented, checking out Harley's expensive cord slacks and cashmere sweater—a sharp contrast to the denim jeans and T-shirts worn by the others. He gathered up his equipment, a long pole with a hook on one end, and followed Gretchen to the cache under the overpass. Harley and Kristin followed at a safe pace, then stopped close by to watch the proceedings.

"Don't disturb anything, Roscoe," Gretchen ordered. "I don't want Einstein mad at me. We only want the knife. It's in a plastic grocery bag."

Roscoe glanced at her. *She really believes.*

He wondered how he'd gotten trapped into chasing a psychic dream, but hesitated only a moment before crawling on his belly to the spot Gretchen indicated—the exact spot she'd determined the cats entered for their Halloween trip. He angled the pole into the opening, pushing the weeds from his face, trying to ignore the flying insects looping around his head as though buzzing their resentment of his invasion into their territory.

"What I don't do for money," he consoled himself. In spite of his discomfort, he began bringing various objects to the surface.

"I'm almost afraid to look," Gretchen said to Kristin and Harley as she recognized bits and pieces of cat memorabilia falling around Roscoe as he brought them out one by one to the surface.

"A plastic bag, you say?" Roscoe asked, rummaging through the collection of items around him. "Well, I'll be damned," she heard him say. "I can't believe it—it is here."

Roscoe dragged out a plastic sack from his collection. It contained a knife. Separating it from the other trophies, he returned the rest of the cat collection to the cave. Then, sliding backward, he crawled out from under the overpass, clutching the evidence in one hand and his pole in the other hand.

"If this isn't the craziest thing I've ever seen!" He looked at Gretchen with renewed respect. "A dream, hmm?"

"Will she need an attorney, Roscoe?" Kristin asked.

Startled, Gretchen turned to Harley. "Oh no, Harley. You told me to let it go, but I was so sure, like the necklace, there'd be a logical explanation."

Sergeant Baguette smiled. "Don't worry, Gretchen. This knife may have been here for years, another time, another murder, that your dream keyed in on. Let's get it to ballistics first and check for identifiable prints. You didn't touch it, did you?"

Gretchen shook her head. "No, Roscoe nosed it."

"Roscoe?" Sergeant Baguette asked.

"A cat—Kristin's—oh no!" Gretchen's psyche made the connection for the first time, "I didn't think—you were all in my dream . . . all of you . . . Kristin, Professor Ipswitch, Shaman, Harley . . . oh, dear, it *was* a dream."

Sergeant Baguette shook his head in protest. "That's enough, I don't want to know any more." Then, catching her apprehensive mood, he quickly reassured her, "It's way too early to jump to conclusions. There may be no fingerprints . . . bloodstains may not match . . ."

"But what if it does check out?" asked Gretchen.

Harley laughed. "Then you'd be a phantom sleuth, my dear, famous the world over. Television shows, talk shows, maybe even asked to write a book about your adventures—all the notoriety accorded a celebrity. Think you could handle it?"

"I'm glad this amuses you, Harley, but it's my head on the chopping block."

She watched as Roscoe transferred the knife into a clean police bag, taking care not to touch it. "Come on, we're through here," he said, stating his part of the job finished. "Let's roll. I'm anxious to see what I have."

He hurried them all into the car, dropped a puzzled Harley and perplexed Gretchen off at their home, and headed for the station to register the knife as police evidence in a murder. He asked the police lab to dust the knife for prints and requested the medical examiner to analyze the stains on the knife. Then he sat back to wait, knowing he'd face a ribbing from his buddies when they learned of his escapade into the supernatural. And he did.

"A psychic, hmm? Where'd you dig up a psychic in this neck of the woods?" his buddies teased. "You been nippin' a few too many at Shaman's?"

Roscoe took the teasing with jolly good English humor. While waiting for results, he decided to question a few of the people Gretchen targeted in her tale to Kristin. He decided to start with Shaman.

Entering the pub, he settled himself at one end of the bar, appraising the Irish décor of the famed establishment. Shaman reigned supreme behind the solid mahogany counter with an array of unusual bottles lining the wall on the rear. Some of the names on the bottles, Roscoe had never heard—not even from his many visits to English pubs in the old country, but they seemed at home in Shaman's Irish pub.

"What can you tell me about the night of October 31st?" he asked the gregarious bartender. "And where were you between the hours of six and nine?"

"Huh?" Shaman stammered, eyeing Roscoe with suspicion. "Me? Why, I suppose I be right here, tendin' my customers. Why?"

"Anything unusual happen that night?"

"No, don't know as it did. What's this all about?"

"I'm investigating a murder that occurred that night," Roscoe told him. "And I'm talking to anyone who might know anything. Your pub seems like a good place to start."

"Ya' don't say. Why's that?" Shaman continued to clean the spotless counter.

"Bartenders tend to hear things."

"Oh? Is that so? And you want to know what I hear, eh?"

"Yeah, something like that. Can you tell me if anything out of the ordinary happened that night?"

"No, don't recollect nothin'—a few strange customers, maybe—that's to be expected on Halloween, I guess."

"How strange?" Roscoe asked.

Shaman shook his head. "They be comin' in from all over, lookin' for treats, bar treats."

"You heard nothing unusual?" Roscoe pressed for more.

"Nooo," Shaman drawled. "Had one strange episode, but it had nothin' to do with my customers."

"What's that?"

"A fight in the parking lot."

"A fight? What time?"

"Early, couple a' guys trying to catch a cat out in the alley. Weirdest thing—fightin' over a cat."

"The cat worth anything? A reward or something?"

"Not in my book, but the professor seemed pretty interested in this particular white cat. 'Had a diamond-studded collar,' someone said. Could be the collar they were fighting over. Never knew cats to wear diamonds, but ya' never know—not in this day."

"A diamond collar, eh? That's what the fight was about? Who wound up with the cat?" Roscoe asked, writing a notation in his book.

"I've no idea." Shaman turned back to washing glasses behind the bar.

"Did you know them?"

"No, didn't see 'em. Just heard the talk," Shaman said, stacking clean glasses on the shelf behind him.

"The professor. Ever ask him about his interest in that particular cat?"

"Nope. I mind my own business." He turned around. Roscoe looked at the man's back and knew the conversation was over. He left the pub.

A cat with a diamond collar, wonder if anyone caught the cat. He headed for the university chemistry lab to check the next man on his list, Professor Ipswitch—the man Shaman said expressed an interest in a particular white cat. Roscoe remembered Kristin mentioning a professor who created some kind of ancient concoction that she sold in her gift shop. *Maybe it's the same one.*

He headed for the university where he discovered the laboratory occupied the top floor of the main building. *Why are laboratories always on the top floor?* Reaching his destination after the long climb up steep steps, he parked himself at the top to catch his breath. *I'm getting out of shape. It's no wonder college kids stay so damned skinny—climbing stairs like these all day long.* He sniffed the air. *Damned stinky up here. Probably the reason they put labs on the top floor.*

He entered the laboratory and found one lone, white-coated individual bent over a beaker, eyedropper in hand, dripping a solution into the vessel a drop at a time. Occasionally, the man stopped long enough to make a notation in a notebook next to him before continuing his observation of the solution.

Roscoe watched the man until he put down the eyedropper and placed his hands on the edge of the counter staring down into the beaker. He took off his glasses, rubbed his eyes, and returned the glasses to his angular-shaped nose, then continued to stare at the bubbling beaker as though expecting it to do something unusual. Roscoe approached, waiting patiently until the man noticed him and turned around.

"Can I help you?" asked the man in the white coat.

"I hope so. What is that you're mixing?"

"Something someone asked me to analyze. There's supposed to be some secret ingredient in it—so the guy says—and I'm trying to figure out what it is."

"Have you?" Roscoe asked.

"Yes, and no. I've isolated something, but can't categorize it. Seems to be some strange form of LSD, but what type is still a mystery." Frustrated, he turned to Roscoe. "What can I do for you?"

"LSD on a college campus? Now that's novel."

"Yeah, I know," agreed the lab assistant. "This one's a different strain though. Nothing I've ever seen here before." He looked at Roscoe. "You're not here because of this, are you?"

"No, I'm looking for a Professor Ipswitch. I'll settle for anyone who can tell me something about him. Do you know him?"

"Sure, who wants to know?"

"Sergeant Baguette from the Ridgecrest Police Department." He flashed his badge. "We're conducting an investigation into a recent murder. You've probably heard about it."

"Yeah, I have. The professor mixed up in it?"

"Not that I know of—just needed to ask him a few questions."

The lab technician turned from his beaker and faced Roscoe. "Professor Ipswitch does some research work for the government—disease control, I believe. Don't know what he's working on right now. His partner told me he's discovered some kind of youth potion."

"That's interesting. The partner or the professor?"

"The partner, I presume. Said he has proof positive it works. The professor plans on writing it up for the next medical review journal. That who you're looking for?"

Roscoe ignored his question and asked, "Where can I find this partner?"

"Check with Professor Ipswitch. You passed his cottage down by the gate. He's probably there now. Let him tell you about his partner. I've never seen him, Just talked to him on the phone."

The lab technician turned back to his beaker. "If you don't find him there, you might check Shaman's Pub. Professor hangs around there a lot."

"Thanks," said Roscoe. "Hope you isolate the magic ingredient and make a million."

The technician laughed. "Don't I wish," he said and continued to stare in the beaker.

Roscoe wandered back down the path toward the cottage, passing the forest where the professor, Harley, and Morgan entered, feeling a cold dampness. He shivered. Reaching the cottage, he located the professor out back—engrossed in stirring some mixture in a black kiln with a fireplace poker. An odor of singed wet feathers filled the air.

Weird. Roscoe approached the little man with the spiked hair and octagon-shaped glasses. "What are you making?" he asked.

"Ashes." The professor continued to stir the foul-smelling contents of the kiln.

Ask a stupid question.

"My fortune is in these ashes." He turned to look at Roscoe. "Do I know you?"

"Sergeant Baguette with the Ridgecrest Police Department. I need to ask you a few questions."

"Shoot," said Professor Ipswitch.

"I'm investigating a murder that occurred this past week. Know anything about it?" Roscoe asked.

"Nope. Should I?" The professor returned to stirring the burning embers.

"I'll ask the questions, sir," Roscoe stated. "That's the way it's done. Where were you between the hours of six and nine, the night of October 31?"

"Right here. Oh, I did go by the pub earlier, but I was back by six," he answered quickly, his eyes darting up the path toward the forest.

"Anyone verify that for you?"

"No, I work alone."

"You have an associate, do you not?"

"No, I work alone. My inventions are my own. I share them with no one."

"Then it's not true, you have a partner?"

The professor faced Roscoe, poker in hand. "When you find proof of that, let me know." He shook the poker in his face, and Roscoe backed up.

"Careful," he said. "Maybe you'd like to come down to the station and take a polygraph test?"

"Why should I?" the professor asked.

"So we can remove you from our suspect list and get on with the investigation." Roscoe eyed the poker waving in front of him.

"I'm a suspect?"

"You are. We'd like to clear your name."

"You put it that way, I'll be glad to," agreed the professor, turning back to his ashes. "How's ten in the morning?" he offered.

"Suits me." Roscoe left the professor stirring his ashes and returned to the police station. Greeted with smirks and snide looks of amusement from his fellow cops, he found his entry into the evidence room on his desk with a note attached that read: "The evidence contained herein does not add anything of value to the case in question. Not only is it devoid of any bloodstains, the stab wounds of the victim do not match. Conclusion, Sergeant Baguette, you've been had." And signed by the medical examiner.

"So much for psychics," Roscoe cursed under his breath and reached for the telephone to call Gretchen.

Chapter Four

The real tragedy of life is when men are afraid of the light.
—Plato

"You can quit worrying about the knife, Gretchen," Roscoe advised when he called. "It isn't the murder weapon. Evidently, it's been under that bridge for years."

Gretchen took the news calmly, but decided to take Julius up on his offer to meet on the chaise that evening. She kept a sharp eye out for him all that day and, about eight o'clock, saw him skulking along the garden fence watching the house. Heading outside, she approached him.

"What did you do with the knife, Julius?" she asked. "Did you pull a switch?"

"You didn't do as I said," Julius replied. "I told you things were not as they seemed. You made a mistake bringing them to the cave."

"I can't do this alone, Julius," Gretchen pleaded. "Besides, I trust my friends. They've helped me."

Julius flipped his tail at Gretchen and jumped onto the fence. He turned to look at her, tail poised straight up and rigid, a stance that Gretchen knew to mean *get moving*.

"Get moving on what?" But Julius had already left, disappearing over the back fence and leaving Gretchen to figure out his meaning. *Does he mean that Kristin and Harley are suspects?*

At Shaman's later that day, Roscoe tossed his notepad onto the table in front of Kristin. "You're not telling me everything," he accused her. "Everything points to you. *Heaven Scent,* Professor Ipswitch, Gretchen, Harley, you were even the instigator of that wild-goose chase we went on last Saturday."

100

"Whatever do you mean?" Kristin hedged. "There's nothing else."

"Why don't I believe you?"

"Because you're a cop. You suspect everyone. I can't imagine how much more I could help you without having my own psychic visions," she teased him.

"Don't be facetious. I want to know what you know about a partner, his associate, or whatever else he's called. Have you ever seen the professor's partner?"

"No, I haven't." Kristin glared at Roscoe. "Professor Ipswitch doesn't talk of his inventions except to say that he has someone who helps him with research. He's never mentioned a partner."

"Did Gretchen ever meet him?"

"The partner? I don't know—maybe in her dreams. Not for real. Why?"

"As long as I'm knee-deep in the occult, I may as well dive in headfirst. Tell me the rest of the dream."

"I can't. You'll have to ask Gretchen that, Roscoe. I won't tell you." Her voice changed as she noticed his dejection. "Look, she's trying to get her life back on an even keel. Harley watches her like a hawk—afraid she'll go off the deep end. If you talk to her, be careful."

"I know. That's why I'm asking you, Kristin. As a friend, she'll talk to you."

"I can't do that. I promised."

"You'd rather see a murderer go free?"

"You got his fingerprints, didn't you?"

"That's what I meant by *wild-goose chase,* Kristin. The knife we found had never been near a murder scene. It's an ordinary, everyday knife used by movers to open packing crates."

"The stains?"

"Paint. Kristin, if you won't tell me, I'll have to ask Gretchen, and I don't want to do that. What can you tell me about the missing associate?"

Kristin stared at her coffee cup and shook her head. "Nothing."

"Look, Kristin," Roscoe pressured her, "I went back up the hill again to talk to the lab assistant, and he couldn't even give me a name. He's never seen the guy."

"A silent partner? Is he the dead man, do you think?"

"That's how I figure it. No one knows him. No one's seen him, and no one can identify him."

"The perfect murder." Kristin laughed. "What a kick."

"You laugh, but that's how it looks. Unless I can learn more, someone's committed the perfect murder." He seemed defeated, and Kristin took pity on him.

"Gretchen saw the dead man, but she didn't recognize him—only relieved it wasn't Harley. That's why she hid the knife. She was afraid Harley had done it. That's crazy though, isn't it?"

"So it seems. You say Gretchen stayed missing for a week then turned up at home unable to remember anything except that she'd witnessed a murder. She professed to know the location of the murder weapon, but can't identify the killer. And the knife we found turns out not to be the murder weapon."

Kristin looked sympathetic. "Is that all there is?" asked Roscoe.

"No, she remembers being a cat and seeing all kinds of crazy things—but as a cat, Roscoe. And she refuses to believe her dream and the murder are connected. You jumped to that conclusion."

"But you know they are, don't you?"

Kristin grinned, amused. "This case is really getting to you, isn't it?"

"Yes, maybe there's something else she's forgetting, and I need to find out what it is. Can't you sort of set up a casual meeting, Kristin?"

"Okay, that I can do," she agreed, adding facetiously. "But it will cost you."

"That I can handle. Whatever you ask, consider it done."

"We're having lunch, Friday at Shaman's. Care to join us?"

"I'll be there."

"Better keep an open mind. Gretchen is like no other. You might even begin to agree with Harley."

Roscoe left, and Kristin plotted. *Wouldn't do for Gretchen to tell Roscoe too much. He's too sharp, and I'm not that certain about her state of mind either.*

*   *   *

"Roscoe thinks there's something you're not telling him," Kristin accused Gretchen. "He's fit to be tied. And I'm beginning to think you made it up too."

"You give me too much credit. I don't have half *that* much imagination. And you *know* I can't tell him *all* my dream."

"We have to give him something . . . something that won't implement Harley or make you a suspect."

"Kristin, you're smarter than me. What do you suggest?"

And Kristin had it figured out. "If we play the game right, Gretchen, we could make a fortune."

"How do you mean?"

Kristin looked absolutely elated. "If there's some way to get hold of the secret recipe, we could mix it ourselves."

"What? Come on, Gretchen. That recipe is a motive for murder . . ."

Gretchen remembered Julius's warning and, for the first time, suspected Kristin's motive. *Maybe Julius is right. She is involved.*

"But if Professor Ipswitch gets nailed for the murder . . . ," Kristin continued. "Can't you imagine, Gretchen, how much we could rake in if we had control of that recipe?"

"Tell me you're not serious, Kristin. You wouldn't try to capitalize on this, would you?"

"Of course not." Kristin sighed and hastened to reassure Gretchen. "I'm only trying to help Roscoe solve his case without throwing suspicion on the rest of us."

"You're sure that's all it is?"

"Oh, come on, Gretchen, don't be so serious. Where's your old spirit? You used to love doing crazy things in college."

"We're not in college, Kristin. We're in the real world. You don't play with people's lives like that."

"Oh well, Roscoe is so paranoid. He's a challenge at times. Anyway, it would break the monotony. Aren't you with me?"

"I'll help you solve the case," Gretchen conceded. "But no profiteering."

"Agreed, spoilsport," Kristin accused.

"What do you suggest?"

"Tell Roscoe the entire story—the way you told me—about what happened to Morgan."

"But it's only a dream, Kristin. You said so yourself."

"Then how do you account for the lapse in time? Alien invasion? You were gone nearly a week." Kristin tried to persuade her. "I'm surprised Harley didn't tear the town apart looking for you. Did he ever file a missing person's request?"

"I don't know," Gretchen looked off in the distance. "I didn't ask."

"Well, you don't have to tell Roscoe everything. That bit about old Ireland and time travel is a bit much . . . but your adventures as a cat can't do any harm. Roscoe needs to solve the case, and I'm willing to pull a few strings to help him."

"Let me think about it," Gretchen promised. "One thing about dreams, they usually mean the opposite of real life."

"I'm banking my future on your dream version," Kristin said.

"After my track record, I don't see how it can contribute to anything other than confusion."

Having won round one, Kristin returned to her antique shop, and Gretchen headed home to dwell on the next step. Relaxing on the chaise lounge on her deck, Gretchen reviewed her rapidly disappearing dream.

Odd, Kristin's using that phrase "Banking her future on my dream." What did she mean, and what did she and Roscoe want from me? Is there something I'm forgetting—something that happened that I don't remember?

The bottle of *Heaven Scent* had disappeared from her dresser, but she understood that. Harley planned to have the secret ingredient analyzed. Did he? *I'll ask him. What else must I remember?* She looked around the garden—so peaceful and quiet. Her strawberries were huge and succulent even in November. *Odors and sounds are so much keener since my dream. Am I still part cat?*

Peeking through semiclosed lids, she observed Julius walking the white picket fence toward her and smiled as he jumped down into her garden. Glancing at Gretchen lying motionless on the chaise, he headed for her strawberry patch and began to dig. Then with his front paw poised in midair as though pointing, he looked back at her before leaping back to his spot on the fence. He watched her pretense at sleep.

The strawberry patch! Why didn't I think of that? I'll bet that's where Julius hid the knife. She moved to the spot where she'd seen Julius digging, aware that he watched her every move. Seizing a trowel Harley had left in the garden, she dug deep into the selected spot until her trowel hit a solid object. *The gun? No, Shaman has the gun.* She pulled out a plastic sack—the very one she'd thought Roscoe found on Saturday. Thinking *evidence,* she didn't touch the knife inside, but tossed the sack in her car.

I don't care what Kristin says. I'm taking this to Sergeant Baguette before I change my mind.

Minutes later found Gretchen heading for the police station, determined to unload her problems on Roscoe's broad shoulders, but walking into Sergeant Baguette's office later, she started to waiver and stopped. *How can I explain to Kristin's boyfriend how I got this package after what happened Saturday? I'll be an idiot for the second time. Maybe I should tell Kristin first.* She had turned back toward the exit when Roscoe entered.

"Hi, Gretchen," he greeted her. "Looking for me?" He motioned to the package in her hand. "What do you have there? Another knife?"

"Oh, Roscoe, after Saturday, I know I shouldn't have come. You'll think I'm crazy . . . but I can't explain . . ." She hedged, backing toward the door.

He stared at the package Gretchen tried to hide behind her. "Is it another knife," he asked, and Gretchen nodded, handing him the plastic sack.

"I think it's the evidence we should have found Saturday. I won't bother to tell you how I got it, but if it is what you're looking for . . . I'll try to explain. Otherwise . . ."

"Let's see it."

A grinning Sergeant Baguette took the package from her and motioned for her to follow him. He headed for the interrogation room and, once there, peeked into the bag. Then pulling on a sterile glove, he removed the knife and placed it in a plastic police bag.

"Now," he told her, "I need the whole story. I've been inheriting bits and pieces of senseless information for weeks. Now it's time to pull it all together." He motioned her to a chair across the table. "Sit, please."

"Do I need a lawyer?" she asked.

"If you're thinking Harley, I don't advise it. He's a suspect too. Anyone else you want to call?"

"No. I know it looks bad for Harley, but he's a casualty too." She bit her upper lip, looked up at Sergeant Baguette, and ventured a question that had been puzzling her ever since her return. "Do you know if Harley ever filed a *Missing Persons* report on me?"

His eyebrows lifted. "Yeah, I found one in the files. We give everyone forty-eight hours to turn up. No one reinitiated the request. Why?"

"I lose a week of my life, and no one cares? It's as if Harley and Kristin knew what happened and won't tell me. Too many things don't make sense . . . I don't know . . ."

Sergeant Baguette sympathized. *I want to believe her.* "I suppose Kristin dreamed up that bit about you being a psychic, in case we found the knife."

Gretchen nodded. "I can't keep up the deception, Roscoe. I'm basically honest, but Kristin does have a tendency to sway me at times. I don't know why I go along with her." She paused as though recalling some fun incident and smiled. "For the rush I get, I suppose. She's not entirely to blame."

Roscoe nodded toward the package on the table between them. "Without giving me a replay of Saturday's fiasco, how did this come into your possession?"

"I'm sorry, Sergeant Roscoe. I know I haven't been completely open with you, but I need someone who'll listen to me, someone who doesn't think I'm making everything up, or that I've flipped. Harley's at wit's end, afraid he'll lose credibility, and after what I'm about to tell you, you'll probably agree with him."

Her remarks surprised Roscoe. "Do you have anything . . . anything at all . . . that will convince me I should listen to you?" When she hesitated, he prodded her. "Go on. You wanted someone to listen. I'm listening." He leaned back in his chair, put his feet on the desk, and closed his eyes. "Talk," he ordered.

And Gretchen did. She told Roscoe about Julius. How Julius indicated to her where he hid the knife, saying, "Julius replaced the knife because I brought in too many people. He warned me not to talk to anyone but you. Maybe because of Kristin's business dealings with Professor Ipswitch."

"Who is Julius?" Roscoe asked. "And how does this Julius fit into the scene? Is he our illusive partner?"

"No." Gretchen looked away, wishing she could disappear. "Not exactly." Collecting her courage, she turned and faced the police sergeant. "He's a cat."

Roscoe's feet came off the desk with a bang. He stared at her. Gretchen waited for the explosion. "Sure he is," he growled. Gretchen turned a smug look in his direction. "Think what you like, Roscoe. You can't know for sure."

"And I'm supposed to believe you talk to cats?" He glared at her, and she laughed.

"Think of the convenience, Roscoe," she remonstrated. "Cats get into places you and I can't, not without raising suspicion." Suddenly aware she's lost him, she adds quickly, "Check out the knife, Roscoe. It's for real."

"Well, why not. Makes as much sense as anything else." He picked up the evidence bag and pocketed the package.

"Trust me, Roscoe."

He stared at her. "Trust, huh? I'm supposed to trust someone who thinks it's normal to talk to cats?"

"What choice do you have?"

"Oh, what the hell. You're right. I'll check out the knife."

As he turned to leave, he looked back as though remembering something. "By the way, Gretchen," he said, "you mentioned a business deal between the professor and Kristin. Is she the partner in this deal?"

"I don't know. In my dream, Professor Ipswitch had a partner. That partner was a dead ringer for the victim. I can't be sure. Maybe Julius can lead us through the maze."

Roscoe shook his head. "I'm sure he can." Wondering if he were being led down a garden path for the second time in a week, he motioned to his coat pocket. "We'll talk again after I've checked this out."

* * *

Chapter Five

Conscience is the traitor that fights the battle of society.

A week passed before Roscoe called Gretchen. "I concede. It's the murder weapon. It fits the stab wounds and the blood matches that of the victim."

"So now, what do we do?"

"You've got to give me more information. Can you come in?"

Gretchen agreed. "Are you ready to listen?"

"Whatever you tell me. I promise to keep an open mind."

As soon as Gretchen arrived, Roscoe led her to the interrogation room and jumped right in with inquiries. "Since you and Julius seem to be my only lead, I need to know everything you know, Gretchen. You say the professor has a partner, and the partner looks a lot like the victim. Did you ever meet this partner?"

"No, but I've seen him. He fits the description of the man you found under the overpass, although I didn't know at the time."

"When did you recognize him as the professor's partner?"

"Halloween night . . . in my dream . . . but he wasn't dead then . . . in my dream, that is. He led Harley and the professor to Dublin." She hesitated as the officer's pen stopped. "Oh, I'm sorry," she said.

"Dublin? You mean, as in Ireland?" Roscoe asked.

"Yes."

"Let me get this straight. First, you talk with cats, then you travel back in time. Explain, please." He listened as Gretchen recited her journey into the *Netherworld.*

"I know it sound crazy—sort of like Alice walking through the looking glass into another world, but it did happen. I walked through a cave into the seventeenth century and met Magus and the devil." She peered at him. "What can I say? You asked."

"Look, Gretchen"—observed a skeptical Sergeant—"I'm a policeman and not into fairy tales. You'll have to do better than that."

"Forget it." Gretchen got up to leave.

"Sit down," he ordered. "You started this. You'll stay until your story makes sense to me." He ran his fingers through his tumbled carrot top. "No wonder Kristin was so evasive."

"She told me to tell you everything except about Ireland. She thought that a bit much," Gretchen said. "I made a mistake. I should have skirted around that."

"That I understand," Roscoe agreed. "Go on. What else did you learn that might help me in *this* century?"

"Isn't there something about dreams—even in *this* century—that are sort of symbolic? You know, like things aren't always what they seem? Shaman and his wild tales of old Ireland, Harley and his overprotection, my need for my own identity, and Kristin's desire to control?"

"The power of suggestion, you mean?"

"Something like that—unfulfilled desires. I can't prove we weren't in Ireland. It may have happened right here in Ridgecrest. Graveyard scenes are pretty much alike, and there are many ancient barns in Connecticut. Like Professor Ipswitch and *Resurrection* . . . his magic potion . . . maybe I've always had a secret desire to be a cat and fulfilled a fantasy."

Sergeant Baguette watched her, surprised by the sudden outburst in her own defense. "Stop," he demanded attempting to assimilate the information into something logical. "I might start to believe you."

"Maybe I should leave before I really confuse you."

"Stay where you are," he ordered, staring at her in disbelief. "I have every intention of getting to the bottom of this."

Gretchen took a deep breath. "Regardless of where it takes you?"

"I'm trying to look at this objectively," he said. "There's been a murder, and you've literally plucked the murder weapon out of thin air. That, at least, makes this conversation a reality. In spite of that, I'm steeled for anything at the moment so make it quick. Tomorrow, I may not be in the mood to listen." He took a deep breath, rubbed his forehead. "What did happen the night of October 31?" he asked.

Gretchen plunged in. "That night . . . Halloween night . . . all the cats met at the Witches' Coven. Being a novice and not knowing where they were heading, I followed them. Evidently, I daydreamed along the

way and didn't realize I'd gotten behind until they were far ahead of me.
I tried to catch up but couldn't find them . . . then I took a wrong path
and lost my way. I kept on walking, trying to guess which path they
took . . . when I saw a light ahead. Believing I'd caught up with the other
cats, I ran faster, but instead of finding my friends, I wound up in an
ancient barn."

"In Ireland." Roscoe interrupted.

"I didn't know that."

"What did you find in the barn?" he prompted.

"Two figures sitting before a roaring fire, wrapped in shawls. They didn't
see me, but I saw a bowl of water in front of the fire. I felt thirsty after my
long trek and took a drink from the bowl. That's when everything turned
topsy-turvy."

"You could have fooled me," Roscoe interjected.

Gretchen ignored his comment. "I recognized one of the figures when
he looked out from under the shawl. It was Shaman . . ."

At that, Roscoe stopped her. "Shaman? The bartender at the pub?"

Gretchen nodded. "The other figure was Elise."

"Who is Elise?"

"Shaman's love from another lifetime. He meets with her once a year."

Roscoe blinked. "Did he tell you that?"

"He told me he'd cut a deal with the devil to bring her back with
him."

"Did he?"

"I don't know. They did leave together."

"Let's get back to the barn. What else happened?"

Gretchen continued her story despite her skeptic listener. When she
reached the part where she woke up in her own bedroom, he stopped her.

"I've got the picture," he said. "Now for the big question. How did
Harley get to Dublin? And don't tell me he went by time machine. I don't
buy that."

"I don't know, but he and Professor Ipswitch and the professor's partner
all showed up at the barn after Shaman and Elise left."

"Through the shield?"

"Yes. Morgan tried to push me into the fire, but he stumbled and fell.
The fire swallowed him up." She stopped talking to see how he took that
part of her story. He seemed resigned, so she continued, "Then the hay in
the loft caught fire, and the entire barn burned to the ground."

"Who's Morgan?"

"The professor's partner, your murdered victim, the hunchback," she explained.

"He's alive?"

"Yes, when I saw him."

Roscoe stopped taking notes. "First, you tell me you saw Morgan killed that afternoon. Then you tell me he's alive and well nearly six hours later. How do you account for the time lapse?"

Gretchen frowned. "You asked me—"

"I know I did. Go on."

"By this time it's nearly midnight, and we headed back to the graveyard."

"You, Harley, and the professor?"

"Yes. That's when Magus showed up in his magic chariot—to lead us home."

"Of course. Why not?" Sergeant Baguette sat quietly. He didn't move, but stared at the woman across the table.

"Please, it's a dream," giving him time to absorb her latest revelation.

"I know I'm going to regret this next question," Roscoe said, running his fingers through his already rumpled mop of red hair and wishing he were anywhere but here. "How did you get back?"

Gretchen hesitated before taking the plunge. "Magus opened the magic door, and Harley and I left, but he kept the professor with him in the *Netherworld*. I don't know how he got back." She looked down at her hands, moving nervously in her lap.

"Don't ask me anything else, Sergeant Baguette. I don't remember coming home." Close to tears, she laid her head on the table. "I can't explain it. I only know it happened." She raised her head and looked up at the cop. "I'm sorry, Sergeant Baguette. I don't blame you for not believing me. It's hard for me to believe."

"I'm trying, Gretchen. I'm really trying." Roscoe sympathized. "You understand my position. I've got to make logical connections between your dream and reality. It leaves me with a lot of questions, such as 'Why did Harley do nothing regarding your disappearance? Why did he call your defense a *loony tunes* defense? Why did the professor deny he had a partner?'"

"I don't know."

Roscoe ignored her. "And what part did the gun play in this scenario? It wasn't the murder weapon. What happened to it?"

"The gun was ancient. When I threw it in the water, it disintegrated."

"Disintegrated?"

"Yes. Shaman couldn't get through the shield until he got rid of the gun. When he dropped it, it fell in the water and disintegrated. It doesn't exist anymore—not in this world."

Noticing his puzzled expression, she felt empathy. "I'm sorry, Roscoe. I don't know the answers to your questions. Maybe Harley didn't want to involve me. Maybe the professor killed his partner. Maybe Kristin knows more than she's telling us. Maybe it's only a dream. See? I've got more questions than answers too."

He ignored her questions with another of his own. "Why did Harley have a gun in the first place?"

"To protect me. He had a client who threatened him, and he got me the gun in case I needed it. I thought he'd sold it, 'til I saw him dig it up from my garden."

"Your garden? The same place you found the knife?"

Gretchen nodded.

"Do you know the name of his dangerous client?"

"No, some guy Harley defended in court. He lost the case. After the defendant was sentenced to a prison term, I gave the gun back to Harley and forgot all about it."

"I need to know the name of the fellow Harley sent to prison. It's possible he's been released and renewed his threat. I'll check that out."

"Will you need me again?" Gretchen asked.

"Not right away, but quit plotting with Kristin. She loves to play pranks."

"And you fall for them."

He grinned. "She does have a way with her, doesn't she?"

*   *   *

Chapter Six

We do not understand Faith until it is tested.

Sergeant Baguette walked into the attorney's office determined to confront Harley with his latest discoveries. Harley sat behind a desk piled high with case files and law books. Roscoe looked for a place to sit, but every chair and table overflowed with files, some sliding off onto the floor. He dumped off one chair to give Roscoe a place to sit.

"We usually meet clients in the conference room," Harley excused the mess. "Image, you know. Don't want people to think we actually work."

He turned his attention to Roscoe. "What's on your mind, Roscoe? I take it, you've been talking with Gretchen?"

"Yes, and she fed me quite a story. I'm not into checking out ghosts and goblins to verify an investigation, but I do need your confirmation on some of what I've heard."

"Shoot," answered Harley. "How can I add to your confusion?"

Roscoe took a deep breath, and began. "First, there's the gun—the one you got for Gretchen. Where did you get it, who did you give it to, and why?"

"And where is it now? That your next question?" asked Harley.

"Yes, but I've a theory I want to run by you. Gretchen says you got the gun to protect her because someone threatened her . . . someone you defended in court. Tell me about him. Who is the guy, and where is he now?"

"Jake Dunbar . . . a petty thief who got in over his head. Thought he could join the big leagues and pull off a bank robbery. He went up the river. Still there, I believe."

"You remember the case?"

"Sure, I defended the guy," Harley told Roscoe. "Never did believe him guilty and surprised at his conviction. But the threats I received during and after the trial . . . they were real. Didn't make sense. Why the sudden interest?"

"Is he still *up the river,* as you say?

"Someone told Shaman recently that he'd been released, and knowing of his threats on my life, he called to warn me . . . promised to keep an eye out for him at the pub. Shaman tell you about the gun?" Harley asked.

"No, the gun doesn't interest me," Roscoe assured him, "except that it keeps popping up in my investigation. No, I'm more interested in Dunbar."

"Really? After Shaman called, I checked with the prison, and the guy's still there. Don't know how the rumor of his escape started. Why do you ask?"

"Last time I talked with Shaman, he gave me some *gobbledygook* about a partner of the professor that no one's seen . . . and whom the professor said doesn't exist."

"So? What's the problem?"

"Time element. The victim died early in the evening, yet he appeared to be in perfect health well close to midnight. How do you explain that?"

"I can't—unless . . ."

"Unless what?"

"Time zones. Have you accounted for time zones?" Harley asked.

"Why would I do that?"

"I know it sounds crazy, but what part of your story isn't?"

"Is that the best you can do?" Roscoe needled him. "I expected a sane answer from an attorney."

"Outside of declaring a perfect murder and accepting the impossible, what choice do you have?" Harley hesitated before adding, "At least, that's what my logical mind tells me."

"Logic, huh?" Roscoe fell silent, staring at the attorney intently. Then he laughed. "By Jove, Harley, I believe you've hit on it. Thanks." His energy renewed, Roscoe rushed from the attorney's office.

"What did I say?" Harley asked the officer's disappearing back. But Roscoe didn't answer. He was halfway back to the station.

*   *   *

Once there at the station, he garnered together his bits and pieces of information. His main concern: *How did Kristin get involved, and why?* He remembered their good times as kids in Yorkshire—her love of a good time, her love of adventure, and his sharing with her in those adventures. She'd had a rare talent for making life come alive. Many times, he'd found himself drawn into one of her escapades, sometimes much to his regret.

He pushed his chair back against the wall, put his big feet on the desk, and reminisced. He hadn't seen Kristin for years until their paths had crossed recently. Outwardly, he'd found her unchanged—the same mischievous glint in her eyes he'd remembered from his youth. Today, a more serious, intense Kristin seemed to use that same devil-may-care attitude as a shield. *Why? What changed her? What made her plot against her best friend?* The entire episode smacked of a Kristin technique—time travel, ancient rituals, secret ingredients—and the final coup d'etat, introducing him, a cop, into the mix.

Why would she take the chance? She and the professor had a good thing going—he creating, and she selling—unless . . . Roscoe pushed the chair back against the wall as his feet crashed to the floor. A sudden thought hit the gregarious lawman as he recreated the scenario. *Aha, that's it! It isn't the professor's invention, it's his partner's grounds for murder!*

Roscoe grabbed his coat off the rack and headed for the door. *That guy at the university lab, he holds the key.* Heading his police car toward the university, he found the lab assistant getting ready to leave.

Roscoe stopped him. "You're the only person I've interviewed so far who makes sense," he told the startled assistant.

"Well, thanks, I guess. What's up?"

"Remember on my last visit, you were analyzing some potion? Did you ever discover the secret ingredient?" Roscoe's enthusiasm bubbled over in excitement.

The lab assistant smiled. "Sure. Didn't I mail you a copy? Come on in, and let me check. I can run you off another copy in a sec, if you'd like."

"If it isn't too much trouble, I'd appreciate it . . . and I'll wait for this one." Roscoe followed him into the lab. "You'll probably need to explain it to me anyway," he said, having no intention of returning to the station empty-handed.

"That illusive ingredient quite surprised me," the assistant told Roscoe, "although, I don't know why it should. You hear about drugs on campus all the time, but you seldom get involved in the business end of it." He pulled out a file from his desk drawer. "Here it is. I ran this for an attorney here in town, Harley Dandrich. He has the original, I sent you a copy." He grinned at Roscoe. "You should check your mail oftener."

Roscoe ignored him. "What does it say?"

"It's relatively harmless, but it's a derivative of LSD and shouldn't be sold over the counter," he informed Roscoe. "There's always someone who overdoes a good thing. When I didn't hear from anyone, I considered the matter closed."

"You didn't question the attorney?"

"No, why should I? I did contact the marketer and advised her of its potential danger."

"The marketer?" Roscoe asked.

"Yes, an antique shop, **The Brass Ring.** It markets the potion under the pseudonym, *Heaven Scent.* The owner is one of the partners, as is the attorney. He's the one who requested I analyze its so-called *secret* ingredient."

"Thanks. You've been a big help." Roscoe put the copy of the report in his pocket and headed back to the station, his mind reeling with facts now instead of suppositions. He knew how close he'd come to ignoring Gretchen and her input, but things were beginning to fall into place. *If that lab technician hadn't discovered the secret ingredient, I'd have absolutely nothing to base my suspicions on. And if Gretchen hadn't been so susceptible to suggestion, I'd probably still believe in phantom sleuths and psychics.*

He checked his watch. *Time to confront Kristin.*

*　　*　　*

Kristin nibbled on hot, buffalo wings, Shaman's specialty, as she occasionally dipped celery sticks into his special dressing. She looked from Roscoe to Gretchen seated across from her. They'd met as she'd prearranged, at their weekly Friday luncheon, but things weren't right. Roscoe didn't look happy, and Gretchen looked strained. *What's going on?*

Worried, catching Gretchen's expression, she directed her attention to Roscoe. "When did you figure it out?" she asked in a low voice.

"Did you really think you'd get away with it?"

"Get away with what?" Gretchen asked, looking from one to the other. "What are you talking about?"

Roscoe ignored her and waited for Kristin to answer.

"Yeah, I guess I did. What tipped you off?"

"*Heaven Scent.* If you and Professor Ipswitch wanted fame and fortune, that's fine, but you enlisted the innocent participation of Gretchen and Harley in your scheme."

"That's preposterous. I don't even know Professor—" She stopped talking at Gretchen's expression. "Well, we did have a business relationship," she admitted. "That doesn't mean anything."

"Not in itself, it doesn't. You had me fooled. That is, 'til Gretchen told me the rest of the story. My suspicions started when Harley unwittingly made a comment that didn't make sense . . . unless he knew something I didn't," Sergeant Baguette told her.

"What did he say?"

"He asked me if I'd checked time zones. He meant it to be facetious, I'm sure. Time travel didn't make much sense to me, but the disappearance of Gretchen for a week, that did make sense to me."

Kristin shrugged. "Doesn't prove anything."

"Not until I talked to the lab technician who'd isolated the secret ingredient. He warned both you and Harley of its potential danger . . . warnings you both ignored."

"Harley?" Gretchen interrupted.

Sergeant Baguette ignored her, his attention focused on Kristin. "My bits and pieces began to make sense when he named the secret ingredient as *psilocybin.* It's an hallucinogenic drug originating from a mushroom known to grow only in Mexico."

"What does that have to do with me?" Kristin asked.

"You wrote me you'd vacationed there last summer. Did you bring anything back for the professor?"

"Kristin, you didn't!" Gretchen stared at her friend in disbelief. Kristin concentrated on the wine in her glass.

"He asked me to bring him back a particular kind of Mexican mushroom. I didn't know why he wanted it, and I certainly didn't know his plans for *Heaven Scent* at the time. I figured it a *pie-in-the-sky* fantasy and indulged him. That's all."

"What did he promise you, Kristin?" Gretchen prodded.

"Marketing rights to *Heaven Scent* . . . and a percentage of the gross."

"Then things got out of control, all hell broke loose, and you had to regroup. I understand, Kristin," Roscoe said softly. "Now I need you to fill me in on the details. What happened to your big plans?"

"I'm not involved in any murder, Roscoe. You can't pin that on me."

"No, I don't believe you are. What happened was unintentional—a string of unexpected circumstances. My guess is the partner created the potion, and the professor laid claim to it, that is . . . until the partner complained. Am I right?"

Gretchen looked at Kristin accusingly. "Kristin how could you?"

"I'm sorry, Gretchen. I didn't know anything about a partner, and I didn't know of any murder until I read it in the newspaper. Even then, I didn't tie the two events together."

Gretchen turned to Roscoe. "I'm inclined to believe her, Roscoe. Who did kill the professor's partner?"

"I've no idea. We don't have a positive ID. He may or may not be the partner. That's why I need Kristin's input. I think she knows more than she's admitting."

Kristin was silent.

"Maybe she'll remember at the station," Roscoe threatened, glaring at her. "Shall we go, my dear?"

"You're going to arrest me?" she asked as Roscoe showed her a pair of handcuffs. "Don't cuff me. I'll go with you."

"Wouldn't think of it." He pocketed the cuffs and prepared to leave. "Coming, Gretchen?"

*   *   *

Later, at the station house, Sergeant Baguette guided them to the interrogation room, now equipped with a recorder. He closed the door. Gretchen wondered why she'd been included in the questioning. She could add nothing. Roscoe settled back in his seat and glared at Kristin.

"Okay, Kristin," he said, "let's have it from the beginning. Why?"

Kristin shrugged. "Why not? The professor had a product. I had a gift shop and clientele. It sounded like a marriage made in heaven. When he offered me a partnership in exchange for a few mushrooms from Mexico, that didn't sound like any big deal. I already had plans to vacation there. How could I refuse?"

"Knowing you, I don't suppose you couldn't. Didn't you consider that crossing the Mexican border with drugs could land you in a Mexican prison?"

Kristin laughed. "Never gave it a thought. It was a *kick*."

Gretchen listened from a comfortable distance as Kristin disclosed how the professor intended to try out his new creation at **Shaman's Pub** that evening, and how she'd advised him against it. "I suggested he experiment on an animal first," she told Roscoe. "He ignored me. I didn't know he'd used it on Gretchen until too late."

"His new creation, *Resurrection,* not the one Harley had analyzed?" Gretchen asked

"Yes, *Resurrection,* his latest experiment . . . an age-controlling potion. That's the one he gave Gretchen at the pub," Kristin told him.

"Is there a difference?"

"I don't know. He didn't confide in me. I gather it's the same, but stronger."

"Did Shaman know what he'd done that night?"

"Not until later."

"How much later?"

"When Gretchen disappeared, Shaman started questioning Harley . . . and the professor got nervous. He'd planned to keep Gretchen at the cottage and observe her reactions, but lost track of her. He got pretty scared after that." She glared at Roscoe before continuing her story. "I didn't know anything about Gretchen until Harley came by Monday morning wanting to know if I'd seen her."

Gretchen's mind drifted back to her dream experience—*so that's how I became a cat*—as she tried to match Kristin's nebulous account of what happened with her own experience.

"The professor's partner." She heard Roscoe ask. "No one except Gretchen and her cat friends seem to have met him. Who is he?"

"I've no idea. The professor claimed they were his inventions . . . *he* created them. I never saw a partner. I did business with the professor." Kristin dropped her head on the table. "You've got to believe me, Roscoe, I honestly don't know any more than I've already told you."

"The dead man, ever see him before?"

"No."

"Anything you can add to this, Gretchen?" asked Roscoe interrupting her daydream.

"What?" Gretchen stirred from her reverie.

"Can you add anything further to Kristin's version of events?"

Gretchen searched her conscience. *Would anything I say now help the situation?* "Professor Ipswitch isn't the murderer, Roscoe. Morgan killed his partner for the potion, and he's already paid. He burned up in the fire."

"There you go again, Gretchen. Disassociating yourself from reality." Sergeant Baguette looked disgusted. "Tell me, who is this partner? Where did he come from? I have to deal with facts here . . . not illusions. I live in this world, not your *Neverworld.*"

"*Netherworld,* Roscoe. Please don't convict the wrong man."

"I don't intend to." He gathered up his papers and prepared to leave. "I'll leave you two to settle your differences," he said and left them alone. *Maybe they'll talk if I'm not in the room.*

As soon as Roscoe had left the room and the recorder turned off, Kristin faced Gretchen. "You have to believe me, Gretchen. I never met a partner.

The professor told me he met this weird chap in trouble with the law and befriended him. He swore the guy was innocent, even though he'd been sentenced to prison."

"What about *Resurrection?*

"He discovered *Heaven Scent* from an ancient recipe he discovered in the prison library. For the fun of it, he mailed it to the professor, the *Heaven Scent* I sell in my shop."

"I repeat, Kristin. What about *Resurrection?*"

"I didn't know he planned to use those Mexican mushrooms in his new mix, Gretchen. You've got to believe me."

"Is he still in prison?"

"I don't know . . . and that's the truth." Kristin answered. "If he is, maybe he and the professor fought over who'd get the lion's share of the profits if it were a success. Whatever happened, the professor didn't kill him."

"How do you know, Kristin? He could very well be the killer . . . if what you say is true."

"He had nothing to gain by killing the goose that laid the golden egg," said Kristin. "Could just as easily have been Harley or Shaman. They both have reasons for wanting the professor out of the way."

"Harley? Why would you say that?" *She's changing her story.*

"Harley's on the board of directors too."

"As an attorney for a corporation the professor set up. That's not a motive for murder. Who else is on the board?"

"That's it. Me, the professor, and Harley . . . it takes three to form a corporation."

And Roscoe has three suspects. "Go on. Where does Morgan fit in?"

"I've no idea. I told you, I never saw a partner."

"My guess is that Morgan and the partner are one and the same."

"That's the way I figured it," agreed Kristin.

"Are you saying that the professor's partner broke out of prison, and Professor Ipswitch hid him out at the university? That's why no one's seen him? Why would he do that?"

"To keep him from gaining control of the potion."

"Didn't the potion belong to Morgan?"

"No, he sent it to the professor. That's why they fought. The professor tried to reason with him—to tell him there's enough for everyone, but Morgan wouldn't listen."

"So the professor killed him? You told me he had no reason."

"I'm guessing, Gretchen, the same as you are. I suppose you could say that the professor had all the necessary credentials to create and patent the potion himself. He didn't need Morgan anymore. Maybe he hired Shaman to do the honors, and Harley provided the gun."

Gretchen interrupted her. "I don't believe you," she said. "Shaman has absolutely no interest in the professor's creations. Nor does Harley."

"Shaman is the assassin," she said.

Gretchen looked at her longtime friend in disbelief. "Why didn't you tell Roscoe?"

Kristin is silent, her mind traveling in high gear. Then something clicked. *Gretchen isn't going to help me.*

"It won't work, Kristin. Roscoe will identify the fingerprints on the knife and prove that neither Harley nor Shaman were involved. That ruse won't work."

Kristin voiced her thoughts. "You're not going to help."

"Not so," Gretchen assured her, "but I find it difficult to forgive you and Harley for leading me on when you suspected something all along."

"I'm sorry, Gretchen, we didn't expect *you* to get involved in a murder, talk about dumb luck."

"That isn't luck, that's reality. Murphy's Law, whatever can go wrong, will—you know that one, Kristin." As Gretchen digested what Kristin told her, she added, "I don't believe you're responsible for the murder, Kristin, but you did allow money to influence your decisions. And you did attempt a cover-up in league with the professor."

"What do you intend to do?" a penitent Kristin asked.

Gretchen hesitated before voicing a suggestion. "If you tell Roscoe what you've told me, I'll help you in any way I can, but you have to level with him, otherwise the deal's off."

When Sergeant Baguette returned, Kristin related an entirely different story to him. On the basis of her new revelations, he rescheduled interrogations with Harley and Shaman and allowed Kristin to return to her antique shop. And he incarcerated Professor Ipswitch, pending further investigation.

Chapter Seven

Whatever can go wrong, will go wrong.
—Murphy's Law

Once again, Sergeant Baguette visited Harley Dandrich in his office. This time he intended to compare Harley's version of what happened to the story Gretchen elicited from Kristin. He found Harley deeply involved in reviewing the Jake Dunbar case file, his coat tossed on a table, his shirt open at the collar, and his tie askew. *I wonder if he knows that Kristin accused him and Shaman of the murder.*

"I thought we verified that Dunbar's still serving his sentence," Roscoe said.

"We did, but you know, there's something odd about that old case of mine."

"Oh? How come?"

"Well, I never could understand why the threats continued *after* Dunbar's sentencing. I've been checking his history, and guess what I've discovered?" He turned and grinned at Roscoe. "Sit down, I'll fill you in."

"I'm listening." Harley cleared a space on a chair, and Roscoe filled it, waiting expectantly. "What's the big news?"

"Jake Dunbar had a twin—an identical twin brother. I'm thinking we sent the wrong man to prison."

"You think the victim is the one who should have been jailed?" Roscoe asked.

"According to what I've been able to find out, they were separated at birth and adopted by different families. Neither one ever met the other."

"You understand what that does to my case, don't you?"

"Yeah, but if there are two of them, it answers a lot of questions." Harley squinted at Roscoe over his wire-frame glasses. "We'd need birth records to prove there's more than one person in the mix."

"Seems the professor knows more than he's telling," Roscoe said.

"Yeah, think you can squeeze the professor enough to make him talk?"

"It's what I do best," Roscoe assured him.

"Now, what else is on your mind?" Harley queried. "You didn't come by for a friendly chat, did you?"

"No, I needed to know how involved you are with the professor and Kristin. Is there some diversionary tactic you two cooked up to keep me off guard?"

"Not at all. I'm trying to clear Kristin. Granted, she's a little *harum-scarum* at times and thrives on suspense, but she's basically honest. I'd hate to see her railroaded, like Dunbar."

"You'd better convince me," Roscoe said. "I've known her for years, too, and I think this time she's stepped too close to the edge."

"That doesn't make her a criminal or even a worthy accomplice. She wanted success. There's no crime in that. She saw her chance and took it. If that's guilt, we're all guilty." He peered at Roscoe. "Let me show you what I've found."

"I hope you're not trying to head me off in another direction. I'm confused enough."

Harley grinned and began his tale of suppositions. "What if I'm right? And there are identical twin babies—Jake and Morgan—adopted at birth by different parents? They could live their entire lives without ever knowing they had a twin."

"That's your theory?" Roscoe asked. "Then they met accidentally and figure it out?"

"Something like that, or maybe one knows and the other doesn't. I'm more inclined to think that's what happened. Dunbar spent a lot of time digging through the prison library. Maybe he found out more than that controversial recipe."

"I see where you're going," Roscoe agreed. "Morgan discovered he had a twin brother when Jake's picture, as the accused, hit the newspapers. He decided to let his twin take the rap. Meanwhile, Morgan had his own reasons for keeping his silence and used the knowledge to his own advantage. That about it?"

"That's one theory," Harley agreed. "Or maybe our illustrious Professor Ipswitch, who knew Morgan, recognized the startling resemblance to his partner, a known criminal, and took advantage of the situation. He hid the real criminal from public view, using Morgan's expertise for his own purposes."

"You think the professor knew Jake was innocent, but pulled the switch and allowed the wrong twin to go to prison?" Roscoe asked. "Kinda far-fetched, isn't it?"

"I'm trying to prove a theory, Roscoe. What if Morgan knew he had a twin, but the professor didn't? Or that Jake didn't?"

"And Morgan sat back and watched while his innocent twin went to prison? As long as you're only supposing, I might go along with that," Roscoe agreed.

"Answer me one question, Roscoe. Why did threatening letters continue *after* the trial?"

"I don't know, but without the letters, we may never have known." He got up to leave. "It's been an interesting meeting, Harley. You think the professor's involved in the scheme, and you may be right. I've arrested the professor on the information I have. It's circumstantial, but maybe this information will help squeeze him." *If you're right, I may wrap up my case.*

"How about Kristin?" Harley asked. "What are your plans for her?"

Roscoe hesitated. "Kristin? I don't know. It's a stretch, you may be right about her." He dug his hands in his pockets, "Maybe, Harley, I'm too moral to believe she's completely innocent. She's a big girl . . . she knows right from wrong."

*   *   *

Professor Ipswitch went on trial for murder later that spring. Harley testified that the victim's twin brother, the man he'd sent to prison five years ago due to mistaken identity, was innocent of the charges brought against him at that time. He therefore requested a full review of the charges based on new information. The court agreed.

Gretchen testified on the professor's behalf, believing that Morgan killed his twin to keep the recipe from being exposed to a profit-seeking world. He then escaped into the *Netherworld.* She knew Morgan would never be found to prove or disprove her theory, but her testimony did help Kristin. The court exonerated her from any liability after she confessed to her part in the marketing scheme.

Facts brought out during the trial failed to prove Roscoe's theory, that the professor murdered his partner in order to gain full control of a very lucrative product. And the court refused to accept Harley's theory that Morgan, the supposed twin brother of Jake Dunbar, robbed the bank and disappeared leaving Jake to take the rap for his criminal twin. Evidence as to the existence of Morgan, the professor's partner and Jakes' twin, could never be verified. The lab assistant had never seen him, nor had anyone else. Shaman denied all knowledge of Morgan ever being in his pub, and Harley could not positively prove that Dunbar had a twin, although new evidence garnered from Professor Ipswitch did clear Jake with the court.

The victim's body was never positively identified, and town officials buried him in a pauper's grave outside town. The jury acquitted the professor for lack of evidence since none of the story Gretchen told Roscoe could be admitted as evidence. No one except Kristin and Roscoe believed her fantasy, and Roscoe—although he preferred fact to fantasy—accepted the results of the trial.

Harley felt justice had been served in the case of *Jake Dunbar v. the State of Connecticut* when the court pardoned Jake Dunbar in light of additional evidence presented by Professor Ipswitch. Morgan was never seen nor heard from again.

All in all, everything turned out as well as could be expected. Gretchen returned to writing books, Kristin continued to sell *Heaven Scent* at her antique shop, but *Resurrection* was put on hold pending further research. Sergeant Baguette became involved in another case that he hoped wouldn't include witches and hobgoblins.

At times, Harley wondered who sent the threatening letters that caused him to buy a gun in the first place, but a grateful Gretchen discovered she didn't imagine her escapade into the *Netherworld*.

Epilogue

Some months later, Gretchen cleaned out her closet intending to contribute clothes she no longer wore to her church. "They're out of style," she consoled herself. "I'll never wear them again." Pulling a few dresses from their hangers, she pushed back the remaining clothes to check those she hadn't worn in years. That's when she noticed a pile of dirty garments on the floor pushed way back into a corner.

"Hmm," she said, "Wonder how long these have been here?" She pulled them out of their hiding place and sniffed. "Wow, filthy! They smell like smoke." She sniffed again. "Fireplace smoke, not cigarette smoke." *Where did I ever wear these?* She plopped herself on the floor and dug deeper into the cluttered corner of her closet.

She inspected a pair of weird-looking silver slippers. *From another planet. I don't remember buying these, and this dress . . .* She picked up the sheer froth of material vaguely resembling a dress and examined it. *Looks familiar in a strange sort of way, but I'd never buy anything this flimsy. It isn't me. Where did it come from?* Gretchen nearly tossed the dress aside when she felt something solid in a pocket. Conscious of the smoky odor emanating from the folds of the dress, she gingerly put her hand into the pocket. Grasping a solid object, she pulled out a small vial of liquid.

"My magic potion," she said, recognizing the bottle. "I've had it all the time."

She placed the bottle on her dresser. Undecided what to do next, she sat down in the middle of her bedroom floor and looked at the strange pile of clothes. "Now what?" She tried to recall details of her cat adventure that she'd nearly forgotten.

Then, picking up the pile of tacky clothes, she placed them into a zippered plastic bag and tossed the bag into the farthest recesses of her closet—*in case someone else tells me it's all in my imagination.* She picked up the bottle of magic potion and placed it in her pocket. *I wonder if it still works.*

Closing the closet door, she gathered up the clothes she planned to give to her church and placed them in the trunk of her car. The vial she tossed into the glove compartment. *I promised Julius.* And later, digging a hole near her strawberry plants, she buried the vial.

*   *   *

PART III

For Money The Monkey Dances

Trilogy Three

Chapter One

*Behold! What you crave shall be yours to your uttermost dreams
and beyond.*
—Olde Irish Faery Tales

"For money, the monkey dances," promised the man behind the music
box. He invited the children to come closer as he turned the organ-grinder
handle and spewed out his comedic tunes. "Drop the money in the hat
and watch the monkey dance," he smiled his toothless smile. As the crowd
gathered around, the parents found coins to give their kids. The kids, in
turn, dropped the coins in the monkey's hat.

Lauren Calloway watched from the sidelines, waiting for the crowd to
disperse and for the man behind the music box to gather up his collection
and climb the steps of the Capitol building. She watched as a New York
senator met the music man at the top of the steps. They spoke a few minutes,
and the Senator dropped his offering into the monkey's hat.

Did the senator pass a message or make a contribution? Lauren couldn't
be sure. As the senator disappeared into the Senate office building, the
music man gathered up his gear. He slammed a battered hat on his head,
and the monkey leaped onto the man's shoulder. At the street, the music
man hailed a cab.

Taxi? Must have had a good morning. Lauren glanced at her watch. *He's
leaving early today—before lunch.* Hating to admit defeat, she noted the cab
number and headed for her car. From her car she watched for the cab carrying
the music man and found it at the next stoplight. The cab headed for the
opulent Watergate district close to the Capitol and stopped in front of an
expensive-looking apartment complex. The man and his monkey exited the
cab and entered the building.

"Well, what do you know," Lauren mused. "The monkey business pays more than I thought." She noted the address and drove on, returning to the Senate building to check on the senator, but he had left. She returned to her office.

Lauren had been working as an agent for the FBI for the past year and looked forward to her assignments. She'd been detailed to this watch for the past few months ever since the September 11 bombing in New York City when a money trail led them in this direction. So far, her assignment had been to observe. She had no idea why she watched the music man, but that was okay. All her life she'd loved watching people.

During her teen years in Ridgecrest, Connecticut, she'd watched kids in cars watching kids on foot—keeping up on high school gossip that way. Lauren didn't tell anyone how she got her information for the school newspaper, not even her best friends, Gretchen and Kristin. She treasured her high school friendships and elated when both she and Gretchen were accepted at the University of Connecticut. They resumed their close friendship and added Kristin, a young English emigrant from Britain, to their list of favorite people.

Gretchen, now a homemaker and married to an attorney, had recently published her third book. Kristin had bought a tiny antique shop in Ridgecrest after her college days and built the shop into a now-thriving business. And Lauren transferred her love of people watching to her new job as FBI agent. Her sharp eye for detail helped her remember faces and numbers, and out of the ordinary phenomena, enabling her to make connections older and more seasoned veterans of the force missed. That same eye for detail caused her to notice an estrangement between her two best friends. Nothing Lauren could put her finger on—more an instinct, a tone of voice when she mentioned Kristin. Then out of the blue last week, Gretchen called to ask if she could impose on her friend for a few weeks. She needed to research life in the Capitol—the setting for her next novel. *She's arriving Thursday morning.*

Chapter Two

Love seeketh only self to please . . . And builds a Hell in Heaven's despite.

—William Blake

Day 1, Thursday

Agent Carlton glared at the man in front of him. *What right did he have to tell him he'd done it all wrong? He wasn't there.* He could barely hide his contempt for this inferior being, his boss and head of the FBI and from whom he took his orders. He tried to stay calm. "You would have done it differently?"

"I would. You're living in the past, Carlton. This business no longer kills for no reason. Had you used a little more *finesse* and less brute force, you would not be in the situation you're in now." Gadsden stared in the cold ice-blue eyes of the man before him. The scar on the side of his face pulsed in anger, telling Gadsden that he'd trod on shaky ground. Carlton, the epitome of good breeding, killed as easily as he drank his Scotch whiskey. Hard as nails, impeccably dressed in pale buckskins and Australian bush jacket, Gadsden acknowledged that for all his toughness, he did attract the gentler sex. He also knew his weaknesses—one of them being his inability to accept criticism for his work. The guy before him seethed with rage.

"What did you do with the body?"

"Left it. It's at the morgue now. I left my phony credentials and took his. There's no way the police can connect the guy to this office. He doesn't exist."

Gadsden leaned back in his chair, silent and in deep thought. He turned and looked out of the window as though gazing upon the calming green of the landscape. He let the man in front of him stew. Then he turned back to Carlton and asked, "Did anyone see you?"

Carlton snorted, "No, of course not!"

"You're sure of that."

Carlton didn't answer, and Gadsden continued. "My report tells me that an unidentified person gave an eyewitness account of the killer."

"No one saw me. Let me see that report."

Gadsden handed the report to Carlton who smiled his mirthless grin. "They'd never find me with that description," he assured Gadsden and handed the report back.

"Nevertheless, you'll need to take a long vacation for a while. Pick up your paycheck and don't come back until the coast is clear."

Carlton turned on his heel and left the room. Gadsden pushed a button on his intercom and said to his secretary, "Contact Calloway and get her over here."

* * *

Leaving her office at lunchtime, Lauren Calloway headed for the airport terminal to pick up her friend Gretchen. She thought about Gadsden's reaction to her surveillance report on the music man. It had certainly piqued interest at FBI headquarters, especially when she'd told her supervisor about the incident on the Capitol steps and related the senator's reactions. Perhaps she'd never learn the final results of her surveillance or how the pieces fit together. That's how the bureau appeared to operate—each agent responsible for his or her own assignment. Lauren could only hope that someone in authority would connect the dots. Little did she know she'd soon find herself in the position of connecting her own dots for a seemingly senseless act.

Arriving at the airport, she gunned her car into a vacant spot in the underground parking garage and raced into the terminal. *Her plane will be landing any minute now.* In the viewing room, she watched the American Airlines plane land then taxi into its designated docking area. Outside the secured area, Lauren spied Gretchen walking toward her, juggling her carry-on luggage. The limit of two bags and an oversize purse to boot took some maneuvering. After passing the secure area, Gretchen dropped her bags on the floor and embraced her friend.

"Ooh, it's so wonderful to see you again—it's been sooo long," she gushed.

"Hey, don't overdo it, Gretchen, you'll spoil me." Lauren relieved Gretchen of one of her bags. "Why didn't you grab a cart?"

"Never saw one, or gone by the time I got there," Gretchen answered, picking up the other bag and following Lauren to the parking garage. "Someday I'm going to get one of those suitcases on little wheels and a handle, if I have to keep traveling. These old relics require a male companion."

"I agree." Gretchen traveling alone did surprise Lauren as Harley had a way of keeping her on a tight leash. "Speaking of male companions, where's Harley? Thought you two never traveled alone."

Amused by the comment, Gretchen smiled. "Harley's a different animal these days," she said. "My husband has *loosed* the reins, so to speak."

Lauren popped the trunk of her Ford Focus, and the two dumped the luggage into the spacious trunk. Slamming down the trunk lid, she asked, "Interesting. How so?"

Gretchen shrugged. "Who knows? Success maybe? Gives one a whole new perspective."

"You'll have to tell me about it."

"Later. First, let's find a place where I can grab a bite to eat. My treat—the airlines have become quite stingy lately—particularly on short hops." Gretchen climbed in the car, noting its newness and remembering the *clunkers* Lauren drove in college. "Nice wheels," she commented. "New?"

"Goes with the job." Lauren maneuvered her car out of the parking garage and onto the streets of Washington, DC. "Big improvement over the days we poured ourselves into my broken down old Volkswagen, hmm?"

"Sure is." She turned to Lauren and smiled. "Hey, congratulations on landing the job of the century, Lauren. You're the envy of UC grads."

"Thanks. More important, though, I love my job." Lauren steered the car to a charming little café in the out-of-the-way Watergate area.

"I'm impressed," Gretchen said, noting the ambiance as she viewed the café. "Almost as charming as Shaman's Pub."

"Almost," agreed Lauren. "Shaman gets the edge though. His place is a piece of history. In comparison, Watergate is young yet." The two ordered wine and lunch and settled down to shortening the gaps in their lives since their last visit.

"Gretchen," Lauren asked as she takes a sip from her glass of Chardonnay, "whatever happened in Ridgecrest last year? I read all the newspapers, those that carried the story, but they left me with more questions than answers."

"Shouldn't wonder. They tossed out my testimony as irrelevant, but Kristin's the one who really shocked me, and I thought I knew her so well."

"How so?"

"Oh, we kept up our weekly luncheons after you left, but I lost a *confidante* last year." Gretchen stopped as the waitress sets lunch in front of her and waited for her to leave before continuing. "Remember in college, that old dogma we quoted? *Never trust anyone over thirty?*" At Lauren's nod, she continued. "We thought that pretty smart, didn't we? But you know?" she shook her head as if in disbelief. "It's not funny anymore."

Puzzled, Lauren broke in, "I don't follow. What did that have to do with you and Kristin?"

"Kristin and Harley betrayed my trust. I lost a whole week in my life, and the people I trusted most let me down. We're the *soon-to-be-over-thirty* crowd, Lauren, and we're worse. We don't trust each other."

Lauren laughed. "You lost a week—a whole week? What were you drinking?"

"It's not funny."

"Sorry." Lauren struggled not to laugh. "Go on."

"Someone knows what happened, but no one's talking. Lauren, I don't trust Harley anymore. We tiptoe around the subject as though we were strangers—it's like living in a box. It can't continue."

"You mean . . . you can't talk about it."

"Right. Harley and Kristin prefer to pretend nothing happened . . . that I dreamed it all . . . and perfectly content to leave it at that."

"And you can't?"

"I hate mysteries unless I'm writing them."

"Anything I can do?" Lauren asked.

"I don't know." She looked at Lauren, her meal momentarily forgotten. "I used research for my new novel as an excuse to get away and collect my thoughts. I never thought I'd look forward to getting away from home, but Harley's become my bogeyman."

Lauren, in the process of removing her napkin ring, stared at her friend, wondering if she'd slipped into her own fantasy world when Gretchen laughed. "You should see your face, Lauren." She stifled her laugh. *She's not ready.*

Lauren, relieved, choked out. "You had me scared, Gretchen, I didn't know whether to laugh or cry." She recovered quickly before she shot out, "I must say, though, I don't much appreciate your pulling my leg."

"Hmm? Oh no." Gretchen shook her head and fiddled with her silverware. "I didn't mean to do that." She continued in a softer voice. "I really do need your honest counsel, Lauren. Goodness knows I don't get that at home, not now, anyway."

"Then there really is something wrong, between you and Harley, and Kristin?"

"Let's discuss it later, Lauren. Right now, it's time to relax."

They concentrated on eating—Lauren more puzzled than ever, and Gretchen hoping Lauren had answers to her puzzling questions when Lauren's cell phone broke the silence. Fishing in an oversized purse for her cell phone, she checked the sender. "Excuse me, Gretchen. It's my office. I've got to answer it."

"Anything wrong?" Gretchen asked when Lauren snapped her phone closed. "You look as though you'd seen a ghost."

"Maybe I have. My assignment seems to have committed suicide, and I'm evidently the last person to see him alive. I've got to go by my office."

Gretchen ventured to ask, "I take it, you don't think it's a suicide?"

"I don't know, but if it's true, what happened to his monkey?"

"Monkey? Gee, Lauren, I know you can't discuss your job with me, but what's this about a monkey? Maybe I can help you worry about him."

Lauren laughed, and the two friends finished their lunch. Leaving the charming little café, Lauren took Gretchen back to her small garden apartment before heading to her office.

"I'm glad you're here, Gretchen. Make yourself comfortable, and I'll see what Gadsden has on his mind. You'll be okay?"

"Sure, I'll appreciate the downtime. Do what you have to do. I'll be fine." She dragged her luggage into Lauren's spare bedroom before calling out, "Oh, and good luck."

Lauren threw back a "Thanks" as she headed out the door. "Make yourself at home."

After she'd left, Gretchen toured the small neat apartment, appreciating Lauren's taste in her selection of art. She wandered into Lauren's bedroom and spied a Siamese cat curled up among the pillows on her bed. The cat opened one eye and peered at Gretchen.

"Who are you?" she asked the blue-eyed Siamese, a replica of Einstein and Ming. "Do you have a name?" The cat rose from the pillows and strolled over to her, nuzzling her outstretched hand. Gretchen petted the gorgeous animal and checked the collar around its neck.

"Oh, so that's who you are," Gretchen said, looking deep into the clear blue eyes. "I'm happy to make your acquaintance, Cyrus. I'm Gretchen."

Back at the office

Lauren knew as soon as she walked into her office that trouble brewed. Mr. Gadsden waved her to a seat while he continued to talk on the phone. Lauren fidgeted, waiting for him. Something's definitely on his mind and whatever it is, it involved her. Finally he finished his call, leaned back in his chair, and turned to look out the window behind him. Lauren waited and wondered. *What is he thinking?*

Philip Gadsden, a Harvard graduate and under the age of thirty she surmised, had an aura of success about him. A short well-muscled young man whose well-tailored suits camouflaged his bulkiness and whose simplicity of language hid a well-muscled mind. *A man to be reckoned with,* Lauren knew. She watched him turn over in his mind how best to handle his latest problem—her.

When he finally turned to her, he confirmed her fears. "Lauren, I'm going to put you on administrative leave 'til we clear up this situation. At the moment, you're a marked target. If you have a place to go away from Washington, I advise you to leave."

"Huh?" a surprised Lauren asked. "What happened, Gadsden? At least I deserve to know why I'm being asked to leave."

"Of course, you do, but your assignment is finished. Your surveillance dug up a *can of worms,* and the brass upstairs are screaming *leak.* And you know what that does to our business. The police want to question you, but the bureau works in secrecy. Only a handful of agents knew about your report, and when one of our undercover men winds up dead shortly thereafter, the finger pointing begins. I want you out of here."

"And I don't want to go," Lauren objected. "Look, Gadsden, I agreed to take my chances when I signed on for this job. So far, I've had nothing but *baby* assignments. I want more than that." Lauren came close to begging. "Don't take me off. Let me in on what you know. What happened to the information I dropped off? Where does it go from here?"

"I don't know, and that's the truth. It could have gone in any direction. You were not the only one to observe that little display on the Capitol steps, but a Senator can't be dragged into the public eye. Our job is to protect the president and Congress, not investigate them."

"Investigating congressmen is a *no-no?* They have access to top security information. How do we know there isn't a traitor in Congress? Who clears them for access?"

"We do, but it's cursory. We trust the voters who elected them. By the time a candidate goes through years of campaigning, there's not much left to discover. Or at least that the way it's supposed to work." Gadsden offered in support of Congress.

"If I'm not involved with the bureau, will I be free to investigate on my own?" Lauren asked. "That way, if I get into trouble, you don't get the blame."

"You mean, like a double agent, Lauren?"

She pondered the question. "Never thought about it, but yes, I guess that's what I'd be."

Phil Gadsden turned back to the window behind his desk. He seemed to do his best, thinking, watching the monument across the square. Lauren waited.

"I'm going to recommend your release from the bureau." He turned to face her and grinned. "Because of your involvement in politics."

"My what . . . ?"

"That's right," he says. "We can't have political activists in the bureau—too dangerous." He picked up her report from his desk and handed it to her. "Don't come near the office. Report to me by cell phone on my secure line. That's your new assignment."

Pleased, Lauren took her report. "Thanks, Phil. I'll do my best."

Later that evening

Gretchen and Lauren stretched out in the apartment prepared for a lively chat. Lauren wanted to know all about Kristin and Harley—and life back in Ridgecrest. Gretchen wanted to know more about Lauren's new assignment. She hoped Lauren didn't consider her a spy for wanting to learn every detail of her secretive job. With Cyrus vying for their attention, Gretchen told Lauren her story. Lauren questioned her, digging into aspects of Gretchen's story that she'd previously slid over.

"When did you first realize your dream had to be more than a dream?" Lauren asked. "Did you wake up one morning and say, '*that wasn't a dream,*' or did it hit you when you were being questioned in court?"

"You're making me analyze. Why?"

"Don't worry about *why*, answer the question. When did you first decide you were NOT dreaming?"

Sitting on the bed, her pajama-covered knees drawn to her chest, Gretchen thought back to her first suspicion. "When I met Julius at the overpass, and he warned me about Kristin. I didn't believe him, but he knew."

"Who's Julius?"

"A big handsome black cat I met in my dream."

"You talked to a cat *after* your dream?"

"Yes."

"And you didn't think that strange? Did you tell anyone?"

"No."

"Not good enough," Lauren decided. "You could have fallen asleep and dreamed that, or been so tired you dropped into the delta level, in which case you'd be susceptible to dreamlike thought waves. Any other time?"

"Yes, when I found the dream potion in the pocket of a dress I never bought, stuffed in the back of my closet, along with the weirdest pair of silver slippers I'd ever seen."

Lauren came to attention. "You found what?"

"The antidote, the one I brought back from the *Netherworld*."

"Did you bring it with you?"

Gretchen laughed, enthused for the first time since the questioning began. "No, I left it for Julius, buried in my strawberry patch. In case I needed it again."

"In case you *needed* it again," Lauren repeated. "Hmm. Why would you *need* a love potion?"

"Not *Heaven Scent, Resurrection*. It's Professor Ipswitch's new serum, and it's supposed to defy the aging process," Gretchen explained. "As a matter of fact, I'm building my new novel around that potion."

"Love it," Lauren laughed. "I want to try your potion." She stopped at the look of shock on Gretchen's face. "I'm thinking along the lines of solving cases and finding a missing monkey, but if I can extend my life span in the process . . ."

"You'd take that chance to find a monkey?"

"He's more than a *monkey* . . . he's my job. Besides, I'm on administrative leave, indefinitely . . . and advised to stay away from the bureau. We could drive to Ridgecrest and dig up your potion."

"What if you couldn't get back?"

"We'll be two this time." Lauren's enthusiasm bubbled over. "I'm *hot copy* right now. If reporters learn about me, I can't think of a better cover."

Gretchen watched her friend in amazement, loath to burst her bubble. *She doesn't think I'm crazy.*

"Think about it, Gretchen. We can sneak into places and observe like mice in a corner. Come on. It'll be fun." Gretchen, having been a victim once, tried to dissuade her.

"My little bottle won't last forever. What if we run out of the antidote?"

"I thought you had a recipe."

"No, Professor Ipswitch has it."

Lauren didn't budge. "I'll take my chances. It's already been analyzed at the university, hasn't it? If we need more, we'll make more."

"I hope you're right," a reluctant Gretchen said.

That decision reached, Gretchen and Lauren spent the rest of the evening plotting and planning—Cyrus nosing in wherever possible. "We'll check out the murder scene first," Lauren told Gretchen. "The newspapers never mentioned a monkey. He may have run off."

"You said, *we,* does that mean I can come?" Gretchen asked. "I'd love to help, if I can."

"Sure. It's not as though I'm on assignment . . . administrative leave covers a multitude of possibilities," Lauren decided. "Right now, let's get some sleep. We've a big day ahead."

"Looking for a monkey? Yeah, a big day," Gretchen agreed.

Chapter Three

Money can buy the husk of many things, but not the kernel.

Day 2, Friday

The next morning after an early breakfast, the two sleuths headed for the apartment of the music man and his monkey. The place appeared vacant; no police barriers anywhere in evidence. That surprised Lauren.

"Well, what do you know?" she said. "I'll bet the FBI doesn't know this. Then again, maybe that's the reason there's no barrier." She rang the manager's office and a pleasant-looking young man opened the door. "What can I do for you?" he asked. "Looking for an apartment?"

Lauren hesitated, wondering how to begin when Gretchen made a snap decision. "Yes, I am," she said. "I'll be in Washington for about three months . . . doing research for a book I'm writing, and this looks like a nice, quiet place. Will you accept a three-month's lease?"

Lauren stepped back, puzzled. *What's she doing, asking about an apartment?*

The young man smiled at Gretchen. "You're in luck. I've had a recent vacancy. That particular apartment is being cleaned at the moment, but I can show you a similar apartment.

"You two together?" he asked, looking at Lauren.

Lauren hesitated then said, "No, I'm looking for a monkey. I heard that its owner, an elderly gentleman, committed suicide. Do you know what happened to his monkey?"

"Suicide? Here?" The young man looked puzzled. "I think you have the wrong place. Mr. Alexander Dumant did have a pet monkey, but he checked out a week ago. Took his monkey with him, I suppose. It's his apartment that's for rent, but I assure you, there's been no suicide here."

He turned back to Gretchen. "Are you still interested?"

"Oh yes, definitely," and to Lauren, "sorry about your friend. Did you know him long?"

"No—a business associate. I'm glad he's okay." She stole a look at Gretchen who winked. "Thanks for your help," Lauren told the young man, and left.

"When will the apartment be ready?" Gretchen asked the young man after Lauren left.

"Tomorrow. You need the furniture too?"

"It's furnished?" Gretchen asked, surprised. "I didn't know." Then before the young man could change his mind, she rushed on. "Of course, I'll need furniture. What's the matter with me?"

"I thought so. Come, I'll show you my apartment. It's identical. This way." He led her to an adjacent two-bedroom apartment.

Gretchen noted exits and entries, and asked, "Do all apartments exit into the courtyard?"

"Not all, the rear apartments open onto the pool area. Would you prefer to wait for one of those?"

"No, this is fine. I'm here to write. I prefer quiet to pool noises."

"Well, I'm sure you'll find this a peaceful place," he assured her as they returned to the office. "Are you ready to sign a lease?"

Gretchen signed and received a key in return.

Leaving the office, she wandered around the apartment complex and found Lauren parked near the pool area. "Pretty slick," Lauren told her. "When did you learn to operate like that? Or does it come naturally to writers?"

"Impulse, maybe. I don't know," she said, climbing into Lauren's car. "Never know how or when inspiration—call it intuition if you wish—whatever. I accept it, and don't challenge the source."

"Wow, sounds like we have a winning team."

Gretchen grinned. "We'll need it. Since we seem to have no suicide, no murder, and no monkey, what's next?"

"We check the coroner's office. Maybe he can tell us what we want to know."

"Okay," agreed Gretchen. "Although without your ties to the FBI, aren't we sort of working in the dark?"

"Afraid of a little challenge, my dear?"

"Not at all. But if it's another dead end?"

"We'll try something else . . . like cranking up the old computer to check up on the missing Mr. Alexander Dumant. I must say, when my office cleans up a mess, they really clean up."

"Makes one wonder, doesn't it? What if you're part of the clean up?"

"Now there's a thought. What if?"

"Sorry, Lauren, but things like that fuel the imagination of us *madcap* mystery writers. Maybe we should be watching the senator instead of heading a manhunt."

"We'll do both," said Lauren "Now that you have your own apartment, do you plan to rent a car, or do your sleuthing on foot? We've good taxi service here . . . bus service too."

"All of the above, as needed," Gretchen decided. "Is the coroner's office on the way?"

"No, it's across the bridge. Let's hit the Senate ofice first," she suggested, heading out into the morning traffic. "At least we have my special parking permit. They didn't take that away . . . yet." A few minutes later, Lauren pulled into the underground parking where they took an elevator to a balcony overlooking the Senate room. "We can talk here without interfering with the proceedings . . . and keep an eye out for the senator."

The two settled into plush seats at the rear of the balcony. A group of students and obvious vacationers occupied the lower seats. Lauren pulled out binoculars. "I spend a lot of my time here," she told Gretchen.

Gretchen looked down on the floor of the Senate. "What are they doing?"

"Voting on a bill. See over there?" Lauren pointed to a scoreboard on the Senate floor. "A monitor keeps you informed of how the vote's going. Sometimes it takes hours. But if you love boredom, listen to the debates before the votes. They can discuss anything for hours on end, regardless of relevance."

"I know, I've watched C-Span. I can clean the entire house while they discuss some moot point," Gretchen agreed. "I get the impression it's more important to be seen on television than score a point."

"It's the name of the game. They know the outcome before they cast a vote. See that guy down there?" She indicated a young man on the floor of the Senate.

"The one who talks to everyone? Sure, why?"

"He isn't talking to them—he's polling for votes. He screens the votes for the majority leader of the Senate. If it isn't in his party's favor, he keeps it from coming to a vote."

Gretchen watched the scoreboard recording the votes. Republicans piled up *no* votes while the Democrats voted *yes.* "Why vote if they know the outcome?" she asked.

"A formality . . . to get the votes on record."

Gretchen watched the voting process. "How can they be split so perfectly? Don't they agree on anything?"

"You noticed?"

"Partisan loyalty?"

"You could say that."

"After they're elected, it seems they should forget party and consider what's best for the people."

"They do. They just have different ideas of what's best. It's a tossup."

"It's a logjam," decided Gretchen.

"That too. The rules change after every election. This year, Democrats are in charge."

"It really is a game, isn't it?"

"Hey, don't knock it. The party that gets the privilege of playing the game depends on your vote. That's why everybody should vote."

"Looks more like a popularity contest than an election, like in college when we voted for class president."

"It's called *checks and balances,* and it's worked for over two hundred years."

"I didn't consider its implications at the time," said Gretchen. "I will in the future." She scanned the headlines of *Capitol News,* a paper Lauren had picked up on their way into the building. "Says here, Senator Traficante is testifying before a House Ethics Committee today. Should be interesting."

"Personally, I think he's being railroaded, although where there's smoke—"

"He didn't follow the rules?"

Lauren laughed. "He's a cowboy, definitely not the darling of the Senate. More the Marlon Brando waterfront-type . . . gets a kick out of shocking the Teddy Kennedy button-downs."

"You don't like him, Kennedy, that is."

"He's a letch. Are women the only ones who see that?" She got up to leave. "Let's go. Our senator didn't show."

"Where to now? The coroner's?"

"Right."

The two left the Senate office building and headed across the bridge. The girl at the desk of the coroner's office snapped her gum and leafed through a register she pulled up on her computer. "Don't have a suicide," she said. "Sure you have the right place?"

"No," said Lauren. "Any other place they'd send a suicide?"

"No. We did have one admission under unusual circumstances . . . Alexander Dumant. That the one?"

"That's him," Lauren said. "What were the unusual circumstances?"

"No idea. You'll have to talk to the medical examiner working on him. Hold on, I'll call him." The girl punched a button on her phone, and a red light glowed. "There's someone from the FBI to talk to you about Dumant," the girl said into the telephone, then pushed the speaker button.

"Send him in," a voice answered. "I'm ready for a break."

The receptionist ushered them to a closed door. "I didn't tell him you were females," the girl explained, opening the door for them. "He's antifeminist. You're on your own."

"Thanks." Gretchen followed Lauren into the forensic lab in time to catch the coroner's startled expression, but he recovered quickly and introduced himself.

"Good morning," he said. "I'm Dr. Ghoul." Lauren's eyebrows shot up, and the coroner explained, "I'll thank you not to give me the usual Dr. Hyde jokes." He returned back to his work. "What can I do for you today?"

"I understand you have one of our agents here, an Alexander Dumant," Lauren said. "Do you have a cause of death?"

"Not yet . . . your office in a hurry? Tell them I'd have a report later today."

"Any guesses?"

"Suffocation. Kind'a hard to breathe with a plastic bag over your head."

"Then why list it as a suicide?"

"The DA called it. He wants confirmation. Likes his cases wrapped up ASAP. Since there's no next of kin to complain, that's how it gets reported." He looked at Lauren, adding, "I've an idea that suits your office too. Never know what kind of mud can get stirred up when the press starts to dig."

"I take it you disagree," Gretchen interrupted. "Why?"

The medical examiner turned to her. "You with the press?" he asked.

"No, I'm a writer, and any, *maybe, maybe not,* suicide interests me. Off the record, can we work together? Strictly fictional . . . with a twist?"

He looked at Lauren, then back to Gretchen. "Talk to your friend here, she's the FBI agent."

"It's her fiction," said Lauren. "What will your report say? Suicide?"

"The facts, ma'am, only the facts. Let the chips fall where they may. My job is over when I submit my report. What they do with it is of no concern of mine." He grinned at Gretchen. "But writing a novel of hypotheses, that intrigues me. Always wanted to be a character in a book."

Gretchen grinned back. "I'll be talking to you," she said.

The two turned to leave when Lauren hesitates. "One more thing," she said. "Do you know what happened to his monkey?"

"Don't know anything about a monkey." He paused before adding, "If your office mopped up, maybe they know."

"I'll find out," Lauren promised.

"Evidently, the monkey's the key, Lauren," Gretchen said as they left. "Now where?"

"Let's check the zoo. He couldn't just disappear."

Delighted the first phase of their plan went so well, Gretchen suggested, "Let's have lunch first then worry about the monkey. I've an idea we won't have to go to the zoo. That monkey's hiding out close by."

Later that day

"Gretchen, remember the summer we went out West? There were six of us who wanted to experience the spacious forests and prairies we'd only read about in history books?" The two settled down a chat, Cyrus curled between them, attentive to their conversation, and accepting attention from each in turn.

"Yeah, what about it?" Gretchen asked wondering how the events of the day reminded Lauren of that particular trip. "Thought we agreed to forget what happened."

"I know, but it comes back to me every time I see a corpse. Do you realize we're the only ones remaining of that group? You, me, and Kristin?"

"No, I never really thought about it. Kristin did make a return trip last summer—to pick up some mushrooms for Professor Ipswitch. I didn't know that until the trial. She never mentioned it." Gretchen stopped peeling the orange she'd selected from a fruit basket in Lauren's kitchen. "That experience never affected her the way it did the rest of us. Makes you wonder . . ."

"About what?"

"Where reality ends and fantasy begins. What did happen to those kids?"

Lauren stared at Gretchen. *Why would she question what happened years ago?*

"They were accidents, Gretchen. What else could they be?"

"What if they really were abducted?"

"Not likely."

"No? They were missing all of three hours, and when authorities found them, they told fantastic stories of being abducted by aliens." She looked at her empty glass. "Do you have any more of this wine?"

"Sure." Lauren changed her comfortable position and reached for the wine bottle and emptied it into the proffered glass. She headed for the kitchen and returned carrying a freshly chilled bottle of chardonnay.

"I happened to believe their stories. Don't you think it's odd that they all died under unusual circumstances?"

"Must I remind you again, Gretchen, accidents, not unusual circumstances." She refilled their glasses. "I believe the police reports."

"Right."

"You're back into fantasy versus reality again, Gretchen. Do you get some kind of vicarious pleasure in doubting your sanity?" she chided, returning to her comfortable place on the sofa.

"Don't I wish . . . I'd give anything not to be bugged by nagging doubts, but too many weird things have happened to me not to believe there's more to this universe than our small minds can comprehend . . . or can accept."

"Okay, that's enough of that. Let's see if we can do something that's constructive. To start with, write down everything you dream—no matter how crazy—and we'll do our own sleuthing. Concentrate on the monkey tonight and fantasize where he could be. Too bad you didn't bring *Resurrection* with you. We could dose you with a little of that"

"I doubt I'd need it. It isn't my sanity that's in doubt . . . and it doesn't take *Resurrection* for me to drift into fantasyland." She peered into her glass thoughtfully. "Sometimes I use my dreams to plot my stories . . . if I can remember them. Usually, they don't make much sense until I straighten them out."

"Well, one thing's for sure . . . there's been no UFO sightings in Washington. We've a lot of weirdoes here, but they're our own weirdoes . . . not from outer space." She nervously twirled the chilled bottle of wine in the ice bucket.

Annoyed, Gretchen asked, "What are you doing to the wine?"

"Sorry." She pulled away. "How did we get on this subject anyway?"

"You started it . . . by remembering something we swore we'd forget," Gretchen reminded her. "What made you think of it?"

"We've had a strange day, and it seemed to fit." Lauren avoided her steady gaze then shrugged. "How should I know?" she finished lamely. "No, that's not true. When I heard about the *accidents*, I began to wonder if there weren't a connection."

"Yeah, me too."

"What about Kristin . . . she ever mention it?

"No, we never discussed it." Lauren refilled Gretchen's glass and her own. "She shocked me at the trial. I never knew until then that she'd returned to the scene. She never told me."

"Why?"

"I don't know. Until the incident with the potion, I had no reason to question her. She never told me about her association with Professor Ipswitch either . . . not even when she gave me a bottle of her *Heaven Scent.*"

"*Heaven Scent?*" asked Lauren. "Is that a potion too?"

"Yes, the professor's first. Harley sent it to a lab to have it analyzed. I don't remember what happened to it after that." She laughed. "Too busy staying alive as a cat to worry about what Harley discovered."

Unexpectedly, Lauren switched the subject. "Are you still into reincarnation and other worlds, Gretchen?"

Startled at the sudden shift in conversation, Gretchen stared at her then recovered enough to answer her from the heart. "No one's ever explained otherwise to my satisfaction," she answered. "Are you still an atheist?"

"Until someone proves otherwise." Lauren laughs. "I know you'll think this a stupid question, but what religion believes in reincarnation?"

"I've no idea, but it makes sense to me in this otherwise senseless world. Why do you ask?"

"Because you accept abduction in spaceships as natural phenomena, life as an animal as a possibility, and you accept dreams as premonitions. Add a belief in reincarnation to the mix, and I wonder how you justify the whole madcap mixture. Doesn't one need to make a choice at some time between science and religion?"

Gretchen searched her thoughts in an attempt to explain her views to a nonbeliever. "No, they're both right as far as they go. You see, I think you're an atheist because religion has never been able to justify the hereafter to your complete satisfaction. You accept the scientific version of evolution. For me, science has never been able to fully justify the beginning of life as a normal progression from the big bang theory and evolvement of life from the ocean bed. That's an elusive mystery no one can answer specifically. I do believe, though, that someday science and religion will merge and become one and the same."

"And you believe reincarnation explains both religion and science?"

"Yes, even though each peers through the looking glass from different angles."

"Looking glass?"

"For want of a better word—different spectrums—if you prefer. Before my mother died, I thought like a child. After her death, I seemed to absorb some of her wisdom. Maybe she reincarnated herself through me. Isn't that crazy?"

Gretchen looked at Lauren for reassurance, but Lauren didn't answer. Instead, she picked up the empty glasses, stored the wine bottle, and headed for her room. At the door, she turned to face at Gretchen. "It does not compute," she said.

"Oh, dear," Gretchen worried. "Why do I expect others to accept my crazy theories . . . even if they do make sense to me."

Chapter Four

All glory comes from daring to begin.

Day 3, Saturday

Next morning, the two intentionally forget their discussions of the previous evening and set about the business of collecting items Gretchen would need to set up temporary housekeeping—dishes, towels, linens, etc., adding a few purchases from local shops. By the time they finished, Gretchen had pictures on the walls, pillows on the sofa, and food and wine chilling in the fridge.

"Looks great," Gretchen decided, surveying their handiwork. "Like I've lived here forever. I'll set up my computer, install a telephone, and I'm in business. What's the first order of the day?"

"Why ask me? You seem to have all the answers," said Lauren, a touch of sarcasm in her voice.

"You're upset."

"Yes, I'm upset. You never said . . . I don't understand . . . Why did you sign that lease?"

Gretchen ignored her question. "Let's have lunch. I'll fix a salad and break open the Chardonnay."

Lauren continued. "I did, so look forward to your staying with me, especially since I won't be working for a while." She pouted as she helped Gretchen prepare the lunch. She knew that Gretchen would tell her in her own time, but later, munching on Caesar salad and croutons, she became impatient. "You didn't answer my question."

"I'm sorry, Lauren, but there's a few things I didn't tell you yesterday."

"Such as?"

Gretchen ate quietly for a time. Finally, she said, "I've left Harley."

"You? Wow! Talk about a bombshell . . ."

"I know. I can't believe it myself. Maybe it isn't permanent—I don't know."

"What happened?"

"Kristin. I tried to ignore it . . . wait it out . . . but it didn't go away. I felt like an intruder in my own home, so I decided to get as far away as possible and think it through. Maybe we needed distance. At first, I buried myself in my writing . . . that's supposed to be great therapy, but it didn't work. So here I am. I got the apartment because I may stay here permanently."

"I'm sorry," Lauren said. "When did it start?"

"I don't really know . . . I presume it blossomed during my disappearance. At least, that's when things seemed different. I think Harley was relieved when I decided to visit you."

"That does explain the apartment, and I'm not sure your being alone is good."

Gretchen grinned at her friend. "Oh, but that's not the only reason I chose this particular apartment. Call it intuition, if you wish, but I think the key to your disappearing monkey is right here in this complex. The little devil may come home when things settle down, and someone should be here when he does."

"Ahh, the pieces are sliding into place. You do have a method to your madness. Maybe I should spend the night in case he returns to the scene of the crime. I've heard the first night in new digs is quite revealing."

"Good idea. Then we're in sync. Besides, your boss advised you to get out of town. Pack a bag, bring Cyrus, and take that vacation."

"You're right. Then you can tell me the rest of your story about you and Harley, and Kristin."

"It's a deal . . . if you'll do something for me."

"Whatever it is, I agree."

Later that Evening

After revisiting Mr. Ghoul, the medical examiner, and learning that he had submitted his *suicide* report to Lauren's office, they settled down to read the revised report he'd handed Gretchen. "For your novel," he'd said with a twinkle in his eyes.

"I knew it couldn't be a suicide," Lauren said after reviewing the report.

"It isn't the real report, Lauren," Gretchen informed her. "It's revised for fiction. What makes you think it's the real one?"

"I don't know, but I do. I think our Mr. Ghoul wants protection in case his suicide report backfires."

"That's crazy, Lauren. Official is official, and the *official* report said *suicide*. This is a fabrication created strictly for my book." She frowned. "Isn't it?"

"I don't think so. I can't outguess the agency, but I'll bet the official report doesn't even list the correct name. How do we know we saw the body of Alexander Dumant? The super at the office said he and the monkey checked out. Dead men don't check out."

"Can you call your office?" asked Gretchen.

"Sure, if I had anything to report. I don't. I've only a suspicion."

"But if the monkey shows up, you'll have proof, won't you?"

"That's a long shot."

Gretchen, sitting next to a lazy Cyrus curled up between the two girls, stroked his neck, and Cyrus responded with deep purrs. "Maybe a shot of *Resurrection* will bring the monkey home?" she teased.

Lauren's eyebrows shot up. "*Resurrection!* That's it."

"Lauren, I'm only teasing."

"I know you are, but I'm not."

"Let's try something else first," Gretchen decides. "If it doesn't work, we'll try the potion, but only as a last resort."

"What do you have in mind?"

"A little hypnotism—see if you can remember a few more details of that morning on the Capitol steps."

"You can do that? I must say . . . you're full of surprises." She stared at Gretchen—her silence a pregnant pause before she asked, "What kind of details?"

"Details you may have missed. For instance, is the man you saw on the Capitol steps the same man we saw at the coroner's office? Or are they two different people?"

"You have doubts?"

"From what I'm hearing, it doesn't compute."

Lauren laughed out loud. "That's rich. *Touche.*"

Gretchen ignored her. "Want to try?"

"What do I have to do?"

"Relax, and follow my instructions."

"That's all?" Lauren emptied her wineglass. "Okay, I'm relaxed. Where do you want me?"

"Wherever you feel comfortable."

Lauren sprawled, relaxing on the sofa, her eyes closed. "Okay, start your magic."

"We begin with your head and work down. As I name each part of the body, concentrate on that area and release all tension. By the time I get to your feet, you should be totally relaxed and under my power. Ready?"

"I'll probably regret this," she muttered.

As soon as Lauren drifted off into a semi-hypnotic state, Gretchen began her instructions. Lauren felt her body floating into space unattached to anything other than the voice that she heard as though from a distance. Cyrus, his cat eyes gigantic pools of liquid intensity, watched his mistress as though poised to protect her.

"You're moving back in time." Lauren heard the voice say. "Return to the spot where you stood in front of the Capitol steps." Immediately, Lauren felt herself transported to the scene of the music man and his performing monkey dancing to the strains of *For Money, the Monkey Dances.*

"Tell me what you see," the voice directed, "in detail."

Engrossed in the scene evolving around her, the voice startled Lauren. She hesitated then began to speak. "It's all so hazy," she said in a voice she didn't recognize as her own. "I can't see too well."

"Move in closer. Does he look like the man at the morgue?"

Lauren tried desperately to move closer to the man on the steps, but people kept pushing her back. Finally, the man broke away and headed up the steps—a man she's seen many times at headquarters, not the man on the slab in the morgue. He stopped the senator who turned to speak to him, and Lauren saw the senator's frustration at the interruption.

"It isn't the man in the morgue," she told Gretchen.

"You're sure?"

"Yes, he's leaving. Should I follow?"

"If you can. Stay with him to where the taxi dropped him off," the voice instructed. "And keep talking, I don't want to lose contact with you."

"He won't hear me?"

"No, you don't have to whisper." Lauren listened to the soothing voice. "He can't see or hear you . . . you're in my apartment, remember? Keep talking . . . nothing can happen to you. Tell me what you see."

"I feel so strange, Gretchen, sort of detached . . . as though I'm watching a scene in a play."

"Is the man talking to the cab driver?"

"No, the monkey chatters, and he answers him. Nothing that makes sense . . . like talking to a pet . . . that's all." The cabbie, music man and monkey, and the unseen Lauren rode in silence. Occasionally, the music man, seated in the front, directs the cabbie to his destination.

"What's happening," a voice broke the silence.

"We're reaching the apartment, Gretchen, and he's arguing with the cabbie. Said he's charging too much, but he pays. The cab's leaving, and he's entering an apartment, the manager's apartment, not this one."

"Stay with him. Is he the same person we talked to yesterday?"

"No, this man's older. Oh, oh!"

"What is it?" the voice asked. "What do you see?"

"He's the man in the morgue, the one we saw yesterday."

"The manager? You're sure?"

"Yes, they're arguing about something. The monkey. They're arguing about the monkey, and the monkey's getting mad . . . the music man does nothing." Suddenly, Lauren screamed and Gretchen awakened her. "It's all right," she soothed her. "You're safe."

Lauren returned to reality. "I think the monkey killed him," she told Gretchen.

"Did you see him kill the old man?"

"No, but he's dead, isn't he? Now the monkey's missing and so is the manager." She sat upright, bewildered. "What do you make of it? Maybe Alexander Dumant really did check out with his monkey."

"Doesn't make sense," Gretchen intimated. "Why must the manager die? You're sure they only fought about the monkey?"

"No, I'm not sure of anything. I watched a dream happening." She shook her head as though to clear it. "Even that's fading fast. Damn, I shouldn't have panicked. I almost had it. Great agent, I am."

"I think you did great. We know more than we did."

"Where did you learn the art of hypnosis, Gretchen?" Lauren asked. "When you were a cat?"

"No, it's nothing unusual," Gretchen assured her. "Some people are more susceptible to suggestion than others. You were easy."

"So I'm easy. Where did you learn it?"

"It's not hypnosis, it's parapsychology. Harley uses it when he has a particularly difficult case. Sometimes I think he tries to use it on me."

"Really? He can do that?"

"Not without my consent. You consented."

"Yeah, I did, didn't I?"

"Even under hypnosis, you're in control. I couldn't get you to do anything you wouldn't do normally," Gretchen said. "And you did very well without resorting to drugs."

"*Resurrection* is a drug?"

"Has to be. How else could I lose control so easily? Kristin brings home a rare strain of Mexican LSD, and the professor uses it in *Resurrection*. You really want a repeat of what I went through?"

"Oh, I don't know. Sounds like fun."

"You may not be so lucky."

"Anyway, we're a few steps closer to understanding what happened to the monkey. Let's get some sleep." Cyrus, already asleep and curled on the sofa, awoke instantly as the two broke for the night.

Lauren had a restless night. She tossed and turned, her mind continually returning to her hypnotic dream state. She tried desperately to recreate the scene in the apartment. What else happened that night? What did the monkey do? How did he do it? Was someone else there?

Gretchen slept peacefully, assured that all answers come in time, and Cyrus stood guard over the two, spending time in each room, protecting his caretakers.

Chapter Five

Friendship doubles our joy and divides our grief.
—Swedish Proverb

Day 4, Sunday

"Today, we do touristy things," Lauren announced at breakfast as they relaxed over orange juice and coffee on Gretchen's patio. "Put your jogging clothes on, and we'll take in the local scenery. Washington is beautiful during the fall months, and the park isn't too far away—a great place to jog. We can check out the mansion, the place our local celebrity met her disastrous end, and maybe pick up some clues. Who knows, maybe all crimes lead to Washington—like all roads led to Rome."

"No one ever found out what happened to Chandra. Did your office get in on it?" asked Gretchen.

"No, strictly a local thing. They didn't want our interference," Lauren said. "It's a strange town. Things happen here, and about the time you think a mystery is about to be solved, everything closes down, and you're back to square one."

"Don't you get curious?" asked Gretchen.

"Sure. Like our suicide . . . someone who couldn't be disturbed needed protecting," Lauren explained. "Happens all the time. Some people hate being disturbed. Have you noticed? Particularly, if it's something unpleasant . . . as if Washington prefers its fantasies to its reality."

"Strange you should say that, considering the business you're in." Gretchen finished lacing her sneaks, and looked around for her jacket. "How do you explain it?"

"What's to explain? No one in this town can afford to get tagged with unsavory publicity or unsavory actions, as the case may be, unless it benefits someone higher up in the ranks. Case in point . . . the railroading of Traficante and a slap on the wrist for Torricelli . . . both guilty of the same misuse of public funds. Someday the real truth will emerge . . . as a footnote in history . . . when their exploits no longer affect someone's future."

"Will that happen with Chandra?"

"Already has—her senator's no longer news now that the *whodunit* won't affect Congress. Case solved, closed, and yesterday's gossip . . . except for her parents whom the world forgets. Washington can keep its nails sharp and sheathed for the next crisis."

"What do you think happened to her?" Gretchen asked. "Any ideas?"

"Sure, lots of them. Why? You want the inside skinny?"

"Yeah, if you know. I have enough ideas of my own."

"Such as?"

"I think the senator's wife walked in on *kinky* sex and blew a gasket. That's enough to send any sane wife off the deep end. Tied up, Chandra had no defense, and the senator covers for his wife. How that's for phantom sleuthing?"

"Not bad . . . if that's what happened. Truth is, we may never find out . . . for another decade or so," Lauren decided. "Truth is a rare commodity buried deep in the bowels of propaganda." She tossed a jacket over her shoulders. "Come on, let's go."

The two take an apartment key and some spare cash and head down a narrow jogger's path behind the apartment complex leading to the park.

Later that Day

On their return to the apartment, they're greeted by an upset Cyrus voicing his discontent at the new surroundings. He wanted out. Being locked up in an apartment for hours at a stretch with no relief raised the *cockles* of his ire. He eagerly leaped for the door the moment he heard a key in the lock. As Lauren entered, she felt the brush of feline fur against her legs and realized too late what has happened. Cyrus disappeared around the corner of the apartment into the dark shrubbery and freedom.

"Cyrus, come back," called Lauren, panicking at the loss of her pet in a strange place.

"Let him go," Gretchen consoled her. "He'll be back when he's ready. Why don't we fix a sandwich and go sit out by the pool?" She headed for the kitchen. "Cats are inquisitive creatures. Can't blame Cyrus for wanting to inspect his new territory. He's more human than you think."

"You're probably right." Eyeing her friend, Lauren realized the validity of her statement, and returned to the apartment, closing the door on Cyrus. "I spend far too much time worrying about creatures who can take care of themselves."

"Animals have built-in survival equipment, and no restraints on using them if backed into a corner. We think our animals are helpless little creatures that need humans to care for them. I think it's the other way round."

Startled, Lauren asked, "Really? Why?"

"Haven't you noticed?" Gretchen explained. "We're restricted by rules and regulations and lose more of our freedoms every day. Animals only lose their freedom when they get involved with humans."

Lauren, believing her friend serious, said, "I do believe you miss not being a cat. Do you?"

"Sometimes. I had so much freedom as a cat and didn't appreciate it. Although I don't regret my cat adventure and can't imagine going back, I've had nothing but problems since my return." Gretchen pondered her statement. "You know the irony of the whole thing? We do it to ourselves, build little cages around us, lock the doors, and call it freedom."

"Wow, sorry I said anything." Lauren headed for the bedroom. "Before you really start to complain, I think I'll take a shower and mull that over." She gave Gretchen a strange look. "I like your idea of eating by the pool though. We can discuss the merits of *man versus animal.*" She disappeared.

Gretchen, appalled at her outburst, chastised her self. "Now, I've done it. Why, should I expect others to be as crazy as I am?" She entered the cooling water of her own shower. *One thing I missed as a cat, my showers.* She let the soothing waters relax her frustrations, realizing that showers had become her defense mechanism against troubled thoughts. As a cat, she could find a quiet corner away from the other cats, groom her long white furry exterior, and contemplate. As a *humanoid,* she sought the shower.

"Mmmm." She laughed as the water sprayed her face. "We really are alike."

Later, munching sandwiches and snacks by the pool, Cyrus wandered into view. Trailing close behind him, the monkey in question. The two animals parked themselves on the grass a safe distance away. Lauren reached over and offered a banana to the scruffy monkey. He came close enough to grab the banana, then quickly moved to a safe distance before stuffing it into his huge mouth.

"Cyrus accomplishes while we merely dream," Lauren mused.

"But where's his master?" Gretchen asked.

"On a slab at the morgue . . . the monkey's proof of that. And my hypnotic dream . . . a mere fantasy . . . so much for magic. Gretchen, we're back to square one."

"He doesn't look like a killer." Gretchen eyed the monkey, her first glimpse of him. "What do we do with him?"

"Be logical, Gretchen. He isn't a killer. He's a homeless pet who's lost his master, and his master's lying on a slab in the morgue. That's reality."

"But what if he is the killer, Lauren? That in itself is reason enough for a cover-up."

"We'll have no more of your hypnotic theories, Gretchen," Lauren argued. "Nothing but the facts, ma'am, the cold, hard facts. I refuse to enter your fantasy world again."

"Okay," Gretchen acceded. "But that doesn't solve the *Case of the Errant Monkey,* does it? What do we do with him now that we've found him? Trap him? Leave him free? Or call the zoo to rescue him?"

"None of the above . . . for the moment. He's survived a week without our help. He'll survive another night, and we'll worry about what to do with him tomorrow. Tonight, we make friends with him." She handed the monkey another banana, and it disappeared as fast as the first one. The afternoon passed with Lauren no closer to winning over the monkey than before.

Later that night, Gretchen heard a scratching noise at her window. Looking out, she saw the monkey looking in at her expectantly. When she opened the apartment door, the monkey scooted in, heading for a space behind the sofa. She left him there and went back to bed.

Chapter Six

Reality can be beaten with enough imagination.

Day 5, Monday

"It's been nearly a week, and I've heard nothing from my office," Lauren related at breakfast. "Have you seen our monkey this morning?"

"Not today. He came to my window last night, and I let him in. Probably in his usual sleeping place . . . behind the sofa." Gretchen put down her coffee cup and peeked behind the sofa. "Still there," she said, returning to the table. "You know, we can't keep calling him *monkey*. He needs a name. Any ideas?"

"How do you know it's a *he?* Maybe we should find that out first . . . then name him."

Gretchen ignored the suggestion. "We could give him a neutral name like Tony or Max."

"I know. Let's call him *Alex* after his former owner. That's neutral."

"Good idea," Gretchen agreed and tried it out on their unwelcome guest. "Hey, Alex, would you like some breakfast?"

Alex peeked out from behind the sofa and began to chatter. *Krikkrakkrikrika!*

"I'll take that for a *yes,"* Gretchen said and handed a banana to the hungry creature. Alex grabbed it and returned to his secure spot behind the sofa. "Maybe Alex really is his name."

"Could be. Not that it makes any difference, but it does conjure up questions about Alexander Dumant."

"Yeah," Gretchen agreed. "Could *Alex* be a code word, and Alexander Dumant an alias?"

"Isn't Alexander Dumant the name of a character in a book? Sounds like an alias."

"No, that's Dumas, and he's an author."

"So he is," Lauren said. "Maybe you should pay another visit to the manager, Gretchen. Tell him about the monkey coming back last night and find out if he knows *anything* about a man who checked out with a monkey then left him behind."

"Me? Why me? It's your case."

"We've a spooked monkey in *your* apartment. You don't know me, remember?" Lauren reminded Gretchen how she conveniently separated them when she registered.

"Okay," she agreed. "I'll do it. You see if you can get a picture of the missing agent."

"Done. Sounds like you think my hypnotic dream's a possibility."

"Worth checking out."

Lauren looked at her, dismayed, her mind reeling. *So far, she's been right on target. Is she psychic?* "You may be right," she admitted, getting up from the table. "Okay, you do your thing, and I'll do mine. We'll meet here for lunch."

"Sure."

Later that morning, Gretchen found herself face to face with Hunter in his office. "Hi, Hunter," she greeted the young man. "Is *Hunter* your first or last name?"

"Whichever you wish." Hunter grinned her exuberance. "What can I do for you today?"

"You'll never guess what happened last night, Hunter," Gretchen related to the eager super. "A monkey knocked on my bedroom window."

Hunter looked worried. "A monkey? Impossible."

"That's what I thought," Gretchen agreed. "But I seem to have inherited your past resident. What do you suggest I do with him?"

Hunter, eyes enlarged and mouth gaping, stuttered, "I-I d-d-don't know."

"Did your previous resident leave a forwarding address?" Gretchen probed as Hunter continued to stare as though in a daze.

"I d-d-don't know," the puzzled young man repeated.

"Maybe the computer?" Gretchen waited, but Hunter did not move.

"Then it is true," he finally said.

"What's true?" asked Gretchen. *He doesn't know.*

Hunter collected himself and took control. "Ms. Dandrich, I can't give that out. It's privileged information."

HEAVEN SCENT163

"Okay, you take the responsibility for shipping a lost monkey to wherever it's supposed to go." She listened to the ticking clock, waiting for the dazed Hunter to make a decision. "Maybe I should call the zoo to come get him."

"N-n-no, d-d-don't do that. Let me think."

"He's made his home behind my sofa and won't let anyone near him." Gretchen watched Hunter struggle with his conscience until he finally agreed to violate the rules.

"I guess there's no harm in it." He punched a few keys on the computer. "That's funny."

"What is?" Gretchen tried to see the face of the computer. "Don't you have a forwarding address for Mr. Dumant?"

"No, only a request to forward all mail to the Senate office building in care of Senator Claghorn. Never heard of him, have you?"

Gretchen shook her head. "Are you sure that's all there is? I'd hate to have to call the zoo to pick up Alex."

"Alex?"

"Yeah, it's what I called him for lack of a better name. Did his owner leave his music box behind, or did he take it with him?" she asked.

"I don't know. Why?"

"Well, if he left under mysterious circumstances, it may still be here and might tell us something about our mysterious stranger."

"We could check the storage room if you like. We hold anything we deem of value for thirty days, then dispose of it," Hunter said, finally coming to life.

"I'd like," Gretchen said.

Hunter selected a set of keys behind him, and Gretchen followed him out of the office and down a hallway. Hunter stopped at one of the doors, slid the key into the lock, and opened the door. Empty.

Gretchen came out of shock first. "But it's only been two days. Did *Good Will* come by?"

"Not that I know." Hunter turned to Gretchen. "Believe me, I know nothing of this. The maid cleaned your apartment two days ago and picked up the key to store the stuff left behind. No one else picked up the key."

"The maid. Did she give the key back?"

"She left it on the counter."

"Did you check to see what she stored in the room?"

"No."

"Do you have a name for the maid?"

"No, she's with a cleaning company. It's not always the same one, depends."

"The name of the company? Do you have an address or phone number?"

Hunter answered her questions in a monotone, as though in shock. "Let's go back to the office," she said. A stunned Hunter locked the door and followed Gretchen back to the office. He checked the address for the *Merry Maids Cleaning Company* and handed it to her.

"Will you let me know what you find out?" he asked.

"Sure. Call ahead first and tell them I'm coming. I may need confirmation from you."

"I'll do that. Anything else?"

"Yes, would you call me a cab? I've no transportation."

"Oh, that's right. You don't, do you? Why don't I lock up, and we'll both go?" he offered. "It's only a few blocks away."

"No need, I can walk. Tell me how to get there and call them when I'm about there. Don't want to give them time to dispose of anything."

Hunter's eyebrows formed an arch. "Why?"

"If someone went to that much trouble to cover-up what happened, others might be involved. They'd have their instructions too, don't you think?"

His mouth dropped. "Do you think? Hunter stared at her. "Then m-maybe I'd better go with you," he stuttered in disbelief. As she hesitated, he became resolute, turning brave. "If what you say is true, I can't let you go it alone. We'll take my car in case we find something to bring back."

Their trip to the *Merry Maids* proved futile. The FBI had beaten them to it, arriving at the precise time the *Merry Maid* picked up the key. "They insisted I give them the key," the maid told Hunter. "And they promised to drop it off with you when they finished. Did they?"

"They may have," Hunter said. "I wish you'd called me. They cleared out the entire storage room. I've no idea what they took. You're sure they were FBI men?" he asked.

"They showed me their credentials," the *Merry Maid* told them. "Why? Is there a problem?"

"The tenant left something behind. We need a forwarding address."

"Oh," said the vivacious *Merry Maid*. "That's no problem. I found this envelope behind the sofa after they left. I forgot about it . . . until now." She pulled a letter from her spacious pocket and handed it to Hunter. "Will this help?" she asked.

Hunter glanced at the return address on the envelope and gleefully planted a kiss on the rosy cheek of the stunned maid. "Oh yes, and thank you. You're a doll." He handed the envelope to Gretchen. "It's all you need. The FBI can have the rest."

Later that evening

The two sleuths met at the pool to exchange findings. Gretchen related her discovery of the empty storage room to Lauren. When she'd finished, she said, "Now, it's your turn. Did you get any pictures of our mystery man?"

"No mystery. Only a picture of a corpse my boss swears is the slain FBI agent. That's a fact, Gretchen. You seem to want to turn everything into a fantasy."

"Guilty, but look who's talking," Gretchen defended herself. "You were ready to take a dose of *Resurrection* to prove a point. Hypnosis is a proven technique even if it's not admissible in court, and it's certainly a lot safer than any drug."

"I agree, and I don't object to using whatever facts we have if we get the right answer." She rumpled her hair with nervous fingers.

"What's wrong, then?"

"I'm frustrated. I don't even know why I'm not working, how I earned my undeserved leave. At first, I thought it was for my own safety."

Gretchen picked up on her thoughts. "Now, you don't. Why?"

"I think they wanted me out of the way, afraid I'll identify someone they don't want identified. Then you showed up and threw me another idea, and confused everything."

Lauren looked so despondent.

"I'm sorry, Lauren." Gretchen realized she's stirred up a hornet's nest. "I've had a crazy year, but that's no reason for me to create doubts in your mind. Haven't you said anything to your supervisor about your suspicions?"

"No, he doesn't want to hear. He has his own problems, and I've my instructions. Unless I find something substantive to add to the investigation, I'm to stay away. Maybe he thinks I'm being followed, and maybe I am." Her fingernail pierced the orange she held with a vengeance, and the juice spurted into her face. "Damn," she said, moving back and wiping her face with her hand.

Gretchen watched, feeling helpless. "Maybe the letter we found . . ." she attempted to console her.

"What about it? It gives you a return address, that's all . . . probably a dead end."

"Oh ye, of little faith," Gretchen said. "Didn't you notice the return address? It's in Connecticut, a town close to Ridgecrest."

"Really?"

"Some farm in Redding. We could be there in a day."

Lauren hesitated. "What about the animals?"

"Take 'em with us. They seem compatible. Besides, it may be Alex's new home."

Lauren mulled it over. "It would be nice to go home for a while. She grinned mischievously. "Where would we stay? With Harley or Kristin?"

"Neither. There's a great *bed-and-breakfast* place not too far away that I've been dying to try. We could stay there."

"Like thieves in the night?"

"Why not?

Lauren laughed. "Okay, Gadsden suggested I leave town, and I'd love to meet your cat friends. When do we leave?"

"Do you need to tell him?"

Lauren considered her question. "No," she decided. "I'm following instructions. How about you? You need to tell Hunter, or Harley?"

"I don't think so."

"'Then let's roll. Is tomorrow too soon?"

"Not for me." And the two toasted their new adventure.

Chapter Seven

You can do very little with faith, but you can do nothing without it.
—Samuel Butler

Day 6, Tuesday

"Looks like you plan on working." Lauren watched Gretchen pack up her computer. "Don't you ever go anywhere without that scourge of tranquil living?"

"It makes life easier," Gretchen explains. "You'll see. I can check and send messages from wherever I am without having to disclose my whereabouts. As long as my friends hear from me, they don't worry. They don't need to know where I am. That's what I like about e-mail, total secrecy."

"I never felt the need for a computer at home," Lauren replied. "I have one at the office that holds a wealth of valuable information, but I prefer to write my personal letters by hand and put a stamp on them. More personal."

"Do you have an e-mail office code?"

"Sure, one I use at the office, but . . . oh, oh . . . I see what you're getting at," she answered as she realized where Gretchen was heading. "You know, I could pull up files from my office on your computer, couldn't I?"

"Unless your office has blocked your access. Do you think they may have?"

"I don't know. I'll check it out when we get where we're going. Which is where, by the way?" Lauren asks. "Did you make reservations?"

"Yes, for the animals too. Next problem, how do we get Alex into the car? He's used to riding, but not with us. He only comes out from behind the sofa for Cyrus. Any ideas?"

"Cyrus has a Pet Taxi. We might find another for Alex, then tempt him inside with a banana," Lauren suggested.

"I hoped we'd find one in storage, but your office cleaned out everything."

"Sorry about that."

"Yeah, sure. So far, we've only two leads, Alex and an address on an envelope."

"Right. Time is getting short, and we haven't made much headway."

"I know, we may be on a wild-goose chase," Gretchen admitted. "So think of this as a vacation, Lauren. How long since you've been home?"

"Three years. After Mom died, I never went back." She goes back to packing, amused. "This will be my first vacation since I started work, and I'm not even sure it's voluntary." She continued packing. "Do we look up Kristin or Harley?"

"That depends," Gretchen decided, setting up her computer on the table. "What we need to do first is find out what kind of access you have on my computer before we leave. There's some reason you've been grounded, and you need to know why. I suggest you check your office files now before we leave."

"You're right. I should have done it right away. Maybe I wouldn't have needed hypnotizing." She opened up the computer and began pulling up information from her office. Gretchen left to shop for a Pet Taxi for Alex and to stock up on bananas for the trip. When she returned, she found Lauren still on her computer.

"I found my earlier files, Gretchen, but everything since I left is blocked. Cut off at the crucial point. Damn, I did want to find out who that guy in the morgue really was."

"Ah," teased Gretchen, "then you do accept your hypnotic vision." She put Cyrus into her lap and pulled at his ears. Cyrus protested and nipped her finger. "Ouch, I'm sorry, Cyrus." She kissed his injured ear, and Cyrus jumped down, retreating to his basket.

"I'm not making friends with Cyrus," she said. "I think he reads my mind."

"What makes you say that?" Lauren asked absentmindedly as she continued pulling up information from the computer. "Got it! We were right."

"About what? The body exchange or the music man?"

"The music man is no more. He's gone—shed his identification when he left Alex behind. The old manager is now the dead agent. They did pull a switch, and your hypnosis was dead center."

"How did you break in?"

"I'll never tell. It's my secret." She printed out the information and closed up the computer. "There's even a picture of him, but, Gretchen, you know what this means."

"No, what does it mean? You're the agent. I'm only trying to write a story."

"It means we can't let on we know anything about it. I'll bet the man at this address is the missing agent who is living under the assumed name of the missing landlord."

"But who killed whom?" Gretchen asked. "The FBI? Is this the way they work? And what about the old man's family . . . won't he be missed? Someone's bound to ask questions."

"Evidently, he's expendable. Like Chandra, people forget as soon as the next crisis hits the fan. Except for family, we really are expendable. Life goes on—with or without us."

"And yet, we all think we're so important in the world. I suppose that's the reason we have a God. Someone to care for you when no one else does," decided Gretchen. "How do you survive without that lifeline?"

Lauren laughed at a serious Gretchen. "You learn to live without crutches," she said. God's a crutch. People create all kinds of crutches to help them throughout their lifetime—drugs, alcohol, cigarettes, sex, politics, music, or religion—pick your poison. Religion is probably the most widely acceptable crutch. Your belief in reincarnation—that's an unusual crutch I grant you, but a crutch, nevertheless. You'd be surprised how easy life becomes when you've only yourself to depend on."

Gretchen observed her friend, recognizing her logic, but unable to accept the fact that her own deeply held faith in God could be little more than her particularly chosen crutch. "I've never heard you talk like that before, Lauren. I guess I never believed you actually viewed a world without God."

"Remember, I studied philosophy in college," Lauren reminded Gretchen. "Sorta makes one question accepted ideologies."

"So did I, but it didn't change my conviction of a Supreme Being in charge of the universe," Gretchen countered. "How does your philosophy explain evil then? Do you deny evil exists? After 9/11, how can anyone doubt there isn't a devil?

"Man is good. Man is evil. Man chooses. Face it, Gretchen. Good and evil will continue to struggle throughout mankind. But to blame some nonexistent figment of the imagination with crime is futile. Neither God nor the devil has a thing to do with it. Some guy wants to rule the world—all in the name of Allah—and convinces a whole nation they will meet virgins in paradise if they commit suicide by dive-bombing planes into American towers. How nutty can you get?"

"But I've met the devil. He does exist," Gretchen said, refusing to accept Lauren's logic. "Maybe you do need to take some of my potion—to get you in touch with God."

Lauren laughed. "That'll be the day, but I accept your challenge."

"Oh, my God," Gretchen mused. "What evils have I wrought upon the earth?"

Meanwhile, at Lauren's Office

Philip Gadsden glared at the man standing before him. "You're supposed to be dead," he accused him. "What are you doing in my office?"

"We need to talk. That perfect agent of yours is getting in my way. She suspects something."

"Oh? How so?"

"She's been snooping around what's none of her business. I thought you took care of her." Agent Archibald Carlton stood before Agent Philip Gadsden with determined fury, his dark eyes blazing with righteous indignation. His newly grown black beard barely hid a snarl beneath its sparse camouflage.

"You're paranoid. I had an e-mail from her. She's out of town and out of the way. I've told her nothing, and she's never met you," Gadsden reassured him. "I don't know what kind of damage you're talking about."

"Where did she go?" asked the irate young man.

"She didn't say." Gadsden turned to look out of his window wondering at Agent Carlton's sudden paranoia. "Hey, you're the one who dreamed up this little scenario, 'the better to find the killer,' you said." He turned from the window and faced his agent. "I gave you that chance against my better judgment. I hate subterfuge. I assure you, Lauren knows nothing."

"I left my kid in charge of the apartments, and he tells me he's leased the place for the summer. Thinking it may be your agent I went by to check.

"And . . . ?"

"Wrong female. This one's blond, but she has my monkey. He must have come home after his scare. Damn, I hated having to give him up."

"You didn't make arrangements for the monkey?"

"I didn't have time. He got loose and took off, and I didn't have time to search the grounds." He paused. "Just as well, I guess. He'd be a dead giveaway. Anyway, Hunter assured me the monkey has a new owner and is well taken care of. Maybe, after it's all over . . ."

"You're sure the old manager had no family. What if someone comes around asking questions?"

"No problem. He's a loner—no next of kin. I checked."

"You'd better find out why he was in your apartment. Did he learn of your connection to the FBI? Maybe your senate friend isn't really a friend."

"Now who's being paranoid?" The agent grinned for the first time since his entry. "Where did you say your agent comes from? Connecticut?"

"She attended school there. I believe her only remaining parent resides in New Mexico." He watched the bearded man and tried to read his thoughts. "You planning on chasing her down?"

"Not if she really doesn't know anything."

"She doesn't, and we've cut access to her computer. You're safe."

Chapter Eight

Doubt questions, 'who believes?' Faith answers, 'I.'

Day 7, Wednesday

Rolling into Ridgecrest the next day, Gretchen and Lauren checked into the Red Mill Inn, a previous country residence that had been converted into a respite for weary travelers. The inn, famous for its fabulous meals and soft piano music in the evenings, boasted a stable complete with riding academy, a freshwater spring for the horses, and a separate home for traveling pets.

After settling the animals into their new quarters and dragging their luggage in their room, they visited the innkeeper, hoping to learn the location of their quarry. She could add nothing more than their maps showed, but perked them up by offering a snack from the luncheon menu after they had settled in their rooms. Later, Gretchen suggested, "I think we'd better check this place out right away before someone here recognizes me." She looked at Lauren. "You're safe, but I'm too well-known to escape detection for very long."

"Then it's time to set the stage," Lauren said. "You've got to let Harley know you're back. Why you insist on staying out of town, I don't understand. You've a perfectly nice home here."

"No, I want to do some sleuthing on my own for a while . . . then I'll let Harley know I'm here," she said as she unpacked her computer.

Lauren ceased her unpacking and startled Gretchen with her penetrating inquiry. "I suspect another reason. What is it?"

Ignoring Lauren, Gretchen opened her suitcase, tossed some clothes into the dresser, hung her dresses and robe in the closet, and stored her suitcase on available floor space. Lauren waited until Gretchen finished. Finally, she sat on the edge of the bed and faced Lauren. "Because I want to observe first and relieve my nasty little mind. I want to find out for myself what's been going on in my absence. Do you blame me?" She didn't wait for an answer. "Don't answer that," she said. "It's Friday and lunchtime, and I'm wondering who Kristin is lunching with today. Maybe Roscoe—"

"Or Harley," added Lauren. "That's why you're hiding?"

Gretchen eyed her in silence. "I'm hungry, Lauren. Let's feed the animals and take Mrs. Warren up on her offer for lunch. If I remember, they have pretty good food here."

"You aren't up to Shamans?" Lauren teased.

"Not today. I'm curious about that address we found . . . and how it's connected to my Washington apartment."

"Great." Lauren locked the room, and they headed for the dining room downstairs. "Glad to see you've got your priorities in-line."

Mrs. Warren, the young brusque innkeeper, soon provided the two girls with a substantial meal of lunch leftovers, all the while, entertaining them with century-old tales of the inn. "Why, at one time," she told them, "even rebels took advantage of our services . . . right here in Ridgecrest. And George Washington and his troops stayed here . . . he right there in the room where you are now. My family has owned this piece of land for over two hundred years—that's how long we've been here in Connecticut. 'Course, the days of affording that much land are gone forever, and it became impossible to keep the place going. We had a choice—either sell or make the place profitable. We chose the latter, and we've never been sorry—such a wide array of guests we've had. Why I could tell you stories . . ."

With appropriate "oohs" and "ahs," and an occasional nod of acceptance, the two girls listened and learned. Mrs. Warren, like a young actress on stage and in her element, entertained them with a running history of the Revolution—doubtless stories handed down from past generations. How much truth and how much merely a figment of a fertile imagination, Gretchen and Lauren didn't know. They didn't question her veracity, but before leaving, asked her about the address on their envelope.

Checking the map and the address, she narrated another story. "The place at one time belonged to a member of the British Parliament. They returned to England some centuries ago when they lost the war. And since then, the place had changed hands quite often. A friend of mine tells me some young Hollywood actor bought the place recently. She's never seen him, and I don't know if it's truth or rumor, but I see no reason to question the source of my information. I'm busy here at the inn and don't have time to check up on what never makes the newspapers." She eyed them, satisfied. "Have I been of any help?"

"Enormously," the girls agreed. "You've been of tremendous help. Thanks so much."

Back in their room, Gretchen asked Lauren, "What do you think? Are we on a wild-goose chase?"

"Could be, but I think it's a chase worth pursuing, don't you agree?"

"Right! Come on, let's go feed the animals."

Chapter Nine

Faith makes yesterday a stepping-stone, today a new beginning,
And tomorrow a limitless possibility.

Day 8, Thursday

The next day found them heading for the farmhouse Mrs. Warren told them about, not knowing what to expect. They'd brought Alex with them, hoping he would indicate in some way a familiarity with the surroundings. He'd become quite the conversationalist and chattered nonstop during the ride 'til Gretchen wished they'd left him behind.

"Sounds as if he's trying to tell us something, but I don't know what it is," Lauren said. "What do you think?"

"Maybe he can show us when we get there. Do you think an actor really does own that place?"

"Why not? I think the big question is how an envelope with his address wound up in a Washington apartment complex. What's the connection?"

As they neared the farmhouse, Alex's chatter took on a new dimension, increasing in volume as if that were possible, and tearing back and forth across the back seat of the car.

"Look! He recognizes the place. He's been here before."

"Maybe we should have brought his Pet Taxi," Lauren said.

"What to do? Take him back?"

"No, leave him here if he wants to stay. It's probably his home. Anyway, I don't particularly like taking care of a monkey that's not ours."

"Maybe you're right. It's why we're here, isn't it? I only hope we can control him long enough to complete our investigation."

As they drove into the yard, Alex went berserk. And as soon as the door opened, he darted out and rushed in the direction of the barn. Helpless, Lauren and Gretchen watched. "Let him go," Lauren said. "We'll worry about him later."

Gretchen turned her attention from the barn to the house in time to see a good-looking young man approaching them. He didn't look surprised to see them as though he expected them. Dressed in an expensive riding habit complete with French-cut boots, he looked the picture of a man of leisure. The two girls hesitated.

"Wow!" said Lauren.

"Cool it," Gretchen answered. "Remember, we're working."

"You're here early," the young man said. "I don't have your horses saddled yet."

"Oh," Lauren stuttered. "We're not . . ."

Gretchen interrupted, "Can we look around the farm while we wait? You've such a charming place here, and I've never seen a real farm in action before. Would you mind?"

Flattered and eager to show off his place, the young man agreed. "Well, it isn't really a farm. It's a riding academy now. No one's lived here for a number of years, and when it finally came on the market, I picked it up, mainly because it's within commuting distance to New York. I think you'll find the only animals here are horses."

"Did you restore the place?" Gretchen asked.

"No, I don't know who did that. Probably whoever owned it at the time." He headed for the barn. "Look around, if you wish, while I get the horses ready," he offered.

"Do you know who had the place before you?" Lauren asked.

"No, I bought it through a receivership. I paid the cash—they gave me the deed. That's all I can tell you, although I hear it has quite a history. Always planned to research what caused the fire . . . maybe I will some day . . . but you know how that is . . . it's in the future. Right now, I'm busy getting my academy rolling."

"Maybe we could help," Gretchen offered. "We've the time, and it looks as though it could be an interesting undertaking."

"Really? You'd do that? Why?"

"Because this place has a history, and I'm a writer. Who knows what would be uncovered during a search, don't you agree?"

"Well, yes, I suppose so." He thought it over before stating, "You're not here for riding lessons, are you?"

"No, we're interested in old historical places like this one. I'm surprised someone hasn't covered it already, especially after the fire. How did that happen?"

"The fire? I've no idea. All I know . . . that's the reason given for restoring the place. At least that's the story they gave me when I bought it." He looked at Gretchen. "You say you're a writer. Do I know you?"

"Probably not. I'm Gretchen Dandrich. And you are?"

"Christopher Martin. Are you the same one on the *best seller's list?*"

"Guilty," Gretchen admitted, introducing Lauren. "My friend, Lauren Calloway."

"Go ahead and do what you have to do," he told them as he noticed his students arriving. "I've some horses to saddle. Where do you want to start?"

"The barn . . . we can help you saddle the horses since we've made you late. Lead us to them."

"Not necessary," he laughed. "That's part of the lesson today—grooming and saddling their own mounts." He led them into the barn. Lauren hoped they'd find Alex before the students did, but they needn't have worried. Alex was nowhere to be seen.

"Where do you suppose the little rascal went?" Lauren asked. "Maybe we shouldn't have brought him."

Gretchen ignored her. "What do you think about Christopher?"

"I wish he didn't have students today. There are a million questions I'd like to ask him."

"What kind of questions?"

"For instance, what relationship he is to the old man in the morgue? Do you think he could be a son or a nephew? And does he know what happened?"

"Not likely." The two helped Christopher lead out three horses from their stalls and watched as he demonstrated to the students the correct technique to prepare their mounts.

"We could help," Gretchen suggested.

"He's doing fine. Besides, those girls already know. They're taking advantage of a handsome instructor."

"Jealous?"

"Not at all. I only wish they'd step on it and get out of here so we can look for Alex."

"They're not paying any attention to us. Let's go look for him." The two disappeared into the barn and climbed the ladder to the loft. "Reminds me of the barn in my dream," Gretchen said. "You don't suppose—no, couldn't be."

"It burned up, didn't it?"

"Yeah, a barn in Ireland, not in Connecticut."

"Oh, Gretchen. Get real. You don't get to Ireland through a hole in the ground. You probably weren't any farther from home than next door."

"You think I made it up, too, don't you?"

"Too? Who else questions you? Harley? Kristin? Shaman?"

"Never mind. I thought you believed me."

"Let's explore the loft . . . maybe Alex is up there."

But they found nothing in the loft other than a few bats sleeping upside down on the rafters, and a few birds pecking away in the hay for seeds. The two sleuths poked into corners, lifted up hay, dug into dark corners, and eventually decided to give up the search.

"There's nothing up here," Lauren decided as she continued to dig into the hay. "Maybe in the house. Any ideas?" But Gretchen had already started down the ladder.

"Maybe we should check the town archives," she suggested, stopping halfway down the ladder to view the spot where she last saw Elise and Shaman. *Amazing, the similarity! Whatever did happen to Elise? Did Shaman bring her back with him, or did she retreat to her grave for another year?*

From her view on the ladder, Gretchen spied Alex jumping up and down and chattering wildly as though he'd made a big discovery. "Here he is," she called to Lauren and moved on down the ladder toward the empty stall to see what had excited the monkey. "Alex, where have you been?"

Meanwhile, Lauren, having satisfied herself that nothing of importance could be gained by further investigation in the loft, started back down the ladder. She reached the bottom rung before she realized Gretchen was no longer in the barn. *Where could she have gone?* She wandered around the stalls, but couldn't see her.

"Gretchen?" she called. "Where are you?" Hearing nothing, she ran outside and called again. "Gretchen?" Racing around the perimeter of the enormous barn, she found herself back where she started. Gretchen had disappeared.

She reentered the barn and climbed to the loft. "Gretchen? Gretchen?" Nary a sound interrupted the quiet desolation of the deserted barn. She headed for the house and knocked on the door. A maid answered.

"Did a young blonde woman come here within the last few minutes?" she asked.

"No," the young maid told her. "No one's been here since Mr. Martin left. Who are you?"

"Never mind. I'll go find Mr. Martin." Thinking of secret passageways and underground caches, she wondered if Gretchen had found something of interest. She returned to the barn. Empty. The quiet worried her. *Did Gretchen say something to me from the ladder, and I didn't hear her? Maybe she's pulling her disappearing act again.*

Roping a horse from the corral, she saddled the gentle bay and climbed onto the English saddle. *I've got to find Chris.* Giving her mount a gentle pat on his neck, she headed in the general direction she'd seen Chris take the class. She found the group relaxing under a tree, Christopher the center of attention as he related Hollywood adventures to his attentive students.

"Come on, join us," he invited her. "Where's your friend?"

"That's why I came looking for you," Lauren said. "I can't find her. She seems to have disappeared. You don't have any secret passages or anything in that barn, do you?"

"Not that I know of," Chris laughed. "But then I haven't had much time to look around." He checked his watch. "We've got a few more miles to go before we stop," he said. "Why don't you ride along? By the time we get back, your friend will probably be waiting for us."

Lauren agreed, and the girls remounted their horses for the remainder of the lesson. An hour later they returned to the barn and unsaddled their mounts. As the stabled animals ate and drank their fill, the class, fascinated by the story Lauren told them, spread out into every corner to examine the barn. They searched in vain, but like Lauren, found nothing.

"I've got blueprints for this spread. Come on in. Maybe they'll show us something," Christopher invited. The students left reluctantly, and Lauren followed Chris into the farmhouse. "Can I fix you a drink?" he asked, digging into a pile of papers in a basket near his desk.

"Yes, please. I think I need one," Lauren agreed.

"Wine okay?" At Lauren's nod, he asked his maid to bring two glasses of wine.

"She's done this before, you know," Lauren ventured.

"Who's done what before?" Chris asked automatically, still rummaging through the basket. "Oh, here's what I'm looking for." He spread the blueprints across a table, leafing through the many pages as the maid brought in a chilled bottle of wine and two glasses. Chris poured a drink for Lauren and handed it to Lauren as she joined him at the table.

"Can you read those?" she asked.

He poured himself a drink before answering. "Sure, they're easy to read." He explained to her how the prints were set up. "This is an overall blueprint of the property. The other pages give detailed instructions for the builder to follow as he restores the buildings. Here's the one for the barn. As you can see, it required extensive work. See? It gives you the size of the beams, how they're joined, and smaller detailed sketches of the rafters, loft, stalls, and manger. Everything . . . but I don't see any places for secret passages."

"Neither do I," Lauren agreed uncertainly. "But Gretchen and the monkey are gone. They had to go somewhere."

"Monkey? You never said anything about a monkey."

"We found him . . . and your address in an apartment in Washington," Lauren started to explain. "We thought maybe the two were connected . . ." Her voice trailed off as she realized how foolish she sounded. "Never mind, there has to be a logical answer."

"Maybe Gretchen found the monkey, and he led her astray." He grinned at her. "From my experience with monkeys, they're guilty of doing that."

"You're teasing me. Do you know anything about monkeys?"

"My uncle had a monkey. He loaned him out to children's parties and special events. Even loaned him out to an FBI agent as a cover while he staked out some low life. Smart as the dickens, that monkey."

"Your uncle doesn't happen to live in Washington, DC, does he?"

"Yeah, how'd you guess?" Chris turned to her. "Oh, FBI . . . the tip-off."

"I think we should talk," said Lauren.

"I thought we were talking." Then noticing Lauren's serious expression, he stopped bantering. "What are you saying?"

"You haven't heard? How long since you've seen your uncle?"

"Not for some time. After he learned I'd bought this place, he planned on making the trip, but it's hard for him to get away."

"Because he managed an apartment complex in the city, was on call for the monkey, and kept a low profile?"

"That's right. You know him?"

"I guess it's time to tell you why I'm really here. As Bette Davis once said, 'Fasten your seat belt. It's going to be a bumpy ride.'" She poured herself another glass of wine, refilled his, and started her story. She began her story with the wild tale Gretchen told her, the strange dream and unsolved murder, and ended by telling him the reason for their trip to his farm.

Christopher sat stunned. "Whew," he said. "I feel like I'm in the middle of a Hollywood plot? You think my uncle is that man, the one in the morgue? And that he's not a suicide?"

"We came here hoping to find your uncle. When we learned that some actor had bought the place, we didn't make the connection."

"Maybe you should leave it be. Let it remain a suicide. I don't think I like the idea of his being murdered. Opens up all sorts of devious activities I'd rather not know about."

"We can't now . . . because of the monkey . . . and Gretchen. I think it's all tied in. Where's the monkey? Where's Gretchen? If the monkey's as smart as you say he is, he found something and took Gretchen with him to wherever he went. I wish I'd gone down the ladder when she did, instead of . . ."

"Don't blame yourself," Chris consoled her. "It probably had to happen the way it did." The two sat in silence each lost in separate thoughts with only the sound the maid's activities emanating from the kitchen. Chris broke the silence.

"This friend of yours, she seems to have some kind of connection to a *Netherworld*. I've heard of people like that . . . highly sensitive to ethereal vibrations. Never met one before, except in the imagination of Hollywood writers. They're imaginative creatures—open to all kinds of weird fantasies, always looking for something unique and different, a new twist."

"Tell me about them . . . the imaginative creatures."

"Yes, now here I am—right in the middle of a real live spook movie." He laughed as the absurdity of the thought struck him.

"I must say you're taking this lightly. I can't be quite that cavalier about the supernatural. I'm an atheist, and fantasy plays no part in my life."

"I prefer logic myself, but I keep my options open. This excursion may hinge on that, but first, we wait for your friend to return. If she doesn't, then we'll decide what to do."

"You wait. I have to feed Cyrus, my cat. Call me? If Gretchen shows up on your doorstep?"

"Will do, but if she isn't here by morning, you'd better plan on staying here. Bring Cyrus with you. He'll be right at home with the other animals."

"We won't be a problem?"

"No, I'd appreciate the company. Besides, I'm fascinated. Maybe Gretchen found a lead and is following it up. Maybe she'll be knocking on my door before morning."

Absorbing his consoling words, Lauren left the farm to return to the inn. Once there, she managed to escape Mrs. Warren's many questions about Gretchen and their visit to the farm. She fed Cyrus and settled down for a disturbing night in her lonely room. Eventually, she fell asleep, wondering what really did happen to Gretchen.

Chapter Ten

Dreams are rudiments of the great state to come. We dream what is about to happen.

—Bailey

Day 9, Friday

Lauren awakened the next morning feeling as tired as if she hadn't slept. She'd dreamed about a strange Gretchen who kept trying to tell her something. Whatever it was, it eluded her by morning. She couldn't remember. *Maybe after I've had my coffee.* But coffee didn't help.

As through in a haze, she seemed to recall Gretchen in an unfamiliar place and having trouble returning, her lips forming words Lauren couldn't connect. *Archives? Check archives?* What archives? *Land records? Early building plats.* She didn't make the connection at the time, but there had to be a history of landowners dating way back to the time man first laid claim to property ownership. Could that be what she meant? *When I get a chance, I'll quiz Mrs. Warren about survey plats. It's worth a shot, and the courthouse is open today.*

Enthused, Lauren selected an old pair of jeans and her riding boots. *In case, I have to ride another horse today.* Dressed, she headed downstairs for breakfast and found Mrs. Warren presiding over the kitchen.

"Where did you leave your friend?" Mrs. Warren asked, supervising a plate of bacon and eggs. "Doesn't she eat breakfast?

"She's with friends," Gretchen lied. "I promised her I'd check out the town records on that piece of property. It's very important."

"Oh, is it now." Mrs. Warren answers filled with curiosity. "You were out there, were you? Did you find out who lives there? Is it that Hollywood character?"

"It's a riding academy . . . for future equestrians," Lauren says. "Do you know anything about possible hidden passages or tunnels on the place? Maybe built back in revolutionary days?" she asked the woman.

"Why could be, you know," Mrs. Warren mused. "Come to think of it, I did hear something about them having to fill up sink holes when the old barn burned down. Nearly took the main house down too, but they caught it in time."

"The barn burned down? When?" *Maybe Gretchen didn't dream it.* She shook her head to clear it. *No, it's a coincidence.*

"Oh yes, about a year ago . . . quite a mystery about it at the time. You know, they never did learn how the fire started."

"Really?" Lauren pressed the woman to keep talking. "Wasn't there an investigation?"

"Oh sure, but then, it was Halloween . . . probably kids."

"No doubt." *She doesn't know.* "Now, about the archives . . ."

"Oh yes, the courthouse. Go on into town. You can't miss the building. It's off the main drag and quite impressive . . . some two hundred years old—an old historical landmark, so to speak. I believe they store the old records in the basement, if I remember. The women will steer you in the right direction. They're real helpful, but inquisitive . . . I have to warn you."

"That okay. I've no secrets. Gretchen has them all." She left the old lady gaping after her. *That should keep her occupied for a day or so,* and hurried down the steps to her car.

Later that day

The women in the archives department were more than helpful to Lauren. They insisted on furnishing her with copies at no cost. Armed with copies of old land plats and loads of lore about its history, Lauren returned to the academy. The nippy weather told her that winter would be early this year. *Gretchen will need warmer clothes, wherever she is.* She inhaled the fresh, sweet air of fall, remembering how much she loved the pungent smell of burning leaves and the thrill of seeing frost on the pumpkins in her earlier years.

At Christopher's, he gave her the unwelcome news. "Gretchen never showed. I heard nothing, I know because I couldn't sleep."

"She must be hungry and cold by this time, Chris. We've got to find her."

"Did you bring your suitcase?" Chris asked.

"No, I'm giving us one more day to find her. My restless night gave me a new lead, and I've brought something you might be interested in . . . even if it doesn't lead us to Gretchen." She laid copies of old plats on a table.

Ecstatic, Chris viewed the collection. "Why didn't I think of this?" Together they spread the copies out. Choosing the one for the barn, they poured over it, looking for anything different about the barn that didn't now exist.

"Something else I found out this morning," Lauren told him. "Your barn is a restored version of the original—the one that burned down."

"I knew that much," he told her.

"I know, but you didn't know that when Gretchen returned from her disappearing act a year ago, she talked about a barn that burned down, but didn't know the location of the barn. She got it mixed up with other weird dream fantasies that sounded too surreal to be authentic."

"And you think the two incidents are tied together? The fire and the dream?"

"Not exactly . . . maybe . . . I don't really know." Lauren hesitated, not willing to make the connection as yet.

"Exactly . . . what did happen to Gretchen? Maybe you better tell me the story . . . from the beginning. Better yet—" He glanced at his watch. "Have you had lunch?"

"No, and I'm really hungry."

"Then let's go out. It's the maid's day off, and I'm not a cook."

"Could we lunch at Shaman's? That's where the story starts."

"Shaman's? Hey, I've heard about that place. Weren't they involved in some big *hush-hush* murder trial a while back?"

"Yes, that's the one where Gretchen testified, and no one believed her—not the jury nor her husband. I'm afraid I didn't believe her either."

"Ah, a mystery. Gretchen lives her own stories, hmm?"

"You don't believe it either."

"I think I'll hold my beliefs in reserve," he answered. "Since Gretchen isn't here to lead the way, we'll start, as you say . . . where it all began."

He helped Lauren with her coat, got into his own, and pulled on an English-style golf cap. "Great disguise," he said to her, patting the cap as he directed her to his Jeep.

"The cap?"

"And the Jeep." He laughed. "People ignore both."

Lauren understood. Ridgecrest had its share of celebrities and paid little attention to them, but occasionally it did happen, and a crowd would form.

At two in the afternoon, they found Shaman's Pub nearly deserted. The regulars had gone back to work, and the once roaring fire had burned low. Einstein and Ming stretched and welcomed the newcomers, then returned to their job of gracing the hearth. A nippy day, Shaman directed his guests to a table near the fire so they could capture the heat from the fireplace.

Chris glanced at the two cats—curled like bookends on the warm stone hearth. "Beautiful decoration for your fireplace, Shaman," he commented.

"That they are." Shaman grinned. "But they're more than decoration."

"I don't doubt." Turning, Chris glimpsed Shaman staring at Lauren.

"You've been here before, have you not?" Shaman asked her.

"Back in my college days, with Gretchen and Kristin. You remember?"

"Never forget a pretty face. Three of the prettiest *colleens* at the university."

"Thanks, Shaman. You've quite a memory."

He helped her off with her coat and hung it on a wooden peg on the far wall. Chris added his to another peg and returned to the table. "We did hang out here a lot in those days," she said as she introduced him to Shaman.

During the introduction, Shaman took their order. "Your place has become a landmark, Shaman. Glad to see you're still in business."

Shaman looked pleased and accepted her compliment. He returned later with their wine and diplomatically left them to their private conversation.

"A landmark?" Chris asked. "How do you figure that?"

"Historically speaking," Lauren explained, "this town dates back to revolutionary days, and a lot of the buildings are that old . . . like the place where Gretchen and I are staying, *The Red Mill.* According to Mrs. Warren, *The Red Mill* housed British soldiers at one time. A private residence then, it later became a refuge for the patriots on their way to fight the British and a stopover for General George Washington and his troops."

"And this place? A watering spot for troops?"

"As far as I know, it's always been a tavern. Shaman seems to have been here for an eternity, which goes back to my story. Gretchen claims he's been reincarnated many times. I know he spins yarns as though he has firsthand knowledge of history even as far back as the 1500s. Most customers accept them merely as entertainment and give them their due."

"And Gretchen? How does she accept his yarns?"

Gretchen told me a story about his meeting an old-time love at an Irish graveyard once a year, on Halloween night, the only time they can meet since Elise, through some twist of fate, is destined to spend eternity there—that is, until Shaman can rescue her."

"And how does he do that?"

"Through Magus, according to the story."

"Magus? Isn't he the fictional character who travels the *Netherworld* chasing evil?"

"You've heard of him?"

"As an actor, you learn all kinds of useless information. Gretchen claims to have been to this *Netherworld?*" Lauren watched the expression on his face, laughing.

"What's funny?"

"Your expression . . . your eyes. They're like saucers." She laughed.

"You're a skeptic who wants to believe," she accused him.

"Hiding one's expression isn't something you learn in acting class. Sorry about that."

"It's okay. I like it. Better than having to guess people's motives as happens in my profession."

"Ah yes, your profession. We only got as far as Gretchen and her career as a writer, I've no idea what you do." He waited for her to answer. When she ignored him, he repeated his request. "What do you do—when you're not sleuthing?"

"That's what I do. Sleuth."

"Must I dig it out of you? What do you sleuth?"

Lauren hesitated, wondering if she should say any more, then answered cautiously. "I work as an investigator for the FBI. At the moment, I seem to be on administrative leave. Somehow your uncle's death is connected to my extended vacation and how I happen to be here." She pulled out an envelope from her purse. "Gretchen found this in her apartment in Washington . . . with your return address on it."

"I see. That's why you two came sleuthing?"

"Yes, to find out if there's a connection between my investigation and your uncle's death. We were about to give up, when Gretchen disappeared."

"And you think there's a connection."

"I don't know. Why didn't anyone notify you of your uncle's death?"

"I've no idea, except—"

"Except what?"

"I changed my name. My given name is Alexander Dumant, the same as my uncle's. I changed it for anonymity in the theater world . . . as well as to protect my uncle."

"I understand the theater reasoning, but why your uncle?"

"He's mixed up in *stooging* for some senator. I don't know the details, but that's how he uses the monkey. In his last letter, the one I answered, he said something about pulling out and returning to Redding. 'Too risky,' is how he put it. That's the last I heard."

"Maybe they don't know you exist. No *next of kin* to notify, that type of thing. Happens all the time, particularly in my business. People do get lost, you know."

"Your business? Spying on an old man?" Chris asked.

"Not me, my office. I'm trying to find out why they cut me out, put me on indefinite leave, and refused to tell me why."

Shaman brought their order of pastrami on rye, replenished their glasses, and disappeared. Chris studied Lauren. *A no-nonsense type, embroiled in something she can't define logically . . . and no way out. She can't afford to be illogical.*

"I'm curious when things don't make sense," Lauren continued as though reading his mind. "Gretchen may stretch the truth and believe in fantasies, but I deal with facts. That's why I'm here. To make sense out of nonsense, so to speak."

Chris stopped eating and roared with laughter.

"I'm glad it amuses you," Lauren said "Look, you've awakened the cats. I don't think they appreciate your humor."

"You're afraid," he accused her, "afraid that cats can really talk, that Einstein is a *familiar*, and you're out to—as you say, make sense out of nonsense." He glanced at the two cats on the hearth. "I do believe Einstein is listening," he teased. "Maybe he has the answers."

"Oh, come off it. You refuse to take me seriously. Look, it's getting late, and this place is filling up. Have you learned enough?" As she spoke, the door opened, and a particularly cold breeze filled the room. The two shivered, and Lauren turned in time to see Professor Ipswitch take his usual place at the end of Shaman's bar.

"Déjà vu," she said to Chris. "Speak of the devil. That weird little man who caused the draught is the esteemed Professor Ipswitch, and the nemesis for Gretchen's fantasies. I wonder if he and Kristin are still in business?"

"I think we should stick around and get to know the old coot," Chris suggested. "You've piqued my interest, my dear. So he's the inventor of weird potions, hmm? He looks harmless enough."

Lauren laughed. "Chris, you look absolutely rapt. It would serve you right—" She stops as she realizes he isn't listening. "What are you thinking?"

"Let's have a nightcap with the professor," he said, a roguish expression on his face.

"Be careful, Chris, you may be his next victim," Lauren mused, gathering up her things and following him to the bar. Chris propped himself next to the eminent professor with Lauren next to him.

"Shaman," he said, "how about a *crème de cocoa* for the two of us before we leave?" He turned to the professor. "How about you? Will you join us?"

"Be delighted," said the professor. "By the way, I don't believe we've met. I'm Professor Ipswitch from the university . . . and you?

"Christopher Martin, and this is Lauren Calloway. We've heard about your inventions."

"If it's a nightcap you're seeking," the professor said, "I've the perfect aphrodisiac. It's my latest invention, guaranteed to make dreams come true." He handed a small vial to Chris. "One drop is all it takes for a peaceful, undisturbed rest."

"Why, thanks." Chris examined the vial the professor handed him. His eyebrows rose to a question mark as he read the inscription on the vial. *"Behold! What you crave shall be yours. To your uttermost dreams and beyond."*

As Shaman set the drinks before them, Chris asked, "Is this guy for real, Shaman?"

Shaman shrugged. "Hasn't killed anyone yet."

Chris held the vial as though it were poison and looked at Lauren. "Are you game?" he asked.

"Why not? Looks harmless." He added a drop to Lauren's drink and pocketed the vial.

"You don't want to dream?" she asked.

"One of us has to stay sane to pick up the pieces." He winked.

Chapter Eleven

*Sweet dreams, my dear. May you find all the happiness you crave
and beyond.*

Day 10, Saturday

Lauren felt rather than saw the escape route Gretchen had taken. Vaguely
aware of her encounter with Professor Ipswitch at Shaman's Pub the night
before, she seemed to hear his voice in the distance. *"Sweet dreams, my dear.
May you find all the happiness you crave and beyond."*

"Where's Chris?" she wondered, looking around and floating on what
looked like a giant lily pad. A frog croaked at her invasion of his property.
"What are you doing on my lily pad?" the frog asked.

"I'm sorry. I seem to be lost. You didn't by chance see a tall, blonde female
wandering around here, did you?" Lauren asked the frog.

"You mean that intruder Alex brought back with him?" He looked
toward the shoreline. "She's over there. Evidently, she likes our mortal enemy,
the cat, more than she does us frogs. Take her away."

As Lauren turned, she noticed a giant playground built offshore for
animals. There were swings and chutes, ladders and sandboxes, and weird-
looking buildings giving shelter to various animals, each separating various
species of animals and reminding Lauren of a giant zoo. A monkey hanging
on a banana tree contentedly peeling his fruit caught her eye, thinking Alex.
No, he's too big for Alex.

Next to the monkey, she saw Einstein and Ming, the Siamese cats from
Shaman's hearth, contentedly curled around a huge cauldron. Einstein
raised his lofty head and opened his big blue eyes as Lauren came out of
the water. Satisfied she presented no eminent danger, he returned to his

sleeping position. *Where does Gretchen fit into this scene? And Einstein, is he the talking cat Gretchen told me about?*

*A*s she walked around the outside perimeter of the playground, she noticed a wide assortment of various wild animals. *Must be some type of invisible barrier separating them; otherwise, they'd all be fighting.* She moved from one animal to another, from the lion perched on a grassy mound to a lamb nursing at his mother's side. *No barriers, how is that possible?* Finding neither Gretchen nor Alex, she turned to the sleeping Siamese on the hearth, a hearth that looked very much like the one in Shaman's Pub.

"Einstein," she asked the sleeping cat, "have you seen Gretchen?" *Why am I asking a cat?* Einstein muted, turned, and looked in the direction of the forest. "She's in the forest? Where? Could you show me?"

Einstein arose, stretched his magnificent loins, and, after sniffing in his companion's ear, glided toward a path leading into the foliage. Lauren followed. In the darkness, she heard loud animal noises that muted as Einstein approached the opening of the glade ahead. There he paused, his nose directing Lauren to a structure that appeared to be an entrance to a mine. She looked at Einstein, puzzled by his meaning, but sensing that he expected her to enter the opening.

"You want me to go in there?" she asked, her skin crawling in fear. She looked ahead into the darkness. *Wish I'd thought to bring a flashlight!* But as she entered the opening, the passageway became as light as day. At the end of the passageway, she found herself in a room furnished in early Colonial and adequately appointed as though ready for occupancy at any time. *Have I slipped into the seventeenth century?* As she looked back, the door closed, replaced by a solid, impregnable wall. She's alone. About to scream out in terror, Gretchen appears at her side.

"Lauren, you found me. When did you get here?"

"Gretchen, I'm so glad to see you're okay." She looked around the room, noticing the old-time spinning wheel by the fireside and the huge black cauldron hanging over a fire that burned low in a massive stone fireplace. "We seem to have stepped back in time. How did it happen?"

"You shouldn't be here," Gretchen said. "But I'm glad you came."

"I'm dreaming . . . but how did you get here?"

"I followed Alex. When I saw him in the barn, I caught hold of him at the same time he disappeared. I must have lost consciousness for a while. When I came to, I found myself in this room. Alex seemed familiar with the place, but he can't get me out 'til it's over."

"What do you mean . . . 'til what's over?"

"It's an underground movement to change the world, and your outfit is mixed up in it whether they know it or not."

"Are you sure? Why haven't I heard about it?"

"You're the logical one, Lauren. Think about it. It makes sense, the senator, an FBI agent, and the mixed-up of bodies in the morgue . . . all part of a gigantic plot for global control. *A new beginning,* they call it. New books printed to replace our present glossed-over and war-infested history books. Peaceful coexistence taught in schools to students . . . the world a safer and better place to live. Peace for all eternity."

"Sounds like someone's been smoking the funny stuff . . ."

"No, these people really believe it's possible. Can you imagine? A perfect world! What more can one ask for?"

"I don't know, Gretchen. It would be funny if it weren't so serious. Who are the good guys and who are the bad ones?"

"Must there be good guys and bad guys?" Gretchen queried. "Peace doesn't involve good or bad if aggression is erased. If we know nothing about violence, it doesn't exist. It's that simple."

"Too simple. Denial doesn't change history, Gretchen. I rather like the world I live in. Besides, isn't it better to face reality?" She sat down on one of the uncomfortable antique chairs, and Gretchen perched on the hearth beside her.

"Well, I must admit," agreed Gretchen, "it does sort of sound like a movie plot, but isn't it a great idea?"

"No, it isn't. It's struggle that makes life worth living. It builds character. Besides, who'd want a world full of *peaceniks*?"

"There you go again . . . being rational, Lauren. I think it's a blast."

"Who's in charge of this nefarious plot? Do you know?"

"They call themselves *The New Americans,* and their motto is *Give Peace a Chance.* At the moment, they're in the process of sending out letters enlisting new members who want to live in a peaceful land. I think it's a great movement. They hold protest demonstrations and everything."

"Protest demonstrations? But Gretchen, you've never been politically active before. Why now?"

"Because it's so exciting . . . makes me feel part of something . . . something worthwhile. And I like that."

Lauren watched as Gretchen talked of her new feelings, her involvement, and her acceptance. "You've no intention of returning, have you?" Lauren asks.

Gretchen looked guilty. "There's no reason to return. Not 'til there's a better world."

"But that's my job, Gretchen," Lauren reminded her. "And it can be done. But not by abolishing the past in exchange for some *Alice in Wonderland* philosophy. I ask you again, Gretchen. Who's in charge?"

"I've no idea."

"Can I see a copy of the letter—the one drumming up new membership?"

"Sure." Gretchen left the room and returned with a four-page letter, written in closely typed copy, entitled *The American Way of Life* (AWOL). "See? Even the acronym is synonymous to peace."

"So it is. AWOL from the world! Underground. It's all there, isn't it?"

"I'm so glad you understand, Lauren. In some way, your organization is involved. I haven't figured out how, but I'm sure it is."

As Lauren read the proffered letter, Gretchen sat busily writing. When Lauren finished reading, Gretchen handed her the note she'd written.

We're being monitored. Be careful what you say. Pretend to accept their philosophy, or we'll never get out of here. Lauren tossed the note into the fire and stared at the flames as the note burned. As she wondered how to proceed, she heard a knock on her door, and Mrs. Warren's voice floated into the room.

*   *   *

"Time to get up, Ms. Calloway," Mrs. Warren called through Lauren's door. "You left a *wake up* call on the downstairs counter."

Lauren struggled to open her eyes. Instead of staring into a fire, she faced a brilliant morning sunbeam burning through the bedroom window and into her room. As she awakened, she recalled her dream.

Back at the farmhouse, Chris also awakened, remembering the previous evening and his meeting with the professor. He called Lauren. "I slept the sleep of the dead last night. What do you suppose that professor puts in his potions?"

"Be careful around him, Gretchen calls him *evil*. Maybe she's right."

"Yeah, maybe, but I haven't slept like that in years. He should call it *aphrodisiac*." Changing the subject abruptly, he asked, "Dream anything exciting last night? I'm assuming you did dream, even if I didn't."

"Yes, and I'm trying to interpret it. In my dream, Gretchen spied Alex in the barn and grabbed him, then disappeared into thin air . . . along with

Alex. What happened next is sort of like an old *Star Trek* movie. Chris, I think she's in danger and can't get back."

"Alex? Who's Alex?"

"Your uncle's monkey. We didn't know what else to call him. Do you know his name?"

"No, never heard Uncle Alex call him by name. Sounds as good as any other name. What else?"

"There has to be an opening somewhere in the barn for them to have disappeared."

"We've looked."

"We'll look again."

"Come on over. I'm not going into that barn alone. I may find the rabbit hole and disappear too."

Lauren laughed. "Not much like a scripted Hollywood scene, is it? No prepared lines. No logical endings."

"You make us sound like a bunch of puppets."

"Sorry. It's the public's general concept of Hollywood actors. They tend to believe their inflated press releases."

"You sound like Uncle Alex."

"That why you changed your name?"

"Could be," he agreed. "How long will it take you to get here?"

"As soon as I have breakfast. I've some ideas I want to discuss with Mrs. Warren first."

"Mrs. Warren?"

"Our local historian. I'll fill you in when I get there. It's in the maps I brought over yesterday, and we both missed it," Lauren explained.

Chris hung up the phone and grabbed the maps. He poured over them, trying to figure out what Lauren meant, matching the old maps with the more recent ones. By the time Lauren arrived, he felt he'd figured it out.

Late Afternoon

"Did you see it?" Lauren asked as soon as she entered Chris's study.

"I think so. The new barn didn't follow the same plans, but there is a tunnel under the barn." He looked at Lauren as though expecting her to verify his finding. "The entrance appears to have been covered over. How could Gretchen disappear through a hole that is no more?"

"It isn't sealed up," Lauren assured him, "and it's been there since before the Civil War. At one time, this barn housed slaves escaping from the South.

If they could get to Washington, and link up with underground railroads, they had a good chance of making it to Canada and freedom. This barn served as a refuge and halfway point."

"Where did you learn all that?" Chris asked.

"From the horses' mouth, so to speak. Mrs. Warren, her ancestors lived in this part of the country, and she has records."

"And she remembers the barn before its restoration?"

"Right," agreed Lauren, giving Chris her *are-you-with-me-or-against-me* look as he opined, giving full credence to the lines on the map and the vague possibility of a tunnel under his barn.

"All well and good," Chris finally said. "Now what do we do? Turn the barn upside down looking for an opening that may not exist?"

"But it has to be there. Else how could Gretchen and Alex have both disappeared?"

"Good question, and one that needs an answer. Let's go." He gathered up the maps, grabbed a jacket, and pulled Lauren out the door heading for the barn.

"We're not riding today," he told the spirited horses who expected a gallop on the range. He patted their rumps and gave them an extra ration of oats in their feeders then moved them away from the area of the barn where Gretchen presumably had disappeared. "If Hollywood could see me now," he grumbled.

Lauren headed for the mangers, pulling back the hay in each compartment. "There's nothing here, Chris," she said reaching the last stall. "What next?"

"Over by the door, Lauren. They didn't rebuild as many stalls as previously. The last stall is now the back door." Chris strode over to the door. As he did, he accidentally touched a wall near the door. An opening appeared in the floor. "I found it," he called out to Lauren, struggling to maintain his balance so as not to make the same mistake as Gretchen. He pulled back, trying to remember what he had touched and straddling the opening in the floor.

Lauren rushed to his side, nearly tumbling into the opening. She pulled back in time to avoid falling and teetered on the edge. *So that's what happened to Gretchen!* "What did you do?" she asked, peering down the black hole.

"I'm not sure. I know I'm lucky not to be down the hole too. I grabbed the doorknob to keep my balance. Anyway, we've solved the riddle. Except . . ." His voice trailed off as he questioned his find. He moved away from the opening and the door sprang shut again.

Lauren looked puzzled. "Didn't this area burn up along with the barn?"

"It's been rebuilt by someone who knew its original intent . . . and capitalized on that knowledge . . . but for what purpose?" He turned to Lauren, puzzled. "What else do you know you haven't told me? Did you know anything about a tunnel?"

"Me? I'm as lost as you are." She plopped down on a bale of hay, looking defeated. "At least, we know how Gretchen disappeared."

"But where? That's the sixty-four dollar question. Tell me again what happened."

"I don't know what, or even how, where, when, or why."

"Go back to that first day and the reason you and Gretchen came snooping around my farm. You said you found an envelope in your apartment with my address on it, and you followed the trail. Are you trying to prove that the death of my uncle and the envelope you found are somehow linked? Or that your office is engaged in a cover-up?"

"I don't know. Maybe."

"Maybe." Chris continued his third degree. "How long has it been since you've contacted your office, Lauren? How long has it been since you checked on that FBI agent you claim is posing as my uncle? And how does he fit into this cops and robbers' story?"

"I've told you everything I know. We decided to follow the money trail."

"And that led you here?"

"No, we got sidetracked when we found the envelope and saw the return address. A long shot, but we decided to check it out and make a trip here . . . since it's our home. But to answer your first question, *No, I haven't contacted my office.* That may sound strange, but I don't completely trust my office at the moment . . . at least, not everyone there."

"You do think there's a cover-up, and that it's connected to my uncle."

"I don't know how, but yes, I do. The fire . . . your uncle . . . Alex . . . my office—they're all connected in some strange way. Gretchen and I decided to play it cool, and try to solve a mystery we knew nothing about. As for Alex . . . we thought maybe if the monkey knew this place, he'd find his home here. Otherwise, I'm as lost as you are."

"You think she's in danger?"

"Yes, because of what she knows. We need to find her."

"Good Lord, I've gotten myself smack dab in the middle of a gosh-darned sci-fi movie. Maybe I should be writing a book."

Lauren risked a grin. "Gretchen's beaten you to it, but maybe you can play the lead."

"Okay, let's set up the next scene and let's get back to business. When did a secret passageway for escaping slaves become a secret tunnel?"

"Recently, I believe . . . but there has to be another way to get back and forth. If we go down this way, we may not get back, so we've got to find the other end. I don't know how to do that."

"Another entrance . . . or exit," Chris pondered. "Alex knew this one. He came back, but monkeys can jump . . . and climb, but Gretchen can't. She may not be able to get back, and I doubt Alex would be much help in that area."

"How deep is the tunnel? How far does it extend? Where does it end? Do we have access to a ladder long enough . . . if this is the only entrance?" Lauren had only questions and no answers.

"Well, we'll have to find a way back or we'll be lost too." They headed for the house, back to the maps and to plan strategy. "Your Mrs. Warren gave us hearsay, the archives give us maps. What we need is someone who's been there."

"A hundred and fifty years ago?"

"A historian, maybe. The public library?"

"Or Shaman," suggested Lauren.

"Shaman? The man at the pub?"

"Why not? We need dinner. He likes to talk and claims to be hundreds of years old. What more do we need?" She looked at Chris with an impish grin as though testing his courage. "Afraid of what he'll say?" She waited for an answer.

"Maybe." He hesitated, mulling over her suggestion. "Shaman does like to talk, and we do need dinner. It won't hurt to test him."

"He's closed on Sundays, so it's either today or wait 'til Monday."

"Let's go. Maybe we can lead the conversation to whatever he knows about the old barn." An elated Chris prepared to leave, and Lauren, inwardly pleased, noticed his renewed exuberance. *He's hooked.*

Saturday Evening

They found Shaman at his usual place behind the bar mixing his special drinks. Chris hit right to the point, watching for his reaction. "Shaman, do you know anything about an underground railroad in these parts?"

Shaman didn't disappoint him. He stopped in midair pouring one of his drinks. "Well, that's a right grizzly subject for a Saturday eve," he said, recovering quickly. "What brings that old business to mind? You located one of those old tunnels?" He poured them each a glass of Chardonnay as he mulled over their question.

"Could be," Chris said. "Lauren tells me you've been here forever. We were hoping you could help us locate someone who has disappeared."

"Why not call Roscoe or one of the other coppers? Why come here looking for a lost person?"

"Because of the person lost," said Lauren. "It's Gretchen. She disappeared into an underground tunnel, and we can't find a way to get her back. We need to find another way and thought you might know of one."

"You must be talking about the old Grange Farm. You the one who bought that place?" he asked Chris.

"Guilty."

"That's where she disappeared?"

"Yes, one minute she's there . . . the next minute she's gone. First the monkey, then Gretchen . . . we think she followed him. Now they're both gone."

"A monkey? What kind of monkey?" Shaman asked.

"An organ-grinder type monkey, I don't know the species. Is it important?"

"It is. Some are capable of instruction. Others are not. Which is it?"

"Alex is as capable a monkey as there is, and can follow instructions if need be," Lauren interrupted. "If he could talk, he could tell us what we need to know. He's a witness to a murder."

"Murder?" Shaman glanced at Einstein, curled on the hearth, his ears alert. At that moment, the door opened and Professor Ipswitch entered. Shaman stopped talking long enough to mix a Rob Roy for the professor and placed it in front of him. The professor concentrated on his drink, ignoring Shaman who appeared upset.

"Your table's ready." He led Chris and Lauren to a vacant table by the fireplace. "It's a nippy night out," he explained. He waited nearby until they'd deposited coats, etc., and when they were settled, added *sotto voce,* "Check back tomorrow. I can't talk here."

"But you're closed Sundays," Lauren reminded him.

"I'll be here." He left.

Chris shook off the eerie chill that moved over him despite the roaring fire as he and Lauren waited for their order. "I think the other entrance is here, in this building. Maybe we shouldn't wait until tomorrow."

"You feel it too . . . that chill?" She rubbed her arms 'til the heat from the fireplace took over. "No wonder he keeps a fire burning winter and summer."

"Strange happenings take place in this establishment, Lauren. I fear Shaman's long since disappeared from the world of men and reality, filled with secrets, past experiences, and knowledge that far exceeds our understanding."

Lauren smiled as though amused by his comment. "That's what Gretchen tried to tell me when I didn't believe her tales of a *Netherworld*. You think there is such a place?"

"Nothing's impossible. Did Gretchen tell you anything that could give us a lead?" Chris asked. "Like, how she got back?"

"I didn't take her story seriously. Maybe I should have listened closer, but it was Halloween." Lauren tried to remember. "I looked on it as a ghost story, like Ichabod Crane."

"You don't remember telling Halloween ghost stories? I can't believe that."

"Okay, you decide. She mentioned something about a forest, by the university, an underground tunnel with tracks, like an old mining camp, although at the time I'd never heard of a mine in Connecticut."

"A story, hmm? You still think so?"

"It's becoming reality, isn't it? The underground track, evidently common knowledge by those who've lived here many years . . . Mrs. Warren and Shaman, to name a few, and Professor Ipswitch, although for other reasons."

"Speaking of the professor, why do you suppose Shaman gave us the brush-off as soon as the professor came in?"

Lauren laughed. "I've no idea. Maybe he keeps secrets from the professor."

They batted suspicions back and forth as they enjoyed Shaman's specialty. The professor left as they finished eating, and they heard his motorcycle skid on the gravel driveway. After he'd left, Shaman returned to their table, completely changed. "You need another entrance to the tunnels, do you?" he asked. "I think I can handle that."

Lauren, surprised, looked at Chris. "You know of any?"

"I know of one . . . there may be others."

"You remember Gretchen, don't you?" Lauren asked. At Shaman's nod, she continued. "We believe she unintentionally stumbled into the tunnel and can't find her way back."

"Where? How?"

"At the ranch . . . in the barn."

"But the barn's been rebuilt. There's no entrance there now." Shaman stared at the two questioning faces. "Is there?"

"We found it . . . a bottomless pit. Anyway, our ladder won't reach to the bottom. We can't go down the same way Gretchen did without knowing we have a way out. And we don't know if she's alive down there or wandering around lost. We need to find an entrance from another direction . . . and find out what happened."

Shaman shook his shaggy head. "That girl . . . she can get into more trouble without half trying. How long has she been missing this time?"

"Since Friday afternoon."

They watched Shaman digest the information. "I can get you in." Then he hesitated. "But the tunnel is active again . . . a haven and headquarters for—" He stopped, then added, "At the moment, radicals protesting the war."

Chris laughed in disbelief. "More of your Irish lore, Shaman?"

"Not at all. You're sure that's where she is?"

"We're sure. Can you help us?" Lauren pleaded.

Shaman grinned. He wasn't beyond the age of appreciating attractive young ladies. "Be here in the morning, and I'll take you there."

"You think she's safe? They won't hurt her?"

"No, they'll try to recruit her. If she's smart, she'll go along with them . . . wait her chance to get away."

"That could take months."

"Or years. Those people believe in their causes and can sometimes become violent in defending them. Do you have the necessary protection . . . in case?"

"We will," Chris assured Shaman. He turned to Lauren. "Can you imagine? There I was . . . sitting around, minding my own business . . ."

"When real life hit you in the solar plexus"—Lauren grinned at him—"you'll get used to it."

Chapter Twelve

Sometimes you have to return to the past to understand the present

Day 11, Sunday morning

Sunday morning started out as a beautiful day with brilliant sunshine and a few clouds, but as Chris and Lauren approached Shaman's, clouds suddenly amassed, the sky darkened, and thunder resounded in the distance. Rains poured onto the foothills, soon making puddles on the road. Shaman opened the door, and they ducked into the shelter, shaking off the rain.

"Did you bring this on?"

Chris teased Shaman, selecting a table by the fireplace as Shaman helped them off with their coats. He left them to dry off before the cheery fire and returned with hot drinks for both of them before he answered Chris.

"If I told you, you wouldn't believe me," he said.

"Probably not," Chris agreed.

"The storm will keep people from wandering around town," Shaman explained. "They tend to become a little crazy if confronted with something they don't understand."

"Can't say I blame them." Chris accepted the hot drink. "Now, getting down to business, Shaman. What do you have to offer a novice in the realm of the supernatural?"

Shaman perched on the hearth beside Einstein and Ming and stroked Einstein, his hands moving to the rhythm of the rain that beat down on the windows as he collected his thoughts. Even then, he chose his words carefully.

"There's a difference between this world and the *Netherworld,*" he began. "Everything here is there, but better. All things brighter . . . the sun more

201

golden . . . the flowers smell sweeter . . . and peace reigns in the other world because Magus remains vigilant in his crusade against evil.

"Today, evil again attempts to take control of the world . . . sometimes going underground to hide its nefarious ways. It's become more than Magus can handle alone, and he requests assistance." He stopped, viewing the perplexed faces of his visitors, then explained. "The *Netherworld* is being compromised," he said.

"Compromised? Where's the *Netherworld?*" asked Chris. "And what does that have to do with Gretchen and a missing monkey?"

"My sources tell me they're connected." Shaman stroked Einstein and Ming as he awaited a reaction.

Puzzled, Chris looked at Lauren, then back to Shaman. "Your sources? What sources? Cats?"

"A very special breed of cat," he replied. "A stolen source of wisdom from the ages." He continued to stroke Einstein. "I've never told anyone the story of how Einstein came into my life, but I assure you, his wisdom never fails me."

His listeners, slightly confused, were quiet. "Gretchen wouldn't hesitate. She'd understand," Shaman assured them.

"Then we can do no less," he accepted and turned to Lauren. "Let's go find the secret passage."

As they rose to follow Shaman, Einstein rose to his full height and stretched languidly. They were surprised to see Einstein taking the lead, and Shaman motion to them to follow.

"Why do I feel as though I've entered the Land of Oz?" Chris asked.

"Because maybe you have," said Shaman, and Chris had to be satisfied. "Ready, Einstein?"

Chris and Lauren followed Einstein, and Shaman brought up the rear. Einstein paused before a locked door in the storeroom until Shaman produced a key and unlocked the door. "Don't be surprised at anything you encounter," he advised them before returning the key to his pocket. "Sometimes you have to return to the past to understand the present."

Einstein led them down a dark tunnel toward a brilliant light that shone in the distance. Occasionally, he turned to Shaman and at Shaman's nod would continue. As they approached the light, Lauren became aware of a peaceful aura surrounding them. She sniffed the balmy fragrant air, and looked at Shaman. He, too, seemed to relish the change of atmosphere and appeared years younger. Chris seemed unaffected.

"Where are we?" she asked.

Shaman didn't answer, letting the surroundings speak for him. Towering shapes of pine trees came into view, and he headed for a lovely cottage hidden in their depth—the roof of the cottage, thatched and low. The windows had small panels of glass set into a larger pane that opened to a panorama of verdant forest. Uneven cobblestones led to a rustic door held in place with huge brass hinges.

Shaman led them through the cottage door into an inviting room—a great room filled with peace and light—boasting an enormous black stone fireplace. A cozy, blazing fire enhanced the atmosphere. Dark leather chairs, each with a footstool placed before it, and an inviting rocker facing the inviting fireplace. A quiet lamp glowed on an ancient oak desk.

"Is this your home?" Lauren asked, looking around the cottage and thinking it similar to the cottage in her dream. Unexpectedly, she asked, "Gretchen says you've lived for centuries. That's not possible, is it?"

"Hmmm, what else did Gretchen say?" Shaman asked her as Lauren settled into the cozy rocking chair.

"I never believed her, now I wonder . . ." She looked around the room, absorbing its peaceful vibrations and feeling she'd never felt so contented. Shaman raided the small icebox in the pantry and returned with refreshing drinks.

"You're going to need these before your journey," he advised them, pouring each of them a small glass of lemonade. The two partook of the refreshments, and Shaman began to speak.

"Gretchen knew from whence she spoke," he said, his deep, sonorous Irish brogue a delight to hear. "You are here in the *Netherworld*, Lauren, a world where Gretchen could wander at will if she so desired, but rather than accept her ability to traverse in two worlds, she struggles to find legitimate meaning behind her strange adventures."

"That sounds logical," Lauren interjected.

Shaman smiled. "Ah yes, but sometimes logic creates its own barriers, Lauren. Gretchen questioned and became wiser for the asking." He paused. "A thoughtful question carries its answer on its back, as a snail carries its shell," he said. "Listen!"

He proceeded to tell them the story of his encounter with the fisherman and his friend Fionne. When he'd finished, an eerie silence reigned, broken only by the monotonous ticking of an old grandfather clock in the corner. Chris, the first to break the quiet, commented, "That's a beautiful story, but I still don't understand how your dream can help us find Gretchen."

"Don't think of it as a dream. I made that mistake. At first, I thought I'd had too much of my own spirits the night before. Then I heard a scratching at the front door. When I opened the door, a shadow darted in. I turned around and saw Einstein sitting next to Ming on the hearth. But that wasn't all. Something else happened. Instead of the spirits leaving me with a terrific hangover, I felt this overwhelming sense of peace and tranquility. From that day on, I've had no desire to partake of my own spirits."

"A strange story," Lauren said. She stared deep into Einstein's eyes. "Einstein may be a special cat, but I'm more inclined to believe a homeless animal found a home on your hearth."

"Oh ye, of little imagination," Chris teased. "I'd much prefer it were a premonition."

Lauren ignored him, remembering something else Gretchen had said. "Who is Elise, Shaman? Gretchen mentioned someone by that name. Does she exist?"

"Elise? She existed many centuries ago, when logic as we know it today did not exist . . . a belief in many worlds existed then. But one world or many worlds . . . good and evil, joy and sorrow . . . existed then as they do to this day. For wherever there is life, there is action . . . and many fates to be determined by councils of learned men."

"Is there another story here?" asked Chris.

Shaman smiled. "Of course," he said. "At one such council, the fate of a young woman held sway before a council of learned men, to determine her punishment . . . punishment for a transgression no more serious than that she dared to escape an unkind husband. Tongues clacked at the gall of a woman who elected to live on her own. The council determined her fate and sentenced her to banishment from earth.

"When the woman heard her sentence, she did not weep or wail, but put on her best finery in preparation for the ritual that would be her funeral. After the ritual, and the keening had ended, they placed her in a boat filled with food and a few of her earthly belongings . . . and pushed her off into the sea . . . destined to sail alone until such time as she repented sufficiently to be forgiven by her husband. She drifted for centuries from one world to another, refusing to repent until one day she floated onto an uninhabited island. There she made her home and survived by catching fish and eating of the bountiful fruit provided by bushes and shrubs."

Shaman hesitated as though reminiscing before continuing his story. "One day after partaking of the annual Feast of Shaman in the *Netherworld*, a great wish came upon me to walk along the sea . . . to gaze out onto the desolate waters and listen to the breakers crashing against the coastline. As I wandered beside the sea, a vision appeared before me . . . a woman so beautiful I gazed in wonder and awe. Her long golden hair floated around her, her milk white skin and ruby lips, her sparkling and flashing dark eyes enchanted me. When she told me her story . . . how the fates had determined her banishment from earth and how only Morgan, the magician, had the power to release her. I wanted only to be her savior.

"I met with her every day and every night and came to know her. I implored the assistance of my connection to the *Netherworld,* Fionne. He advised me that only Morgan had the power to reverse banishment of the undeserved. He admitted knowledge of the great man, but cautioned me of the dangers of loving such beauty because, as he said, *Even a magician can be fooled.* He warned that I might have fallen in love with a mortal that could no longer enter the world of man. *One who is lovely can bewitch you into believing she is good as well.*"

"Who is Morgan?" Chris asked.

"He rules the *Underworld* . . . and will do anything for a price . . . but I couldn't be dissuaded. I assured Fionne that I would pay whatever the cost, but he must find a way whereby she would be mine. *I'll tell you on the morrow,* Fionne promised, and true to his word, the next evening he returned. *You must put yourself in the hands of Morgan and follow his instructions. Are you prepared?* I said I would follow Morgan and his difficult demands. He allowed me one day a year . . . only one day a year for my beloved Elise to return to earth and be mine."

At that moment, the cottage door opened, and a beautiful woman appeared on the threshold, her arms filled with the bounty of the forest— nuts, grapes, berries, roots, and herbs. Shaman greeted her, and, taking her by the arm, led her to meet his guests.

"This is Elise," he told his guests, admiring her with adoring eyes. He paused a moment as though wondering if he should say more before continuing. "Last year, thanks to my contacts in the *Netherworld,* Elise needs no longer return to the grave, but may remain with me through all eternity."

After they bade adieu to their two guests, Shaman, taking Elise by the hand, returned down the pathway from whence they'd come, leaving the two skeptics to believe whatever they may.

"Why do you suppose he told us those Irish fairy tales?" Lauren asked.

"Maybe because he knew we wouldn't believe him, do you suppose?"

"Oh, I don't know. I'd like to believe that Einstein is a unique animal, destined to solve the problems of the world. It ties into what Gretchen told me. How else could Shaman have known about this particular cottage? It looks ancient . . . like a stage set for a seventeenth-century scene."

Chris looked around the cottage as though seeing it for the first time. "You fell for his story. Does it look like the cottage in your dream, Lauren . . . the one where you saw Gretchen?"

"My dream?" She finished the last of her lemonade and laughed as she remembered falling off a lily pad and having to swim ashore. "They do look very much alike. Do you suppose it's the cottage where Shaman met the fisherman and Einstein, or the cottage of the banished woman?"

"Maybe neither," Chris said. "Now that the players are gone, what say we take a tour of the area?" He started to rise then sat back down. "I'm beginning to feel a little strange. How about you?"

Lauren looked at Chris. "No wonder. You've shrunk!"

"That drink!" Chris stared at the oversized doll sitting in a mammoth chair.

"We've both shrunk! Didn't you notice, Chris? This didn't happen 'til Shaman and Elise left."

"Why the old coot. That's why he didn't join us. He knew."

Chris accepted his new transformation as part of an exciting adventure. Only Einstein remained the same, their new size giving him the appearance of being a young tiger cub. "Shades of Professor Ipswitch . . . We're bloomin' leprechauns."

"At least we didn't become animals, although I always did want to be a mouse in a corner," Lauren countered, entering into the spirit of the transformation. "I don't mind shrinking, providing I don't regress intellectually. We'll need all our faculties to survive. What did Shaman call this place?"

"The *Netherworld.*"

"Anyway, we didn't go back in time the way Gretchen did."

"I'm not so sure," Chris said. "This cottage is definitely seventeenth-century Ireland, but you may be right." Wandering outside, they found everything in direct proportion to their reduced size, a land of little people. "I think I can handle this."

"We're like everyone else now."

Chris jumped up and clicked his heels to test his agility. "Always did want to be a leprechaun and live in a forest with the animals."

"Aren't you ever serious?" Lauren asked. "We've got to find Gretchen and Alex."

"We can do both," he said as he rushed to keep up with Einstein bouncing down the cobbled stones. "Come on, Lauren. I haven't had so much fun since I played *Huckleberry Finn* in high school."

Lauren gets into the spirit, trailing along behind him, but stopping at the river's bend. She recognized the frog on the lily pad and asked him, "Can you tell me where Gretchen is?"

The frog looked at her, but directed his remarks to Einstein. "Tell her the proper procedure for requesting information," the frog directed Einstein.

Lauren turned to Einstein and asked him the same question. "Can you help me find Gretchen?" *I'm as bad as Gretchen, talking to a cat!*

Einstein turned and walked away. Chris watched the by-play, amused at Lauren's confusion. When he turned and followed Einstein, Lauren followed him. "The frog speaks only to animals," he said. "Einstein wants us to follow him."

The two held hands and followed the arrogant monster cat through dense undergrowth. As he reached the edge of the forest, he stopped and sat down. Lauren and Chris caught up with him and observed the open glade totally populated with little people busily absorbed in creating piles of paper scraps. No one noticed the intruders.

"I wonder if we're invisible," Lauren asked Chris.

"There's one way to find out." Chris ventured with caution toward one of the tables. No one noticed him. A scrap of paper floated from a table close to him. He picked it up and returned to the edge of the forest. "Do you think they can't see me or am I just lucky?"

"They can't see you," Lauren assured him. "But they can see Einstein. One pointed him out, and I stood right beside him. They didn't see me."

"No wonder he stopped at the edge of the forest. He may need a quick exit."

"What did you pick up?" Lauren asked him.

Chris examined the scrap of paper in his hand. "My God," he said, looking at the tables loaded with similar bills. "It's a hundred-dollar bill. What did you say about *following the money?* It's all here, millions and millions of dollars, they're turning them out like confetti on New Years' Eve."

Lauren looked at the bill. "The mystery deepens . . . a counterfeiting ring? His could answer *what and how,* but *why* is another question . . . and *who* benefits?"

"The elusive *why* . . . and *who*. And don't forget *where*. *Where* does the money go?" Chris, scrutinizing the scene before him, spied Alex dancing on one of the tables. "Look," he said, pointing out the monkey to Lauren. "That's Alex, isn't it?"

Lauren followed his gaze. Sure enough, Alex, seemingly in his element here in this underground cavern, danced and generally entertained the workers, moving from table to table. Lauren remembered the organ-grinder's sign—*for money, the monkey dances*—where she first saw the dancing Alex on the Capitol steps.

"If Alex is here, Gretchen can't be too far behind."

"What do we do?" Chris asked. "Grab the monkey?"

"Not yet. We'll let him lead us to Gretchen. Someone has to feed him, and my guess is that's Gretchen." They waited beside Einstein and watched as the workers loaded boxes of cash on a railway tram, preparing to close up shop for the day. "I wonder where they stay."

"Let's follow the tram. Gretchen isn't going anywhere, but the money is."

"I'm concerned about Gretchen, not the money," Lauren retorted. "We've got to get her out of here."

"We will. No one can see us, Lauren, but they can see Gretchen. We can work like mice in a corner, but she can't . . . not without a dose of Shaman's *lemonade*. Even then, they might get suspicious if she disappeared all of a sudden."

"You're right, although I hate to admit it," Lauren agreed. "We'll do what we can before the *lemonade* wears off, as I'm sure it will eventually."

"Didn't think of that."

"Shaman never tells us the consequences of his actions."

"We follow the tram."

They scurried down the track after the disappearing tram and soon see its blinking lights up ahead. Einstein has disappeared.

"If we catch up, we can hitch a ride."

Chris sprinted faster down the track with Lauren in close pursuit. They caught the slowly moving tram and hopped onto the tailgate. The clickity-clack of the tram wheels made talking difficult, so the two watched the rails in silence as the miles disappeared beneath them. The ice-cold tunnel—a deep penetrating cold—reminded the two they needed warmer clothing. Other than the occasional dim lights that flickered at various intervals long the track, they traveled in total darkness.

What if something happens and we can never return? Lauren shivered and moved closer to Chris. The tram—their sole attachment to reality—rattled on.

Chapter Thirteen

To imagine is everything, to know is nothing at all
—Anatole France

Day 12, Monday

Chris and Lauren spent the first night taking advantage of their unique situation. As the workers reveled in the success of their endeavor, the two intruders investigated the surroundings. Uncertain as to how long they would remain in their present state of invisibility, the two fought weariness, seeking an explanation for the hidden enterprise.

"Records have to exist somewhere," Chris said, digging into any place that looked like a possible storage area. "Where are we, anyway?"

"Don't ask me," Lauren answered. "Einstein appears to have deserted us. Gretchen is nowhere to be seen, and we seem to have entered a sort of no-man's land for animals."

"Anyway, since everyone's asleep, this may be our only opportunity to find out what's going on."

"I don't really care right now. I want to find Gretchen. Everything else takes second place."

"You've forgotten your *follow-the-money* theory?" Chris needled.

"No, but priority is priority. Gretchen first."

"I don't think she's here. If she is, I doubt she knows what's going on," Chris said, opening boxes and digging into anything that looked as though it might give him a clue. "Who's that senator you say my uncle worked with?"

"I didn't say. That's privileged information."

"Really . . . couldn't by chance be old Senator Claghorn, could it?"

Surprised, Lauren asked, "How'd you come up with that name?"

"It's on this box," he explained, reading the caption on one of the box. "EXCLUSIVE PROPERTY OF SENATOR EDWARD CLAGHORN—DO NOT OPEN— CONTAINS DOCUMENTS INVOLVING NATIONAL SECURITY.

"Looks like your office, the state department, and my uncle were mixed up in counterfeiting too. Maybe mailing huge donations to God knows who for whatever purpose, do you suppose?"

"Don't jump to conclusions," cautioned Lauren. "I'm sure there's a logical explanation. We don't know it's counterfeit money. Could be legitimate currency."

"And I'm a monkey's uncle. You saw Alex dancing on the Senate steps, and again today, dancing as though he belongs here. I'm opening this box." He pulled out his penknife.

"No, not here." Lauren stopped him. "Let's get it to the tram while everyone's asleep. We can go through it at our leisure if we can get it back to the cottage."

"Good idea. I think I'll take a box of this money too, check it for counterfeiting."

They looked around for one of the small flatcars they'd seen the workers using to load and unload the boxes of money. Locating an empty one, they tipped the box over onto the flatcar, no small achievement for two elfin creatures, and dragged the flatcar to the tram. Not even the squeaking wheels of the cart disturbed the grog-filled crew. No one stirred except for one or two bodies that turned over, then continue to snore, the grog they drank acting like an aphrodisiac to the tired crew.

"How do we turn the tram around?" Lauren asked.

"We don't need to. It goes in either direction, but we do have to find the switch that reverses the power."

As Chris scrutinized the mechanism near the track, he spied Einstein curled up on the floor of the tram surrounded by a motley crew of ragtag cats. "Are you here to help?" Chris asked the sleepy cat.

Einstein looked at him in silence and spoke to the group beside him. "Show him how it's done," Einstein advised his crew, and together they disengaged a hook that hung over the tram. They snagged the box on the flatcar and lifted it onto the tram. Then those ragtag cats sat back looking smug.

Chris laughed. "Well done," he told Einstein. "Now find the switch that reverses direction." And Einstein did. He placed a well-groomed paw on a lever and pressed. Cats and all pile onto the tram and headed back to the cottage in the forest.

"Do you know where Gretchen is?" Lauren asked Einstein as he rode beside her.

He shook his head, but questioned the cats behind him. One large black cat stepped out from the pack, jumped off the tram, and headed back down the tracks. Lauren watched him.

"That looks like Julius," she said to Einstein.

Einstein nodded in agreement as though to say, *Julius will find her.*

When they reached the glade, the ragtag cats helped load the boxes onto a flatcar, then helped pull them across the glade and into the forest to the cottage. With Lauren and Chris safely deposited at the cottage, Einstein gave the cats a nod of thanks, and they all disappeared into the forest.

Weary for lack of sleep, the sight of comfortable beds welcomed Lauren and Chris, and they lay down to catch a few hours of shut-eye. When they awakened hours later, they found themselves back to their original size.

"I suppose we're no longer invisible either." Lauren lamented. "Now what?"

"We drink more lemonade," Chris suggested, "but not 'til it's necessary. We'll have to conserve . . . unless you have that potion with you. Do you?"

"No. I don't know where . . . Oh yes, I do." Her eyes got big. "Oh no . . . Julius is here." She stared at Chris. "Do you suppose?"

"What?"

"Oh, Chris, he might have dug up the potion. If she took some of the potion, she could be any one of these animals we see around here."

"She'd let us know, wouldn't she?" He turned to Lauren. "You know her better than I do. What do you think? Would she use it?"

Lauren recalled Gretchen's reaction when she wanted to test the potion on herself—*a fear of not returning to her human form the next time?* "No, I don't believe so, not unless she were cornered and had no other means to escape."

"Forget that, then," Chris decided. "We wait for Julius's report. In the meantime, let's dig into that box we brought back." He dragged out the box and opened it. "Damn, I sure wish Shaman would show up with one of his famous steak burgers. I'm starved."

"Just like a man. He wants it all spread in front of him. I'll see what I can rustle up."

Lauren checked the cupboard and found it well stocked. She chose a can of soup and a box of crackers. "It's soup and crackers for lunch," she announced. "That okay?"

"Sure, whatever."

"You get started on that box of goodies, and I'll take care of the meals."

"Sounds good to me. Evidently, Shaman didn't intend for us to starve."

"I've an idea Elise has a garden outside, or maybe you can catch a fish from the stream we crossed last night."

"Sure, and maybe I can find the old fisherman and 'catch the special fish that eats of the special bush.' Now, wouldn't that be a kick?"

"You never know. This is the *Netherworld.*"

"It's catching."

"What is?"

"Life in the world of unreality, I suppose."

Chris's voice faded as he dug into the first box, and Lauren concentrated on building a fire in the small fireplace. She found an ancient pot in which to heat the soup and hung it on a spit located above the fire. Soon the room filled up with aromatic odors as the pot bubbled invitingly.

Meanwhile, Julius had his own problems. Returning to rescue Gretchen, he found Alex faithfully guarding her. He tried to entice him away, but Alex had his own orders. He didn't budge. Julius left. *This will take strategy. Einstein will know what to do.*

And Einstein did. *For money, the monkey dances,* he reminded Julius. *Entice him.* But Julius didn't need to entice Alex. The tram, back in operation and in its rightful place after taking Lauren and Chris to the cottage, returned the workers to the glade and the printing press. Alex, not realizing Julius waited to usurp his spot in guarding Gretchen, climbed on board the tram with his buddies. As Julius watched the tram disappear around the bend, he trotted off to the cottage and parked himself on the hearth waiting for Gretchen to notice him. She didn't, and he waited.

*   *   *

Gretchen sighed, her mind on her seemingly inescapable situation. As she sat in the chair by the fireplace, she wondered whether her telepathic thoughts ever reached Lauren, or if she were destined to remain in the underground cottage for the rest of her life. When Julius jumped onto her lap to get attention, she automatically began stroking him.

Startled, she recognized him. "Julius? Is it you?" Julius snuggled against her, purring his delight as she smiled and hugged him to her. He purred, and she heard his mantra: *We could make such beautiful music together.*

"Oh, Julius, it is you. Can you help me find my way out of the forest? I'm being treated like a prisoner, and I don't know why. Alex moves freely, but he's so afraid of losing his *status* with the others, he's absolutely no help to me at all."

Your friends look for you, and Einstein sends me to find you. He and your feline friends return at midnight. Can you be ready?

"Oh yes, yes I can." She grabbed Julius and whirled and danced around the room. "Oh, I love you, I love you, I love you." She kissed Julius on the tip of his nose. "I can't believe I'm really going home." She stopped and dropped down on the rug, suddenly disheartened. "But Julius, there's no exit to this place, and I'm not a cat anymore."

Ah, but you could be. You have only to drink of the potion. The black feline nuzzled against her, purring lasciviously. *You'd rather stay here?*

"I'm sorry, Julius. I buried the potion in my strawberry patch. I don't have it." She ran her hand along the cats arched back. "Does that mean I can't return?" she asked.

Julius moved toward the door of the cottage. *I must report to Einstein.* In dismay, Gretchen watched. He turned at the door, looking back at her. *I'll return at midnight. There's lemonade in the fridge.* And he was gone.

Julius detoured to the rabbit hole located under Chris's barn. Examining the grass under the opening, he spied Gretchen's handbag hidden nearby in the tall grass. Dragging the purse by its handle, he returned to the cottage and deposited the purse on the hearth, then headed for his rendezvous with Einstein.

Meanwhile, Lauren and Chris investigated the contents of the box they'd found. "Just what was your office working on?" he asked, digging into the box.

"Not my office. Gretchen and I decided to check out the money trail on our own."

"Hmmm . . . makes one wonder how many more politicians are involved besides my uncle, and your FBI outfit."

"I can't say. Everything's so secretive at the FBI. Each agent has his own part in a program, and only a very few top secret intellects have authorization to connect the dots and solve the puzzle."

"What happens if those few connect the wrong dots?"

"It's how they work. The idea is, if everyone does his job, the pieces all fall into place, and the result is the solution. Mission accomplished."

Lauren watched Chris digest this piece of information. "You accepted that?"

"Mine is not to question why . . . ," Lauren quoted, "but to answer your inquiry, yes. We take an oath to uphold the laws of the agency."

"Did you realize that your monkey could skew the entire mission?" he asked, pawing through the contents of the box. "Like this box, for instance. How did it get here? Where did it come from? Maybe if your Senator Claghorn had forewarned the president, he could have alerted the NSA, and with them in the mix, there may never have been a 9/11."

"You can't be sure of that," Lauren said

"No, I can't, Lauren, I'm only saying this looks mighty suspicious." He tapped the box in front of him. "This box has information that should have been processed long ago. What else can I think?"

"What you're thinking is impossible, Chris," she argued

"All right, answer me this. Why else is my dead uncle being buried under false pretenses? And why are you on administrative leave if not to get you out of the way? We've run into a situation that has no explanation."

"Counterfeiting is against the law. There'd be an investigation."

"In a perfect world, Lauren, that might be true. But we're not living in a perfect world. Who needs all that fake money? What is it funding? The war? Or campaign funds for the next election? Lauren, we live in a world of liars, cheats and thieves, men who'll do anything for power, and I don't put it past our politicians to play the power game in exchange for votes."

"I guess I prefer to see the best in people not the worst. I prefer an explanation before I condemn anyone."

"A noble gesture, Lauren. Politicians love that philosophy and have more than enough explanations to suit the casual voter, but you're an agent for the FBI, Lauren. You need to be continually vigilant for interlopers . . . despite your inner feelings."

"I am vigilant, as you say," Lauren retorted. "Why else would I be in this position? Certainly, not out of choice. You're the one I had to convince. You treated my story like another scene on your imaginary stage. You didn't want any part of it . . . your uncle notwithstanding . . . even after we told you about the body switch."

Chris stopped and looked at her, taken back by her outburst. "You're right. *Mea culpa.* I stand corrected. I didn't believe you. And you have every right to chastise me."

Lauren grinned inwardly, knowing she's bested him on this round. Now that she'd convinced him, maybe they could concentrate on getting Gretchen back. And with the evidence in the box, they could turn Washington on its heels. She gloated, looking to Chris, very much like a smug Cheshire cat after he'd eaten the last of the cream.

Chris glanced at her. "You don't have to look so superior."

Chapter Fourteen

Fear less, hope more, and good things are yours.
—Swedish Proverb

Day 13, Tuesday

True to his word, a few minutes after midnight, Julius appeared at the cottage. Gretchen, having realized the purpose of the lemonade, was beside herself in frustration. Julius grinned smugly. *Aha, you drank of the lemonade, I see.*

"Why, Julius?" she asked the grinning feline. "Why did you shrink me?" *You're also invisible, except to me.*

"I am?" She climbed on a stool and looked in the mirror on the wall. No face stared back at her. Unappeased, Gretchen complained, "You tricked me, Julius."

She jumped down from the stool then stopped as a thought struck her. "Has that lemonade been here all this time? Does everyone drink lemonade? Is that why they're so tiny here?"

Julius watched her ruminate in silence.

"Who'd have thought that a tiny glass of lemonade would do this to me?" She laughed, amused at her image. "I feel like Gulliver . . . when the little people captured him and hundreds of tiny hands tied him down."

He waited for her to adjust to her new size. *It's the best I could do with what I had to work with.* He gloated as Gretchen glared.

"I feel like a museum piece." She turned and preened before him.

Julius, exhibiting his facetious cat smirk, warned her. *It's temporary . . . we must work fast.*

"Should we take it with us?"

No, follow me. Julius led the way from the cottage, down the mining track, heading for the cottage on the other side of the forest. On the way, they met Alex returning to check on Gretchen. He took one look at Gretchen and Julius, surmised what had happened, and leaped for the nearest tree. Using his long arms for leverage, he swung himself back toward the camp and his cronies.

"What do we do, Julius? He saw me, and he's gone to warn the others."

Hurry . . . he doesn't know about the cottage on the edge of the Netherworld.

Arriving at the clearing, they met Einstein and his renegade pals—a bunch of street cats living by their wits, not the domestic breed Gretchen knew from past cat encounters. Einstein, who took immediate charge of this new cat crew, directed them on how to head the enemy off at the pass.

Keep them busy, Einstein. I know the way from here.

Okay, Julius. We'll stay and guard the entrance to the mine. They have to return this way.

Gretchen ran as fast as her short legs would move, across the clearing, heading for the forest on the other side. *If only I hadn't drunk so much of that lemonade, but I was thirsty.*

Julius, noticing Gretchen panting noisily trying to keep up, stopped suddenly in midfield. *Would you perhaps like a ride, Gretchen? Climb on me. I can run like the wind, if need be.*

Gretchen accepted his offer and climbed on the back of the big black cat. She leaned forward the length of his body with her arms encircling his neck. Julius seemed unencumbered with the extra weight and, at exhilarating speed, headed toward a special opening among the trees. As they neared their destination, they heard a crash and stopped to look back.

"Oh, look what the cats did, Julius," Gretchen said, sliding off his back. "The entrance to the mine has disappeared, it's covered with rocks."

Watch.

"Is that what Einstein asked the cats to do?"

Einstein, his ragtag army swarming around him, gave him their special *tails up* message. Pointing long tails toward the rocks that covered the mine entrance and signifying their success at pinning the little people inside the tunnel, they sent the *mission accomplished* message. It would be quite a while before the merry little people could dig out from under those heavy rocks.

"We're safe, Julius. They can't get to us now."

We're safe unless they return and loose the animals from their cages.

"The animals? You mean the animals I saw when I first came here? They aren't dangerous, Julius. They were helpful to me. Why would you say they are dangerous?"

They haven't been fed today. You and your friends may be their next meal.

"Will Einstein be safe?

Einstein has many lives. He has eaten of the sacred bush. We ordinary cats have only nine lives and must be careful how we use them.

"Oh, I'm sorry, Julius."

That's all right. You have only one.

"But it's a long one, Julius," she advised.

Approaching the cottage, Gretchen stopped and stared, bewildered. "Why didn't I find this cottage? It looks just like the one on the other side of the forest."

You were not meant to find this one. Only Magus can approve entry . . . or exit.

"Magus? Where am I, Julius? Who are these people?

Gretchen talked of Magus. Where am I?"

You're in the Netherworld.

"Why are the little people here?"

They pay penance to Magus and are destined to repeat their vices for all eternity . . . unless given a chance to redeem themselves.

"When will that be?"

If they return to earth and do good, instead of evil, they earn points to heaven.

"Why don't they?"

They refuse to believe.

At the cottage, Julius prepared to leave, but Gretchen stopped him. "No, Julius, please don't go. I need you here."

I must check on Einstein. Enter the cottage. Your friends are there.

And Julius disappeared. Inside the cottage, Lauren had caught sight of Gretchen and rushed to greet her. All thoughts of Julius disappeared when Gretchen saw her friend. Amid hugs and kisses, Lauren ushered Gretchen inside the cottage.

"I see you've already discovered our lemonade."

"And I'm still hungry. Do you have anything to eat here?"

When she saw the opened box and its contents littering the floor, all thought of food vanished. "What's all this?" she asked.

"It's what we were looking for, remember? How it got here is the question of the week. We've no idea how it traveled from your apartment complex storage room in Washington to an underground cave in Connecticut. Do you have a clue?"

"Strange."

"Yes, isn't it?"

"Have you forgotten me?" Chris asked from the sidelines, waiting patiently to be noticed. "I take it this is Gretchen, the missing sleuth?"

"I'm sorry, Chris. Yes, it's Gretchen."

"I'm so glad you're all right. You had us worried when you disappeared without a trace."

"No more worried than I," Gretchen answered. "How are you, Chris? We met briefly, I believe, at your farm. You were not too friendly."

"Sorry about that. I'm not used to having beautiful women telling fantastic tales showing up on my doorstep. And I admit to being less than cordial. Lauren straightened me out." His apology amused Gretchen.

Gretchen looked at herself. "I'm not usually this small, Chris, but it seems the accepted style in the *Netherworld*."

"We had our introduction to that elixir too. Standard equipment in cottages here, I presume. What happened when you disappeared?"

Gretchen looked puzzled. "Disappeared?"

"Chris has been helping me since you disappeared from the barn. You remember . . . the barn on Chris's property?"

"Oh yes, you were in the loft when I fell down the rabbit hole. How did you know where to find me?"

"I picked up on your psychic message in my dream one night and began digging into the archives after you disappeared. We got hold of some preCivil War building plans and discovered an underground railway evidently used by slaves escaping into Canada. The rails ran right under the barn. Then we accidentally stumbled onto your exit, but didn't want your fate to happen to us. We enlisted Shaman's support, and he led us here."

"He's evidently been here before," Chris added.

"Yes, Julius told me I'd been here before too."

"Julius?" Chris asked.

"Oh, dear. Now I've done it. Never mind." She looked at Lauren and then at the box in the middle of the living room. "Can we get this evidence out with us? There isn't much time."

"Why?" asked Lauren and Chris in unison. "What's the hurry?"

"The little people . . . they may already have opened the animal cages. You don't want to be their dinner tonight, do you?"

"What are you talking about?" Chris asked.

"The animals . . . the ones who guarded me. Magus controls the forest, but sometimes his animals are uncontrollable. I'll feel better when we get out of here."

"Chris and I took the tramway to the other side of the forest where we found the box and took the tramway back. Where were they holding you? We didn't even see Alex. Have you seen him?"

"Yes, but I don't recommend we wait for him. He's their spy now."

"What happened?"

"Nothing, that's just it. Alex does as he's told. They're his masters. Can we get out of here?"

"Not until Shaman and Elise return. In the meantime, I'm fixing dinner."

"Elise is here? Shaman did bring her back with him. I'm so glad."

"Yes, this is her cottage. You did say you were hungry, didn't you?"

"I'm more afraid than hungry." Gretchen wanted to believe, but remembered Julius's warning. "You sure we're safe?"

"It's not safe to enter the glade, but the forest is Shaman's territory." Chris explained to her as though an authority on the laws of the *Netherworld*. "Shaman will return for us when we're ready."

"Yes, Elise wanders all over the forest gathering flowers and berries and feels perfectly safe," Lauren assured her.

Looking around, Gretchen spied her purse on the hearth where Julius had placed it, and puzzled, picked it up. "My purse . . . the one I dropped when I fell down the rabbit hole. Where did it come from?" She looked around at Lauren. "Did you find it?"

Lauren shook her head and turned to Chris. He looked as puzzled as Gretchen. "It wasn't there when we came in last night," he said. "Someone must have brought it during the night."

"Did you tell anyone you'd lost it?" Lauren asked her.

"Julius. Maybe he found it and brought it here."

"Who is Julius?"

"A black cat," Lauren answered, "And I'll thank you not to ask too many questions . . . accept it on faith. That's what I've learned to do."

Gretchen looked at the two skeptics and sighed. "What can I say?"

They sat down to Lauren's quickly prepared dinner, and for the rest of the evening discussed the contents of the box, and what it could mean to their future.

Chapter Fifteen

Learn from yesterday, live for today, hope for tomorrow.

Day 14, Wednesday

Gretchen resumed her normal size after sleeping off the effects of the lemonade and appeared no worse the wear after her experience. Waiting for Shaman to arrive and accompany them to civilization, she and Lauren busied themselves in the kitchen preparing breakfast.

Chris returned to Senator Claghorn's mystery box. He found the bill of lading signed by Senator Claghorn that listed the items in the box. He checked them off; they matched, but something didn't look right. *Why is the box bigger on the outside than on the inside . . . a false bottom?* He emptied the box on the floor and turned it over. Opening the box from the other end, he discovered a yellow plastic package with the words HEROIN printed in black letters.

"Well, whatta you know." Surprised, he pulled back, glancing toward the kitchen.

Now what do I do? Bury it and not tell anyone, or wait for Shaman? The others hadn't seen it. He made a snap decision, closed the box and pushed it into the back room. *We need to get rid of this.*

Returning to the kitchen, Lauren offered him a cup of coffee, her eyes questioning.

What did you find?

Chris accepted the coffee but ignored her raised eyebrows, his mind struggling with his own questions. *What did my uncle have to do with this?*

At that moment, Shaman entered the cottage, in time to observe the silent by-play. "You've found something?" Chris nodded.

"What is it?" And Chris took him into the back room. When Shaman lifted up the top few packages, he discovered something else. Tucked under the packets of heroin is a package labeled URANIUM. Shaman sat back on his haunches and stared.

Chris said, "Oh, oh, I didn't dig deep enough. What do we do now?"

"Bury it, deep in the forest," Shaman decided. "It's better the world never knows. Let time work its magic." He removed the correspondence, handed it to Chris, and resealed the box. Together they rejoined the others, Shaman carrying the mystery box under his arm. Gretchen had set out plates of food on the rustic maple table.

"Where are you going, Shaman?" she asked as he headed for the door. She eyed the box under Shaman's arm. "Can't it wait?" She eyed the package. "Eat first, then tell us what we're about to bury."

Chris selected a seat. "Join us, Shaman?"

"I've no time to lose," he said. "Chris can explain."

Gretchen persisted. "Did we miss something, Shaman?"

"Well, you and your friends did help save the free world, Gretchen, at least for the time being." Shaman looked at the box under his arm, heading down the path into the forest.

"Chris?" Two sets of questioning eyes turned on Chris as Shaman left.

"Remember those poppy fields in Afghanistan?" he asked. "Why weren't they burned instead of left for harvesting?"

"It's their survival," Gretchen said. "At least, that's what I thought. Am I wrong?"

"Not really," Lauren said. "The poppy fields fund the war on terrorism."

"Then they should be burned. If we're to fight terrorism, why not cut off their money supply?" Gretchen looked at Lauren for an explanation.

"Depends on who needs funds. Congress isn't too generous with the taxpayer's money in the war department; hence, the senator's intense interest in money . . . the by-play engaged in with Alex . . . and the implication it involved my office. A tricky game, isn't it?"

"A clever game," Chris agreed. "Like the old New York shell game . . . three-card monte. 'Which card covers the booty?' I've an idea old Senator Claghorn hit the jackpot on his last visit with the troops and looked for a safe place to hide the booty and got my uncle involved. Dropping that box into the *Netherworld* must have been like frosting on his yellow cake. He knew nothing of a thriving underground community already holding the world hostage. That old excavation under my uncle's barn must have seemed a safe haven."

"You mean . . . we accidentally fell into a *pot of jam*?"

"Well, Gretchen evidently did. We'd never have discovered that underground railway if she hadn't fallen down the shaft."

"How could the senator get it out of Iraq?" Chris asked.

"Senators have immunity," Lauren explained. "Can even hook rides on Air Force One if it's available—the perfect cover. No one suspects a senator."

"But why would he do that? To use as political leverage before the election?"

"Maybe, or maybe the president planned to release the information at the appropriate time. That's possible, too, isn't it?"

"Anything's possible. Dissenters don't want that box found until after the election."

The three pondered the enormity of the power dropped unexpectedly into their laps. Chris, holding out his cup out for a coffee refill, mused, "We could play politics, too, Lauren, and hold your office hostage until they tell us what really happened to my uncle."

"I've an idea your uncle discovered the senator's find and refused to go along with the plan. When that happened, he knew too much and had to go. Our agent used him as a cover, and my boss fell for his story."

"And your uncle isn't a suicide," said Gretchen. "Anyone for more coffee? I can make another pot." They declined and she poured the last of the coffee in her cup. "What are your plans now, Lauren?"

"Take pictures of our find, and pass the information on to security. Let the President use it for leverage, if he needs to. I'm sure Senator Claghorn is already aware all is not rosy."

"There she goes, taking all the fun out of our discovery," Chris commented. "I had visions of money and virgins at my beck and call. You burst my bubble."

Lauren laughed, and Gretchen teased him. "As though you need it—with all those gorgeous babes in Hollywood."

*　　*　　*

"We've been compromised," Archibald Carlton told Philip Gadsden. "I can't get any response to my calls."

"How's come?" Gadsden queried. "There's no way you could be compromised. The plan is foolproof. You said so." He looked at the aggrieved individual facing him in his office. "What have you done?"

"What have I done?" Carlton flung the question back at him. "I've tried to get hold of Senator Claghorn. He's unavailable for comments. I've called the professor, and he's noncommittal. Said he's not involved. He furnished a place of operation . . . other than that, he's wiped his hands of all responsibility. He knows nothing."

Gadsden laughed. "Aha, the professor. Slippery as an eel, isn't he? I warned you. He builds escape hatches at every turn. How do you think he's survived centuries of turmoil and come out unscathed? If you figured him for a fall guy, you've stepped into deep *doo doo*."

"It's that female agent," Carlton fumed. "You lost touch with her, and somehow she's stumbled onto the whole damned operation."

"You give a novice too much credit. She knows nothing."

"She's the only wild card. It has to be her."

"If what you say is true, she's found professional help. There's no way she knew enough to act alone."

"Can you contact her? Find out where she is? I've tried all morning to contact my sources, and all lines are down in that area, an absolute blackout. Cell phones, computers—all down. It's as though the entire operation dropped off the face of the earth."

Carlton sank into the one chair in Gadsden's office and put his head in his hands, looking the epitome of utter defeat. Gadsden looked at him, feeling sympathy, but only to a small degree. He'd never thought much about the plan at its onset, pouring counterfeit money onto the economy in an attempt to smoke out recipients of the real money being used to fund terrorist organizations. He had no sympathy for trickery. *If it blows up in their faces, they had it coming.* He particularly didn't like having to pull his agents out of the fire when their stupid plans went awry.

"You lost control and your fantastic plot backfired," Gadsden chided him. "Now you need someone to blame. Look in the mirror, Archie. You've been outmaneuvered. I've an idea Agent Calloway did your job for you and deserves your thanks, not your censure."

Chapter Sixteen

Time deepens the wonder.

Day 17, Saturday

"Now that we're home, Lauren, what are your plans?" The two girls had settled into Lauren's apartment in Washington and, over glasses of wine, reviewed their successes and failures. Cyrus, happy to be home, seemed none the worse for wear after his lone vigil at the farm. Alex had not surfaced, but then, he alone knew the location of the escape hatch in the barn. They could only hope he survived.

"I don't know," Lauren said sipping her wine. "After having exposed a nefarious plot to intercept money intended to fight terrorism, I'm no longer on administrative leave. I'm sure some heads will roll and others be crowned, but that's no longer my responsibility. I'll leave that to the top honchos at security."

"What do you think would have happened if we hadn't been so nosy?" Gretchen spoke absentmindedly as though it were of no importance. She caressed Cyrus who cuddled beside her, but her thoughts were on Julius. "Would their plan have worked?"

"We'll never know." Then as though reading her mind, Lauren said, "For a while there, I thought Julius would come with us. What changed his mind?"

"Inasmuch as he likes to visit, he says he's a field cat and would go stir-crazy as a pampered, petted house cat. Says we *humanoids* build our own cages, and he wants no part of that . . . might as well be underground with the rest of the little people. He didn't like that much either."

"Wise cat, if those were his words. Methinks you have a great imagination, giving your felines thoughts beyond their capability." Lauren peered over her glass at her friend.

"And there you go again, doubting what your inner senses tell you."

"What do you plan to do with the apartment?"

"Nothing, at the moment. I'm staying the summer to finish my novel. You'll be going back to work, and it's a nice quiet place to create."

"What about Harley? Any plans to return to Ridgecrest and Harley?"

Gretchen ignored her question and continued as though she hadn't heard. "Hunter is still here. He knew nothing of what happened at the apartment before his uncle hired him. He's completely innocent—a stool pigeon, so to speak."

"Must have been a shock for him when they arrested his uncle." She watched her wine swirl around the glass as she fiddled with it. "Strange how things eventually work out to the good, isn't it?"

"Not strange at all, Lauren. You don't really believe we did that alone, do you? With no help from a higher power?"

"We had help from Shaman and Chris . . . and the plat books. Other than that, *we* did it." Lauren viewed her friend with empathy. "You're not being logical, Gretchen. When will you realize that nothing happens without physical energy?"

"You're so wrong, my dear. God creates that physical energy . . . and true logic. Man creates flawed logic . . . egotistical, flawed logic . . . and screws up everything he touches. God creates harmony . . . the stars, the sun, the moon . . . harmony. The tide comes in . . . the tide goes out . . . nothing ever fails. The sun comes up . . . the sun goes down . . . right on schedule. Everything He touches achieves perfection. He wastes nothing and recycles everything . . . even man's soul after his body fails."

"I accept the universe too, but I also believe in science and that someday we'll understand it all—through provable science, Gretchen, not fantasy. Your fantasies can't be proven."

"You're wrong, Lauren. Science attempts to recreate a better universe, then screws up and destroys what God created. With man, it's a continual struggle to save the perfection that God created. You prepared to settle for a world like that?"

"Sure, rather than believe Magus programs the world's events. You've read too many Irish fairy tales."

Gretchen finished her wine and got up to refill their glasses. When she returned, Lauren changed the subject. "Reality says you'd never have known about Harley and Kristin if you hadn't accidentally walked in on them at lunch," she teased.

"And fantasy says I already knew. Why did you change the subject?"

Lauren ignored her comment. "When you heard Kristin mention divorce, how did you feel?"

"Harley didn't agree, did he? Look, Lauren, I know that Kristin can be quite persuasive when she wants to be, but Harley expects me home at the end of summer."

"What changed?"

"I never realized how easily Kristin pulls my strings. Strange, isn't it? She's my friend, but she does manage to manipulate people's lives." Gretchen put a hand up as though to stop Lauren's self-proclaimed comment. "Don't preach, I know, and you're right. She couldn't do it without my consent."

"True, but that doesn't explain your sudden change toward Harley."

"I don't know. Maybe my experiences this summer has made me realize I can survive on my own, if necessary. Learning that, it's made me more independent."

"That's you . . . using logic," Lauren said facetiously. "You and Kristin can remain friends, and be stronger for the experience."

"Maybe . . . I did get some good fantasy material for my novel . . . and gave Harley something to think about." She grinned at a sudden thought. "Sometimes I think we don't really solve anything, Lauren. We only rearrange the mysteries."

The End